England and Other Stories

ENGLAND AND
OTHER STORIES

Graham Swift

ALFRED A. KNOPF   NEW YORK   2015

THIS IS A BORZOI BOOK
PUBLISHED BY ALFRED A. KNOPF

Published in the United States by Alfred A. Knopf,
a division of Random House LLC, New York,
a Penguin Random House company.
www.aaknopf.com

Originally published in Great Britain by Simon & Schuster, London, in 2014.

Knopf, Borzoi Books, and the colophon are
registered trademarks of Random House LLC.

Library of Congress Cataloging-in-Publication Data
Swift, Graham, [date]
[Short stories. Selections]
England and other stories / Graham Swift. — First edition.
pages ; cm
"This is a Borzoi Book"—Title page verso.
ISBN 978-1-101-87418-9 (hardcover)   ISBN 978-1-101-87420-2 (eBook)
I. Swift, Graham, 1949–.   II. Title.
PR6069.W47A6 2015
823'.914—dc23 2014028381

Front-of-jacket image: *Beachy Head* (detail) by Eric Ravilious, 1939,
private collection/Bridgeman Images
Jacket design by Carol Devine Carson

Manufactured in the United States of America
First United States Edition

For Candice

L—d! said my mother, what is all this story about?

—LAURENCE STERNE, *Tristram Shandy*

Contents

England and Other Stories

Going Up in the World

Charlie Yates is a small compact man with the look such men can have of inhabiting well their own modest proportions. He'd been less at ease, once, with his name. Charles Yates, the proper version, the name he had to write on forms, was a toff's name, a joke name. What had his parents been thinking? But Charlie was a joke name too, a joker's name. A right Charlie. Still, he couldn't wriggle out of it. Charlie Yates. No one else seemed to mind.

He's fifty-seven now. He's not quite sure how it's happened. He was born in Wapping in 1951. The Wapping he can remember from back then was still pretty much the Wapping that Hitler had flattened. Look at it now.

He can look at it now because more than twenty years ago he and Brenda moved to Blackheath. Not very far as the crow flies, but in other ways a different country. They'd made the move because they could. They'd gone up in the world. And Don Abbot and Marion had made the same move at the same time. Don and Charlie were old pals and business partners. Bren and Marion got on with each other too.

Now at fifty-seven Charlie likes to keep himself in shape. He likes on crisp bright still-early Sunday mornings to take a jog. Not such a short one either: across the heath itself and into Greenwich Park, then through the trees to the brow of the hill where you get the view. Then he likes to sit for a bit on one of the benches and take it all in. My city, my London. He's sitting there now.

Jogging isn't his friend Don's idea of how to spend the early part, or any part, of a Sunday morning, even a brilliant crisp one like this, so Charlie has never jogged with Don. He jogs alone. But every other Sunday, even after Charlie has already gone for a jog, Don and Charlie meet up and go and play nine holes. At Shooters Hill or Eltham, even sometimes, if someone asks them, at Blackheath itself—"Royal Blackheath." There, perhaps, he should be known as Charles.

There were never many golf courses in Wapping.

When he jogs Charlie wears a pale grey tracksuit, with a blue stripe, and neat trainers, nothing sloppy or cheap. The simple thin gold chain that it seems he's worn all his life flips up and down at the base of his neck. He has trim close-cropped hair that's now more white than grey, but it's soft and fine and his wife still likes to stroke it sometimes as if she might be stroking the head of a dog.

As he sits for a while he's hardly puffed at all. At fifty-seven Charlie's father, Frank Yates, had been pretty much past it. But then he was a docker—or he had been—just like Don's father. Look at the docks now.

Francis Yates. You could say that was a toff's name too.

One fine morning in Wapping over fifty years ago Charlie Yates and Don Abbot had met in the playground at Lea Road Infants' School and for some strange reason—a big chunky kid and a little nipper—they'd known it would be a lifelong thing. Lea Road Infants' had later got flattened too, though not by bombs.

For his size, Charlie has quite broad shoulders. When he pushes up the sleeves of his tracksuit (or of his red cashmere golf sweater) you notice the tattoos on his forearms and that, for his size, he has large wrists and hands. He also has, for the size of his face, quite a big prominent but well-shaped nose. With his deep-set eyes this can give him, especially when he grins, a slightly wolfish expression which once used to help him with a certain kind of girl.

But Charlie would say—and the jogging, which is sometimes more of a gentle floating run, would back this up—that the most important item is the feet. The balance and the feet.

Once, for three or four years, Charlie was a boxer. Big hands, but it was really the feet. A bantamweight. He won a few fights and is still proud of the fact that he never got his finely shaped nose smashed out of true. Once he worked on an oil rig, which was when, more fool him, he got the tattoos. But tattoos had come back again now—so he's in fashion. Once he was a roofer. That was his main thing. He was never going to be a docker at any rate. Just as well.

A roofer. He could climb like a monkey. He had the physique. Then it seemed that the roofs just got higher and higher and he became something more than a roofer, without really reckoning on it and without knowing if there was any limit to how high he could go.

He went up in the world. He discovered that he had no fear of heights.

Once, if he'd been born earlier, Charlie might have been a steeplejack, but that was a trade, even a word—like docker—that was becoming out of date. Where were the steeples? Where were the tall chimneys? But suddenly, instead, there were the towers, springing up as if it were a race, and Charlie could work at the very top of them on the exposed girders, without a moment's giddiness or fear. A head for heights is what they say, but Charlie would say it was all in the feet. Where you are standing is just where you are standing.

He earned good money and there was no shortage of work. Some people called it danger money. Charlie didn't like to call it danger money because that implied it was dangerous, but he accepted the basic principle: no risk, no gain. Do something special—like boxing—so you might make a bit extra and put something away, not just scrape along till Friday. Don't be a docker.

Some people—quite a lot of the people Charlie has known—like to place bets, to put their hopes in dogs and horses. Charlie has never placed a bet in his life. He became a birdman, helping to build towers.

And there they are now, glinting in the early-September sunshine, the towers that Charlie Yates helped to build. There, beyond the hidden twists of the river, is Wapping. There's Stepney, there's Limehouse. There's Docklands.

One night, when it was still only starting with him and Brenda, when it was still a bit touch and go, Brenda had said, "Charlie, you have lovely feet." It was the clincher. No one had said this to him before. It went straight, not to his feet, but to his heart, not just because it had never been said before, but because it was true. He said, "Brenda, you have lovely everything." And that was that.

Now Brenda and Marion go on shopping sprees together. Now, twice a year, all four of them go on holidays, to faraway places. Last March it was the Maldives. Charlie couldn't say precisely where the Maldives are, but he's been there. You get out of a plane. The others were all for going again this winter, but Charlie wasn't so sure. He'd heard somewhere that the Maldives could be one of the first places in the world to be submerged by rising sea levels. It was hardly likely to happen while they were there. But he wasn't sure.

Funny, the feelings you could get. He had no fear of heights, but he'd never got on with the sea. He'd known it, working on that oil rig. Once was enough. The same perhaps was true of the Maldives, different proposition though they were. And if he was honest, Charlie would say that he'd be just as happy knocking a ball around the local course with Don as he would be sitting in the Maldives. Or wherever. He's just as happy sitting here. It's all the same place, it's sitting in your own body.

He'd said to Brenda, "You don't have to worry, Bren, with these feet." As if his feet had little wings. But there he'd be anyway, safe and sound every night, cuddling up with her again. A thirty-floor tower in the Isle of Dogs wasn't, in that respect as well as others, like being stuck out in the North Sea.

He said, "Aren't you glad, Bren?"

"Glad what?"

"Glad I'm not on an oil rig."

But it wasn't fair to her, he knew, the prospect of his going off every day indefinitely to walk in the sky. He said that when he'd stashed enough away he'd fix something else up. He hadn't a clue what. He'd come back down to earth.

At some point he twigged that those towers weren't just built with risk, they were built for it. It was risk inside and out. They were built, most of them, to be full of people dealing in their own mysterious kind of danger money. Well, that was their business. He took his money and took the risk that one day, though he never did, he might step off into space.

But one day he took another kind of risk. He followed another lifetime hunch.

It was obvious too, once you saw it, like all the big things perhaps are. It was so obvious that his immediate second thought was: If it was so obvious, how many others might already be in on the act? But it was still early days. More and more towers. And what were those towers made of—or what did it look as though they were made of? What was it that sometimes you didn't see even when it was staring you in the face?

He went to see Don, who was then—well, what was Don Abbot in those days? He was a wheeler-dealer, he was a bit of this and that. You might say he was going places, you might say he was all talk. They had a drink in the Queen Victoria. Don listened. He looked his little friend up and down. Then he spoke as if he hadn't really been listening, but that was Don's way.

"So what are you suggesting, Charlie? That you and me should become a pair of window cleaners?"

"No, Don. Don't muck me about."

Then they'd talked some more.

It became the standard story anyway, the standard line. In golf club bars. In hotel bars, by the blue pools, all around the world.

"I'm Don, this is Charlie. We're window cleaners."

He looks at the towers. He'd helped to build them. And then for twenty years or so he and Don had helped to keep them sparkling.

Don had said, "One thing you have to understand, Charlie, I'm never getting in one of those—contraptions, I'm never even going *up* there. I'm not the kind of guvnor who likes to show everybody he can actually do the job."

"Well you can leave that to me. I'll be the one who won't have to bullshit. But don't get me wrong, Don. I'm planning on the same as you. And I've promised Brenda."

Abbot and Yates. No arguing about the alphabetical order. We clean windows, not just any old windows. It took a while to get it off the ground, so to speak, but then . . . All that glittering glass.

Now they live with the gentry in Blackheath. And now it isn't just him and Bren and Don and Marion, but their kids, a boy and a girl each. Who aren't even kids any more. They'd grown up in Blackheath and gone to school there, and then they'd all gone, with one exception, to university. University! It had been a good move, to cross the river.

The one exception was Don and Marion's Sebastian. Sebastian! How did Don and Marion come up with a name like that?

Thank God he was known as Seb. Seb had gone straight from being sixteen, or so it seemed, to working in one of those towers. For a New York bank. At twenty-three Seb was making serious money, or crazy money—take your pick—money that made Don and him look pretty silly. That made getting A levels and going to university look pretty silly too. Or as Don put it, and Charlie was never quite sure how Don meant it, Seb was one of the barrow boys, wasn't he? One of the barrow boys who'd moved on and moved in. Moved on and moved up.

Charlie looks at the towers. His own son Ian is studying in Southampton to be a marine biologist, which makes Charlie feel—in a different way from how Don must feel about Seb—out of his depth. Ha. There was a joke there. And when Charlie had first told Don about Ian's leanings in life Don had said, "My Uncle Eddy was in the marines in the war. I never knew they had their own biologists."

Charlie and Don could say, "My old man was a docker." What else could they say? What would their kids say? "My old man was a window cleaner?" They wouldn't even say "my old man." Except maybe Seb. Seb might say it, and laugh.

Down in Southampton, Ian wouldn't be able to think: My city, my London. He wouldn't be able to point and say, "See—over there." When Charlie and Brenda drive down to Southampton Charlie humbles himself and listens while his son talks. Maybe that thing about the Maldives came from Ian. Of course it did. But it's not difficult to be humble. Perhaps it isn't even humility. Sometimes while Ian talks Charlie feels a little quick whoosh inside. It's like the whoosh he feels when with Don on a Sunday morning he hits a really good drive. "That one's shifting, Charlie." It's like the whoosh he once felt years ago, after a fight, when the ref's arm would go up, lifting his.

My son Ian. A marine biologist.

He sits on the bench in his tracksuit, feeling the circulation in his veins, feeling, as he's always done, good in his own skin. Charlie is a businessman (a word he can find strange) and a successful one, yet he would still say that the most important thing is your own body. It's what you have, what you come with, and to be glad of it and trust in it is simply life's greatest gift.

So it was funny how it was the urge and aim of most people— almost a sort of law of the world—to go up into their heads, into the topmost part of themselves and live there, live in and by their heads, when most people (he was the exception proving the rule) were afraid of heights.

He looks at the towers, a hand screening his eyes from the dazzle, and smiles. Or it looks like a smile. Only Brenda would know that it's not a smile. Only Brenda would see the two little extra pinches at the corners of Charlie's mouth and understand this contradiction in his face. He has no repertoire of frowns. When Charlie's worried or puzzled he smiles, but smiles differently.

He's worried, and has been now for some time, about his friend Don, about how he's putting on weight. Don has always been a big man, but big of frame, not flabby or cumbersome or slow. Now he's spreading, he's simply expanding. It's a sort of joke—that he's putting on pounds—a joke that even Don likes to tell against himself, but it isn't really a joke at all, and when Charlie plays golf with Don now he knows it's not just for fun, but it's important for keeping Don moving. They should play every Sunday. They should play the other nine holes, not just spend them in the bar.

He knows there's no point, there's never been, in asking Don to come jogging with him. And how would it look now, how could it possibly work: Don lumbering and sweating beside him while he, Charlie, just hovered on his toes? It has even come to seem a little wrong to Charlie that he should go jogging by himself while Don has this weight problem—which is completely illogical, even vaguely superstitious. Like thinking you shouldn't go to the Maldives because the Maldives might one day disappear.

But Charlie worries about Don. It's as if all the money is at last turning to fat. Fifty years ago and more, Charlie had thought that he was just a little scrap of nothing and this bigger kid might take him under his wing. And so it was. Though now you could also say it was Don who should be for ever grateful to Charlie. But Charlie feels the strange worrying need, like some unpaid debt, to take his ever bulkier friend under his wing. How?

And now he has the other worry too, this new worry that could knock the first one aside. He's going to talk to Don about it soon. Don will tell him what else he knows, when they play their round in just a couple of hours. By the sound of it, there won't be much concentrating on Don's weight problem or even on the golf. Crisp bright morning though it is.

Charlie is a businessman, yes that's what he can legitimately be called, but, even though he likes to sit and look at them, he doesn't keep his ear close to what goes on inside those towers. That's their business, he just cleans the windows, so to speak. But Don keeps an ear, it's even an inside ear, because of Seb. Charlie has sometimes had the bizarre vision of Don actually cleaning a window, on the twenty-fifth floor say, something Don could never do (though Charlie could, easy-peasy), and looking in and waving at his son.

Don had called and said, "Seb's in trouble, deep trouble."

Trouble? Wasn't Seb making telephone numbers? Wasn't Seb making them all look silly?

Don said, "They're going to pull the rug from under him.

Him and everyone else. Something big's coming, Charlie, something big and bad. If you ask me, from what Seb's heard—it's not
just Seb who's in trouble, it's the whole fucking world."

Did Don have drink in his voice? No. Charlie didn't say anything to Brenda, only that it was Don calling about tomorrow,
though Brenda would have thought: Why did Don need to call?
It was a Saturday night. Charlie didn't hear anything on the late-
night news. Later, cuddling up, he said, "Aren't you glad, Bren?"

"Glad what?"

"Glad I was never a marine biologist."

"What are you on about?"

He didn't really know, himself. There was something about
Don's voice, there was something about that "whole fucking
world."

His instinct the next morning was to get up and do the usual
jog, to be on his feet, to prepare—to prepare his mind by preparing his body. And it was such a beautiful morning, early September, the tingle of autumn in the air.

Now he gets up from the bench and takes a last look at the
towers. They gleam back. Then he turns and jogs again through
the glistening trees, feeling at fifty-seven as light on his feet as he
did when he was seventeen.

Wonders Will Never Cease

When Aaron and I were younger we used to chase women. It's a phrase. How many times do you actually see a man chasing a woman, say ten yards behind and gaining? We were both runners anyway, literally—athletes. With me it was the hurdles. We both did the same PE course at college, and girls were part of our physical education. I'll be the first to say that Aaron was better at it than me. In his case it was more that the women chased him, or crawled all over him. It was how he was made. I tended to get his rejects. But even Aaron's rejects could be something, and one day I married and settled down with one of them. Patti.

After that I didn't hang out with Aaron so much. In fact we hardly heard from each other. Maybe he thought that by marrying Patti and settling down I was also letting the side down. Well, too bad.

I wouldn't have said this ten years ago, but I think I'm the type who sees life like a book, with chapters. In one chapter you mess around, then you marry, have kids, get a place of your own, and so on. I'm not like Aaron. I wouldn't like to guess how many books Aaron's read. But that's the point perhaps with physical education, it's not really about reading.

It was an option anyway. If you did the course and got the certificate you could make a career, a life out of it. It was a chance. Meanwhile we were athletes too.

I never had any illusions about making it to the big competitions. I was just quite good at hurdling, I loved the hurdles. Aaron used to say, "Count me out, man. When I run, I want to run. I don't want to run at something that'll trip me up."

I didn't say, "Doesn't that apply to women?"

They tripped him up and they crawled all over him. And they crawled all over him because he was quite a specimen. It was a vicious circle. But Aaron, I believe—just to talk about his running—could have been championship stuff. I say this as a qualified PE teacher.

Anyhow, the time came, years back, when I'd settled down with Patti, and Aaron and I had almost lost touch. Just now and then Patti and I would have our "wondering about Aaron" conversations. I was always a bit nervous about them, Patti having been one of Aaron's rejects. I sometimes thought this was the reason why the gap had opened up between Aaron and me. It was Patti's doing, it was Aaron's, it was mine. I don't know. Once—we were having Sunday breakfast—I actually said to Patti, "I wonder if those women aren't catching up with him." I might have said "the years" instead. It was just a casual, private-joke thing, but it was a bit careless perhaps.

Patti didn't pick it up one way or the other. She said, "Mmm, I wonder too." She took a bite of toast. Then she said, "If you're worried about him, give him a call, look him up." As if she was daring me.

She was pregnant with Daryl, our first, around this time. She was crazy about marmalade! Maybe she was thinking: Well, if he's hankering for a last boys' night out, he better take his chance while he can. Now we have the two boys, Daryl and Warren, two growing boys. Lots of boys' nights in.

Anyhow, I never made the call. But one day, years later, I get a call, out of the blue, from Aaron. He sounds just like the old Aaron, but he also sounds a bit cagey. It turns out he's called to tell me he's going to get married. I wait a bit, in case I'm being wound up. Then I wait anyway, in case he has some joke to make about it. I wait for an "Okay, man, don't laugh." But the only joke is that he's speaking in a sort of whisper, as if it's top-secret information he can trust only with me.

Then he says he'd like me—me and Patti of course—to come to the wedding. To make things clear, he says it's going to be a "low-key" thing, in a registry office, just the two of them. Except you need a witness. So would Patti and I like to be there, to witness?

All the time, apart from swallowing back my surprise, I'm thinking: He didn't have to tell me this—a witness could be anyone—but I get the feeling he thinks that by telling me and having me as his witness he won't have to tell anyone else. I feel honoured and I also feel arm-twisted, but how could I not say yes? Even though, apparently, it means a trip to Birmingham. That's where he is now. Guess what—teaching PE.

I say, "Yes, of course." Before I've even spoken to Patti. I also feel like saying, "Don't worry, Aaron, I won't breathe a word."

I say, "So what's her name then?"

"It's Wanda."

"Wanda," I say, trying to form a picture of a Wanda. I don't say, "So, is she pregnant?"

Fortunately, Patti more or less has the same thought as me: How can we not? Perhaps she's really thinking: Must we? But she looks all keen and interested, she even makes a joke about it, a pretty good joke too. "Well, Wandas will never cease."

So we go through with it, this low-key, hush-hush event. We manage to park the boys with Patti's parents. We're even ready to book a hotel. But Aaron says, "Nah, man, stay with us, no problem." This needs a bit of thought. I don't like to spell it out: this might be intruding on Aaron and Wanda's wedding night. We aren't at PE college any more.

But I soon get the picture that, apart from the business at the registry office and a few drinks and a meal, nothing much out of the ordinary is going to happen. There's not going to be a honeymoon. Aaron and Wanda have apparently been shacked up together for quite a while. There'd be a spare room in their flat for Patti and me. It's just that they've both decided it's time to get married.

"Okay," I say, slightly wishing it would be easier to insist on paying for a hotel anyway. With the two boys, Patti and me have to watch the cash. But of course what I'm mostly thinking, and so's Patti, is: What's this Wanda like? And, given all the years that have passed: What's Aaron like?

Well, it may put me in a bad light, but I have to say Wanda was a disappointment. At least at first. A surprise and a disappointment. Don't get me wrong. I don't mean she wasn't perfectly—fine. But if all those years of what Aaron once got up to were supposed to be a selection process, so that in the end he'd pick out a real star—well, Wanda was nothing special.

I even felt, which doesn't put me in a good light either, I did better with Patti.

I didn't share this thought with Patti, but I could feel her tuning in to it and relaxing. It put me in a good light with her. I think Patti's fear was that we were about to meet some woman who'd have me, in spite of myself, spending the whole weekend with my tongue hanging out. That this might have been the real purpose of the exercise. Aaron just wanted to show off his trophy.

To be honest, it was my fear too.

Wanda was built along pretty pared-down lines, which wasn't, as I recall, how Aaron had liked them. She wasn't skinny, but she was, well, wiry, with a tough little pair of shoulders. And her face, though it had a cheeky way of making you feel good and want to laugh, wasn't a face that would stop you in your tracks. It could even sometimes look a bit hard and locked up.

She wasn't a beauty, but she had a way of carrying herself,

of moving, an energy, an intensity. I liked her. I was glad I didn't fancy her. And pretty soon I twigged it.

I found a moment to say in private to Aaron, "She's a runner, isn't she?" This was barely an hour after the two of them had become Mr. and Mrs.

"I hope she's not running anywhere, man, after what we've just done."

"You know what I mean."

"I know what you mean." In fact a glint had come into his eyes. We were at a bar, fetching drinks.

"Yep," he said. "Four hundred. Eight hundred maybe." He gave me a quick stare. "Maybe hurdles. She has to find where it really is for her." Then he said, with a certain pride in his voice, and he even looked across the crowded room to exchange a wink with his new wife, "Yep, a runner. She's going places. Same again, man?"

As for Aaron himself, how did he look? Well, he looked good—right then he looked very good—but I could see how the years had affected him. They'd blunted and blurred him a bit, taken off some shine. Enough to make me think: How will he look in another five years? And to make me think: He'll be having the same thoughts about me.

Except I didn't kid myself and I hadn't just got married and I was a father of two. And my viewpoint had perhaps been different all along. I keep people fit for a living, so I keep fit myself, but there are limits, and no one gets any younger. That's why these days I spend a good deal of time with a man called Jarvis who's starting up a sportswear company. It's why I enrolled not long ago on a business course. It's my plan B. For the boys' and Patti's sake. For my own sake.

I could have been a hurdler? Maybe. But, as I said once to Patti a long time ago, I saw the hurdles.

All the same, people reach their peaks, I believe this. They come into their best. There's the book with the chapters, but there's something else. We reach our peaks and we pass them. There's nothing to be done about it, but it's a sad thing if you never even knew the peak you had it in you to reach. In the world of physical fitness you see a lot of this. You see the chances and you see a lot of missed ones.

What I'm really saying is that you might have thought that for Aaron and Wanda their wedding day wasn't their moment of coming into their best. It was important, but their best was somewhere else. Maybe Aaron knew that his had already gone.

Anyhow, after a few drinks—it was a three o'clock wedding—they took us back to their place before we went out again for dinner. It was a top flat, on two floors, and our room was a tiny little spare room under the roof, but I was relieved we wouldn't be sleeping just the other side of a wall from them.

More than relieved. As we went upstairs Patti was ahead. She was wearing a nice outfit for the occasion (maybe for Aaron too, but I'll let that pass). I was carrying our overnight bag, but I couldn't keep my free hand to myself. I couldn't help giving Patti a good goosing. And no sooner were we behind the door and supposed to be, according to Aaron, "sorting ourselves out," than we were at it, quick and breathless and more or less still standing up. A chilly attic room in Birmingham, dark outside. Patti with her skirt up, holding on to the back of a chair. The kids off our hands. Two newly-weds below. Wonders will never cease.

We had a good time—I mean we had a good time, too, with Aaron and Wanda. Because of the head start we had, of having been married for five years already and having two kids, being with Aaron and Wanda was like being with a couple of kids. And, not having our own kids around, it was like being a couple of kids ourselves.

True, when we came back later that night—it *was* their wedding night—our top room, above theirs, might still have been a bit tricky. But we'd all been drinking and then Patti and me—

well, we'd had our head start. All I remember is curling up with her, this time just for warmth, and crashing.

When I woke up I could hear a lot of scuffling below. I don't mean bedroom noises. I mean scuffling, on the stairs and then in the hallway. The sound of people on their feet and busy about something—very early on a Sunday morning, in January. On the day after their wedding.

I heard muffled voices. I think I heard, "Okay, Wan? Keys?" Then I heard the front door being shut with an effort to keep it quiet. Then I heard more voices below in the street. I wondered if Aaron and Wanda were still drunk. And I couldn't help getting up to peep through the curtains of our little front window.

It made me think of getting up once when I'd heard strange noises at home. It was just two foxes, under the streetlamps, mucking around with an upended dustbin. I remember thinking that I wasn't young any more—I was someone who worried about noises in the night.

What I saw this time, under the streetlamps, was Aaron and Wanda. To say they were mucking around wouldn't have been quite right, but not quite wrong either. They were in tracksuits and trainers. On the morning after their wedding night—it was still dark and freezing—they were going for a run. But they were also mucking around as if they couldn't yet get down to serious business. They were laughing. They were like two foxes in their own way. They more than once kissed and ran their hands over each other. I thought: They could be doing all that snuggled up in bed.

Nonetheless I saw Aaron had a stopwatch on a loop round his neck. They actually took up positions, side by side, in the middle of the road, half crouching, as if their toes were on a line. Aaron held the stopwatch, looking at it, then Wanda tensed and

Aaron spoke. I'm sure I heard, "Set! Go!" Wanda sped off and Aaron kept looking at the watch—maybe it was a ten-second handicap—then he sped off too.

His challenge to her, or hers to him? I'll never know. Or what the distance was or the route. It was 6:30 a.m.

Wanda's an eight-hundred-metre runner now. The real deal. It's less than a year to the London Olympics. And she's Aaron's missis.

I turned from the window. Patti had woken up. She switched on a bedside light and stared at me. "What the hell are you doing? What's going on?"

Well, the phrase came to me. I had to laugh. I said, "I've just seen Aaron chasing a woman."

I explained. I explained what I'd heard and what I'd seen and I expected there'd now be some chuckling head-shaking discussion between us about this weird post-wedding behaviour. Or that this might be the time for our in-depth analysis of the whole Aaron-Wanda thing.

But Patti just said, "You mean they're not here, they're not right below us? We've got the place to ourselves?"

And she grabbed my wrist and yanked me back into bed.

People Are Life

"But you have friends," I said.

I don't know why I said it. It was somewhere between saying and asking.

"Friends?" he said.

"Friends. You know."

He was my last of the day. I'd already told Hassan to turn the sign on the door. I was tired, but sometimes the last of the day is different, if only because it's the last. It was a little before seven, already dark.

I snipped away.

"Friends," he said, as if he'd never heard the word before. Then he went silent. "I have meetings," he said.

Now it was my turn. "Meetings?"

"Meetings. I know people and I meet them. People I've known for a long time, but I just meet them. Know what I mean? Time goes by, then we meet, for a drink or something. Then time goes by again. Is that having friends?"

I wasn't sure now if he was saying or asking.

"Well," I said.

Maybe what I'd meant by friends was no more than just that—what he'd just said. People you could talk to. People he could talk to.

"Well," I said.

It's not every day that one comes in and lets you know that since you did them last their mother has died. And who puts it this way: "That's both of them. My dad last year, my mum last week."

Well, that was certainly saying.

I'd never known, or I couldn't remember, about his dad.

"I didn't know that," I said. "The two of them."

And I'd never known till now the truth of this one's situation. He didn't have to say it, I didn't have to ask. I saw it in his face in the mirror, in the way he looked at his face in the mirror.

"Well it has to happen," I said, "sooner or later." I might have said, "When you get to our age," but I didn't.

You see things in the way people look at their own faces. It's not a thing they often do or even want to do, but in a barber's shop there's not much else to do. In a café people pay to sit and look out at the world going by. In a barber's they pay to stare at their own faces, and you see what goes on when they do.

You don't see much in the top of a head. Though sometimes I think: Right there beneath my fingers is their skull, their brain and every thought that's in it.

What this one was telling me, by his look in the mirror, was that he'd lived with—lived for—his mum and his dad all his life. Some men are big children. That was about the whole of it. And he must have been past sixty. One of those big, hefty but soft types. What he was telling me was that he was all alone in the world.

I carried on snipping. What I thought was: Well, what can I do about it? I cut hair.

"Still, it's tough," I said. "How old—your mother?"

"Eighty-three," he said.

"Eighty-three," I said. "That's not bad. Eighty-three's not a bad age."

Then after a silence I said, I don't know why, "But you have friends."

People to talk to, I meant, in your time of trouble. Everyone has friends. But he only had "meetings" apparently.

"Friends," he said, as if the word was strange. "I had friends when I was a kid. I mean a little kid. We hung around together, all the time. We were in and out of each other's homes, each other's lives. We never thought twice about it. That's having friends."

I snipped away. "Well that's true enough," I said.

And how many times do I say that to a customer? "That's true enough." It's what you say. Whatever they say.

"The friends we make when we're young," I said, "they're the ones that stick, they're the ones that matter."

That wasn't quite what he'd said, or meant, and I knew it. It wasn't quite what I meant either. I saw what he'd meant. I snipped away and looked at his hair, but I saw my friends, in Cyprus. In Ayios Nikolaos. All my nine-year-old, ten-year-old friends. I saw myself with them.

Maybe he knew that I hadn't meant what I'd said. I'd said something everyone says, or likes to think.

He said, "It's not the same, is it? Meeting people, seeing people, talking to them. It's not the same as having friends."

I moved the angle of his head. "That's too hard," I said, "too hard." I felt something coming, something almost like anger. I pushed it back. I almost stopped snipping. "You're asking too much," I said. "All due respect—to your mother. All due respect to your feelings. If you have people to see and talk to, then you have friends. If you have people, you have life."

It was late, it was dark. It was the nearest I could get to a little philosophy. It's what some people expect, sometimes, from a barber. A little philosophy. Especially a barber who's turned sixty himself and who's boss of his own shop (me and three juniors) and whose hair is crinkly grey. And I'm Greek too (or Cypriot) and we invented philosophy.

"People," I said. "People are life."

But what I thought was: You didn't have to come and get your

hair cut, did you, after your mum had just died? His hair wasn't
so long, it didn't need a cut.

I put the scissors and comb in my top pocket and switched
on the clippers so we couldn't speak.

People think if you're a barber then you have people, you
have talk all the time, your whole day. The things you must hear,
the stories, the things you must learn from all those people.

But the truth is I like to get away from people. I like it when
it's the end of the day. That's why sometimes I'm different, I say
things, with the last one. I get enough of people. And people are
mainly just heads of hair, some of them not such nice heads of
hair.

I thought: He wants it neat and tidy for the funeral.

My mother and father died years ago, in Cyprus. I hadn't
seen them anyway for quite a time. I hadn't been back. As a matter of fact, my wife died too, just three years ago—my English
wife, Irene. But we'd split up, we'd been split up for years. She
drank all the time. She drank and she swore all the time.

Did I tell all my customers, when she died, when we split up?
Did I gabble away to my customers? Did I close the shop?

I have two grown-up boys who are both in computers and are
embarrassed by their father who's just been a barber all his life.

I'm glad when I get home and can be alone.

Maybe he heard all this in my voice. Or he saw it in my face,
in the mirror. There's always a moment when you stand behind
them, with your fingers either side of their head, holding it
straight, and you both stare at the mirror as if for a photograph.
As if the head you have in your hands might be something you've
just made.

"People are life," I said.

But he could see, in the mirror, that I was thinking: Don't
come to me at the end of the day for wise words or comfort, or
friendship, if that's what you want. What do you expect? That
when I shut the shop in just a moment I'm going to say, "Why

don't you and I go for a drink? Why don't we get to know each other better?"

I'm glad when I get home and can take a beer from the fridge.

One of those heavy but soft types who look as if they've been well fed by their mothers and will end up feeding them. A regular, it's true. How many years? Always wanting me, the boss, to do him, none of the juniors. The years flash by if you count them in haircuts. I didn't know his name. That's not so strange, of course. No appointment system. No need to know their names—unless they tell you—or what they do for a living.

It's how the English are, I learnt this.

They all know my name. It's over the window. Vangeli. And they know what I do. But how many times do any of them ask, "So how did you get to be a barber?"

I tell them, if they ask, I give them the story. I say I was born holding a comb and scissors . . .

The truth is it was something I could do. It didn't need a brain. Then I did my army service. They made me cut the whole camp's hair. There I met some people! There I got some talk! I gave them all the same shaved-rat's face. Then I came to this country and ran around for a while with a crazy bunch who'd made the journey before me. Then I settled down to be a barber.

And now I was the same age, give or take, as this man whose head was in my hands. And yes, in however many years it was, I'd seen his hair grow thinner and greyer, more pink showing through. But of course never said.

There's a joke in the barber's trade: "I'm sorry for your loss."

When my wife died and I went to see her, I mean in the chapel of rest, she was covered right up to her chin in a cloth. All I saw was a head. You can't get away from some things.

I went back to snipping. Outside people were hurrying home. Lucas, one of my juniors—it's what I call them, "juniors"—was sweeping the floor.

Your turn to speak, I thought. But he didn't. For a second or so I thought: He's just glad of the touch of my fingers, through his hair, on his scalp, the flick of my comb. The smell of shampoo and talc, like the smell of being a baby again.

Vangeli. It means "angel of good news," but I don't like to explain this to people, because of the jokes. I don't like to explain that Irene, my wife's name, is really a Greek name too. It means "peace."

Peace!

There's another moment when you reach for the hand mirror and hold it up to the back of their heads. And once again you have to look, both of you, straight into the big mirror, as if you're a pair who go together. It's the moment when it's almost over. Then there's the moment when you pull away the cloth and brush them down and they stand up and you give them the paper towel, then they wipe their necks, put on their jackets and pay. You give them back any change, if they don't tell you to keep it.

Then there's the moment when they turn, and you—or at least I always do it—give them a little pat, a little pat that turns into a squeeze, just half a second, on one shoulder. It means thank you, thank you for the tip, but it also means: there, that's you done, that's you all fresh and ready. Now go and live your life.

Haematology

Roehampton, Surrey
House of Eliab Harvey

7th February, 1649

Colonel Edward Francis
The Council of Officers
Westminster

My dear cousin,

Well, Ned (if I may still so call you and if you will deign to hear from me), we have lived through extraordinary times. Were there ever such times as these? And now I must cede to you that you are of the winning party and may lord it over me who was the close attendant of kings, nay of our late—of our very late—king. Or would you have me name him, if I have it right, "tyrant, traitor, murderer?" Would you daub me with the same charges, for having been so privy to His Majesty—but must I not call him that?—for having ministered to his agues, fevers and coughs? Would you have me place my own head upon the block for having been such a bodily accomplice to tyranny? Then it would be seen, would it not, if my argument of the blood's motion held true? Physician, prove thyself!

But was it not proven when that royal blood—may we even call it that?—spurted forth but a week ago at Whitehall? And is it not proven when any man's head or limb is severed from his body, as has been the lot of many men—nay, of women and children— in these late times? A king is but a man like any other. Has it needed seven years of war and a trial by Parliament to determine the matter, when any such as I might have attested to it? Anatomy is no respecter. I have dissected criminals and examined kings. Does it need any special statute to claim the one might be the other?

That, Ned, was my grounding and my ground, long before those of your party set out to curb the King's powers, then overthrow him. There are tyrannies and tyrannies, and treacheries and treacheries. There are some even now of my party—I mean among the party of physicians—who would not blench or lament to see my old head removed from my body, to see me cut down for having raised my standard against King Galen. There are many kinds of majesty and rebellion. We were but boys, Ned, when the Armada closed upon our shores, but would we not have rallied round our monarch? Rally, I say! We were more than half the age we have now when Ralegh's head was severed from his body. Did we not then both feel not a little of the sharpness of the axe that smote him? There were many of your party for whom that day, I dare say, marked a severance. It was their beginning, their pretext. So it was with you. It was the beginning, I dare say, of our own severance.

Yet did we not feel also, if we are truthful, that there is a motion, a fluctuation—may not I use such terms?—in the fortunes of men, an ebb and flow, a rise and fall, beyond all issue of government or justice; and that it is into these unrestrained tides—we knew it by then—we enter as we enter the world? We set our little skiffs upon them, as Ralegh set many a fine vessel upon the waters of his ambition. Should I have stepped in, Ned, to bid my former master James withhold his warrant upon so worthy a head? I was but his physician, not his counsellor, and had been hardly a year in his service. And Ralegh went to his death bravely and nobly, as did, but these seven days past, my other late master Charles.

Is that what we must call him now, only Charles? Is that the ordinance? As you and I may still call each other—or so I trust—but Ned and Will, boys who once played at knucklebones and did battle with the wooden swords of our rulers at Canterbury. And quaked in our shoes, no doubt, at the wrath of our masters, or spoke impudence about them, behind our hands, when their gowned backs were turned. They were only our schoolmasters, but it was all our world. Such tyranny, such subjection. Such fledgling revolt. Such nursing of our destinies. And it was the *King's* School, mark you. Though it was still the reign, long to continue, of, as we would call her, even in our prayers, Our Sovereign Lady Elizabeth.

What times, Ned, what times. "That one might read the book of fate and see the revolution of the times"—do I have it correctly? Is it not King Henry IV, deposer himself of kings? But it was you who attended the playhouses and, if I know you as I knew you in your youth, no doubt other houses as well, while I attended my lectures at Padua. You who are now of God's militia, while I, to pass the hours, read more of the poets than I read of the Bible. Is that to speak treason?

That, surely, was our first parting, though we would write much to each other. You were for the law, I was for physic. You were for the Middle Temple, I was for Padua. Was it not indeed the seed of all our future differences and of future offices we would hold as then undiscovered to us? Yet that common seed, that common stirring of the blood—quite so!—was ambition. Should we deny it? I was for anatomy, you, with your lawyer's trenchancy, were for the bones of human contention. It was always in you, Ned, though it was your profession then to fight but with words. You had the mark of a swordsman. One day you might draw a true sword. I had only a scalpel. Even with your wooden ruler you were more often than not, as I recall, the victor. Now I must own again that you, and those of your kind, are my victor. Nay, my ruler! Truly I live now under your rule.

How does it go, Ned? "If this were seen, the happiest youth, viewing his progress through, what perils past, what crosses to ensue." I am an old man. I read by a winter fire. But I freely admit I was ambitious too. My cause was the advancement of learning, but it was also the advancement of myself. Did I marry my late wife because I wished her to be my wife or because I wished to be the husband of the daughter of the late Queen's physician? It opened more doors than my laurels from Padua. Yet how I miss her, my dear Liz. My late Liz. Late! It is the only word now for us, now we have passed our three score and ten. All is late. Though you may think, if God (and your physician) grant you health, that you are now but in your earliness, your newness. Do we not have a new world? Is this not the seventh day of its creation?

Ambition, Ned, it was our common spurring in our separate courses. Shall we confess it? And shall we confess that for a while, for a good long while, my ambition outrode and was better stabled than yours? Now shall we see where the ambition of your master Cromwell—but I must call him master too—will take him and how it may serve and accommodate yours.

What times, what times. It is now I who must sit aside, withdraw and retire, taking shelter as I do in my brother's house. It is I who must content myself with my books and studies, I who once accompanied kings. Yet I want no more. You will perhaps smirk to know that my studies remain upon the reproduction of our kind and of the animals at large. What food for mirth and raillery have I given my enemies and detractors—who are still many and persistent—that I, an old man both wifeless and childless, should dwell upon such stuff. How they must snigger at me as we once sniggered behind the backs of our schoolmasters.

Yet I would know, Ned, perhaps before I die, how we are born, how we are shaped for the world. Leave that, some will still cry, to the doctors of divinity, tread not upon that holy ground. So are we not alike there? Do you not discern it from your present elevation? We both came moulded with the rebellious, some might say heretical, disposition to trespass upon sacred soil. In the interests, to be sure, of truth and justice. And of ambition?

I was no prostrate worshipper in the church of kingship, no more than you, but my interests, or shall I say the interests of learning, made me seek their best protection. Is it not at least food for thought for you that our late king, tyrant, traitor and murderer, who clung so much to his own divine prerogative, was yet the patron of so much that assailed the sacrosanct? And is it not also food for thought for you that those of your party who once so boldly and blasphemously rose up against him are now entrenched in their own sanctimonies? Do I blaspheme now? Will you arraign me?

The bones of human contention! Why did I hold back for some dozen years the publication of my findings, my *De Motu Cordis*? Because I lacked courage, I confess it, because—I should say this!—I was weak of heart. Because I knew it would bring down upon me the learned heavens, if not other powers-that-be. It would bring me enemies. And lose me valued practice. And so it did, and still does. There is heresy and heresy, there is dogma and dogma.

How well I remember, Ned, when we last spoke together. It was some eight years past. It was at your table. There were the bonds of our kinship and of our friendship and of host and guest, yet I felt a broil simmering. There was the whiff of smoke. You said there was a time approaching when every man would have to make his stand. Of whose party was he? I said may not a man make a stand, and a stout one, of being of no party? You said that was no stand at all. Or rather, as I recall, you said it was not the stand of a man but of a tree. Would I be a tree and not a man?

It was late August and your windows were flung open upon the view of your orchard, a whole regiment of trees, hung with blushing apples. "No, Ned," I said, "I am not a tree, but let trees still decide the matter. I too have an orchard. Let us not quarrel over whose apples are the sweeter, though over lesser things men have sometimes come to blows, but here is the true quarrel: if you or any man or any man's party were to invade my orchard, cut down my trees and trample my land, why then I would be of the opposing party. There would be my allegiance."

You would not take this for an answer (nor in all honesty did I think it quite sufficient). You said, "Well there you have spoken wisely, Will, since the King already cuts and tramples through the orchard that is his kingdom, claiming it as his right to do so and that it is no man's land but his own. Is not then your allegiance decided?" There was a smile upon your lips, but there was a smouldering in your eyes. You poured another cup of ale. You said, "There will come a time, Will, there will come a time." I should perhaps have said nothing, but I said, "Then let us hope that time does not come tomorrow, or the day after. And let us hope that when it comes we do not fall out upon our cousinship, no matter which party we choose." I said, "I am a doctor, Ned, I must minister to all parties."

But you would not take that for an answer either, or your eyes would not. I had not seen them burn so before. You plainly deemed, but did not say, that for certain causes even a doctor must throw aside his phials, as a lawyer must throw aside his books of law, and buckle on armour. How little I or you knew, Ned, that one day soldiers of your party would enter my chamber and ransack its contents, casting hither and thither my precious notes, papers and experiments. There was my orchard for you, there was my party confirmed.

But, not to skirt about the nub of the matter, how could I say that my party was already chosen for me? As you knew it was. How could I, who was physician to the King, who knew the King's very body as no other man knew it, be of any party but the King's? It was scarcely a case of cause or principle. But how, equally, could I have said that I noted that fire in your eyes? I noted it as a physician notes symptoms. It was the fire of your cause, I grant you, but it was the fire also of envy. It was the fire of an ambition not yet rewarded, and overtaken by another's eminence. And such was the fire—I can say this, now you enjoy your own eminence—that lit the eyes of many of your ranks, cause or no cause.

Orchards! Kingdoms! How could I have said, without seeming to speak like my master the King in his worst haughtiness, that my party was of bigger things? It is a small entity, the heart, it is a small allowance, the blood of any creature, yet to every creature it is the All of life. I was born, you know this, Ned, in Folkestone, which looks across to the Continent. How could I have said that I was of the Continent's party, I was of the world's party? England is but a small country, albeit my own. Why did I journey to Padua? How could I have said that I was of Fabricius's party, nay of Galileo's, whose noble hand I have clasped? Knowledge is vaster than kingdoms and, while kingdoms come and go, is the only true arbiter of the times. How could I have said this to you, a lawyer and counsellor to members of Parliament (did you not have, even then, your modicum of eminence?), without adding fuel to that fire? I can scarcely claim the licence of old age to speak it now.

I care not for kings. I cared for the King. I knew him well. I was charged with the King's body, not with the body politick. It was a small and slight body, for all its loftiness of position and mien. It was stunted by rickets. It was a body indeed that was sniggered at. How many of your party knew so well your enemy, knew his fleshly infirmities as well as his kingly towerings, knew his private graces? When I attended his hunts he would set aside for me so much of his quarry, his stags, hinds and hares, as I might want as fresh matter for my dissections. He did not trample on the advancement of learning, nor even on the defying of Galen. When he took up his headquarters in Oxford he ensured I should have place and time for my studies. It was his fortress of war, but still a seat of learning. True, Ned, I was a Caius man, before Cambridge was Parliament's school, who found sanctuary in Oxford. Did I choose my party? I was made, by the King's wish, Warden of Merton. You were made Colonel of Horse. We find our places, Ned, we find our colours.

Either way now, the orchard, the kingdom—the commonwealth, the republic, what are we to call it?—lies bleeding and cut down. A commonwealth? Look at its poverty. A republic? A headless body.

When I was at Edge Hill, in attendance, before my days in Oxford, I observed the pallor in my master's brow. It was but a man's pallor, the pallor of any man on hearing the opening shots of cannon, but it was a king's pallor. No other man could have worn that pallor. It was the first battle. Pray God, he must have thought, it would be the only one. It was the first occasion of his leading an army in battle, and certainly the first against his own people.

What times, Ned, what times. We who played at knucklebones. Truly that battle, if such disorderliness could be called a battle, was well named, since was it not a great edge of things, a great precipice overstepped? It was not for me, dissector of corpses and philosopher of the blood, to be affrighted at the carnage and slaughter. In truth I spent much of the time behind a hedge endeavouring to read a book. Yet I was affrighted at the look I saw on almost every man's face, be he for King or Parliament (and you could not often well tell the difference), the look that said, as it were: It is a true thing now, and it is of this sanguinary substance, this thing that was but hours ago still a thing of speech and protestation. It is a thing now of experiment, and such is the experiment.

Had they chosen their party, those green recruits who had not known a fight before? Had they chosen their party, those who turned and ran or galloped for their lives before the charge of Prince Rupert? And had they chosen their party, those of Prince Rupert's command, who knew, it seemed, no command, but charged ever on beyond the field, as if the battle were not a battle but a great chase, a great hunting of men? It almost cost the King the day. It certainly cost his winning it.

Would that he had won it. Do I speak treachery? It would have settled the matter. There would have been a battle only and no war. I believe it was in that pallor that I noted. That he knew he could win. He had the ridge, indeed the edge, and all the advantages. He held the London road. He might prevail, as a king should all at once prevail. Yet it was that day that led to his placing his neck upon the block.

But did you see it, Ned, that look upon the *common* face? I know you were there. That is, it came to my later knowledge that you had been among Sir William Balfour's horse, who led the counter-charge, against an army naked of its own horse, and very nearly seized a victory. It was the beginning of your late-won eminence, not as man of law or even of Parliament, but of arms.

But did you know, even then, that I was there? Did you know how close your cuirassiers came to the King and to those in his attendance? Did we look upon each other, Ned? This I would know. Your face would have been hidden by a helmet, but not my own. Did you see my face? Yet did you see, in any case, or were you blinded by your purposes, that look upon the general face that said all England is a butcher's yard now, a very shambles? All England is a hunting ground and every man a quarry.

I would know it, Ned. I did not fight. I carried no weapon. I carried a book, thinking I might be idle. I attended the King and I tended the wounded, of both parties. It was an October day, bitter cold, and darkness, blessedly, came early, ending the matter in no party's favour but not stopping the flow from wounds. Did we look upon each other? It is seven years past and we were both even then men with grey hairs. I was never a man of arms, but I am haunted by the dream, Ned, that we face each other on a field of battle. I have no potion to drive away the stubborn vision. We both have swords drawn. They are not wooden rulers. It is not apples and orchards. It has come to this. Did you see my face, and should I be thankful I did not see yours?

It is bitter cold this night also. I write by firelight and candlelight. Either way, the land lies ravaged. Soon, they say, Parliament's victory will be further visited upon the people of Ireland. You are surely too old now to command there a regiment. Yet, physician as I am, I know not the mettle of your ageing body. The army is a toughening and late schooling, no doubt; and the heat of battle, so it would seem, is a heater of the soul, even a forger of zeal for the Lord. We are all of God's party now, but some more so. Is it not the case? There were all along in this affair but two parties, the army and the people, that too is now more so, and either the army would be our church or the church our army. Is it not so? We have no civility but a confusion of godliness and war. Such our new world.

Well, Ned, I am of the people's party now, I am only of the people. Though I have served kings, I am, as physician, only of the party and of the care of Every Body. I believe, and indeed can demonstrate, that every man's organs obey the same internal government. I still hold faith in the advancement of learning, if I believe less that by learning we advance.

Yet tell me, did we see each other? And tell me, might we yet, in the time remaining to us, see each other again? We are kinsmen and, whatever the divisions between us, we are now old men. I would have been your physician, Ned, most happily and truly, if you had asked me. And would be so still. Old men require physicians. Unless your Cromwell takes a crown, neither of us, I dare say, will know another king. We are as one there. We have only our allotted years. You would be welcome here at my brother's house. You may view, for your amusement, my experiments. It is not a long journey from Westminster, and but a short way from Putney where you would have held your late debates. Were they not upon "An Agreement of the People?" There is good ale. There is an orchard, be it bare. We should sit and be at peace, Ned, and talk, as old men are given to talk. And remember. What times we have seen.

Your humble servant and cousin,
Will

William Harvey, Doctor of Physic

Remember This

They were married now and had been told they should make
their wills, as if that was the next step in life, so one day they
went together to see a solicitor, Mr. Reeves. He was not as they'd
expected. He was soft-spoken, silver-haired and kindly. He smiled
at them as if he'd never before met such a sweet newly married
young couple, so plainly in love yet so sensibly doing the right
thing. He was more like a vicar than a solicitor, and later Nick
and Lisa shared the thought that they'd wished Mr. Reeves had
actually married them. Going to see him was in fact not unlike
getting married. It had the same mixture of solemnity and giggly
disbelief—are we really doing this?—the same feeling of being a
child in adult's clothing.

They'd thought it might be a rather grim process. You can't
make a will without thinking about death, even when you're
twenty-four and twenty-five. They'd thought Mr. Reeves might be
hard going. But he was so nice. He gently steered them through
the delicate business of making provision for their dying together,
or with the briefest of gaps in between. "In a car accident say," he
said, with an apologetic smile. That was like contemplating death
indeed, that was like saying they might die tomorrow.

But they got through it. And, all in all, the fact of having
drafted your last will and testament and having left all your
worldly possessions—pending children—to your spouse was

every bit as significant and as enduring a commitment as a wedding. Perhaps even more so.

And then there was something . . . Something.

Though it was a twelve-noon appointment and wouldn't take long, they'd both taken the day off and, without discussing it but simultaneously, dressed quite smartly, as if for a job interview. Nick wore a suit and tie. Lisa wore a short black jacket, a dark red blouse and a black skirt which, though formal, was also eye-catchingly clingy. They both knew that if they'd turned up at Mr. Reeves' office in jeans and T-shirts it wouldn't have particularly mattered—he was only a high street solicitor. On the other hand this was hardly an everyday event, for them at least. They both felt that certain occasions required an element of ceremony, even of celebration. Though could you celebrate making a will?

In any case, if just for themselves, they'd dressed up a bit, and perhaps Mr. Reeves had simply been taken by the way they'd done this. Thus he'd smiled at them as if, so it seemed to them, he was going to consecrate their marriage all over again.

It was a bright and balmy May morning, so they walked across the common. There was no point in driving (and when Mr. Reeves said that thing about a car accident they were glad they hadn't). There was no one else to think about, really, except themselves and their as yet unmet solicitor. As they walked they linked arms or held hands, or Nick's hand would wander to pat Lisa's bottom in her slim black skirt. The big trees on the common were in their first vivid green and full of singing birds.

They were newly married, but it had seemed to make no essential difference. It was a "formality," as today was a formality. Formality was a lovely word, since it implied the existence of informality and even in some strange way gave its blessing to it. Nick let his palm travel and wondered if his glad freedom to let it do so was in any way altered, even enhanced, now that Lisa was his wife and not just Lisa.

Married or not, they were still at the stage of not being able to keep their hands off each other, even in public places. As they walked across the common to see Mr. Reeves, Nick found himself considering that this might only be a stage—a stage that would fade or even cease one day. They'd grow older and just get used to each other. They wouldn't just grow older, they'd age, they'd *die*. It was why they were doing what they were doing today. And it was the deal with marriage.

It seemed necessary to go down this terminal path of thought even as they walked in the sunshine. Nonetheless, he let his palm travel.

And in Mr. Reeves' office, though it was reassuring that Mr. Reeves was so nice, one thing that helped Nick, while they were told about the various circumstances in which they might die, was thinking about Lisa's arse and hearing the tiny slithery noises her skirt made whenever she shifted in her seat.

It was a beautiful morning, but he'd heard a mixed forecast and he'd brought an umbrella. Having your will done seemed, generally, like remembering to bring an umbrella.

When they came out—it took less than half an hour—the clouds had thickened, though the bright patches of sky seemed all the brighter. "Well, that's that," Nick said to Lisa, as if the whole thing deserved only a relieved shrug, though they both felt an oddly exhilarating sense of accomplishment. Lisa said, "Wasn't he *sweet*," and Nick agreed immediately, and they both felt also, released back into the spring air, a great sense of animal vitality.

There was a bloom upon them and perhaps Mr. Reeves couldn't be immune to it.

They retraced their steps, or rather took a longer route via the

White Lion on the edge of the common. It seemed appropriate, however illogical, after what they'd done, to have a drink. Yes, to celebrate. Lunch, a bottle of wine, why not? In fact, since they both knew that, above all, they were hungry and thirsty for each other, they settled for nothing more detaining than two prawn sandwiches and two glasses of Sauvignon. The sky, at the window, meanwhile turned distinctly threatening.

By the time they'd crossed back over the common the rain had begun, but Nick had the umbrella, under which it was necessary to huddle close together. As he put it up he had the fleeting thought that its stretched black folds were not unlike women's tight black skirts. He'd never before had this thought about umbrellas, only the usual thoughts—that they were like bats' wings or that they were vaguely funereal—and this was like other thoughts and words that came into his head on this day, almost as if newly invented. It was a bit like the word "kindly" suddenly presenting itself as the exact word to describe Mr. Reeves.

As they turned the corner of their street it began to pelt down and they broke into a run. Inside, in the hallway, they stood and panted a little. It was dark and clammy and with the rain beating outside a little like being inside a drum. They climbed the stairs to their flat, Lisa going first. Nick had an erection and the words "stair rods" came into his mind.

It was barely two o'clock and the lower of the two flats was empty. Nick thought—though very quickly, since his thoughts were really elsewhere—of how incredibly lucky they were to be who they were and to have a flat of their own to go to on a rainy afternoon. It was supposed to be a "starter home" and they owed it largely to Lisa's dad. It was supposed to be a first stage. He thought of stages again, if less bleakly this time. Everything in life could be viewed as a stage, leading to other stages and to having things you didn't yet have. But right now he felt they had everything, the best life could bring. What more could you want? And they'd even made their wills.

He'd hardly dropped the sopping umbrella into the kitchen sink than they were both, by inevitable progression, in the bedroom, and he'd hardly removed his jacket and pulled across the curtains than Lisa had unbuttoned her red blouse. She'd let him unzip her skirt, she knew how he liked to.

It rained all afternoon and kept raining, if not so hard, through the evening. They both slept a bit, then got up, picked up the clothes they'd hastily shed, and thought about going for a pizza. But it was still wet and they didn't want to break the strange spell of the day or fail to repeat, later, the manner of their return in the early afternoon. It seemed, too, that they might destroy the mood if they went out dressed in anything less special than what they'd worn earlier. But just for a pizza?

So—going to the other extreme they took a shared bath, put on bathrobes, and settled for Welsh rarebit. They opened the only bottle of wine they had, a Rioja that someone had once brought them. They found a red twisty candle left over from Christmas. They put on a favourite CD. Outside, the rain persisted and darkness, though it was May, came early. The candle flame and their white-robed bodies loomed in the kitchen window.

Why this day had become so special, a day of celebration, of formality mixed with its flagrant opposite, neither of them could have said exactly. It happened. Having eaten and having drunk only half the bottle, it seemed natural to drift back to bed, less hurriedly this time, to make love again more lingeringly.

Then they lay awake a long time holding each other, talking and listening to the rain in the gutters and to the occasional slosh of a car outside. They talked about Mr. Reeves. They wondered what it was precisely that had made him so sweet. They wondered if he was happily married and had a family, a grown-up family. Surely he would have all those things. They wondered how he'd met Mrs. Reeves—they decided her name was Sylvia—and what she was like. They wondered if he'd been perhaps a little jealous of their own youth or just, in his gracious way, gladdened by it.

They wondered if he found wills merely routine or if he could be occasionally stopped short by the very idea of two absurdly young people making decisions about death. He must have made his own will. Surely—a good one. They wondered if a good aim in life might simply be to become like Mr. Reeves, gentle, courteous and benign. Of course, that could only really apply to Nick, not to Lisa.

Then Lisa fell asleep and Nick lay awake still holding her and thinking. He thought: What is Mr. Reeves doing now? Is he in bed with Mrs. Reeves—with Sylvia? He wondered if when Mr. Reeves had talked to them in his office he'd had any idea of how the two of them, his clients (and that was a strange word and a strange thing to be), would spend the rest of the day. He hoped Mr. Reeves had had an inkling.

He wondered if he really might become like Mr. Reeves when he was older. If he too would have (still plentiful and handsome) silver hair.

Then he forgot Mr. Reeves altogether and the overwhelming thought came to him: Remember this, remember this. Remember this always. Whatever comes, remember this.

He was so smitten by the need to honour and consummate this thought that even as he held Lisa in his arms his chest felt full and he couldn't prevent his eyes suddenly welling. When Lisa slept she sometimes unknowingly nuzzled him, like some small creature pressing against its mother. She did this now, as if she might have quickly licked the skin at the base of his neck.

He was wide awake. Remember this. He couldn't sleep and he didn't want to sleep. The grotesque thought came to him that he'd just made his last will and testament, so he could die now, it was all right to die. This might be his deathbed and this, with Lisa in his arms, might be called dying happy—surely it could be called dying happy—the very thing that no will or testament, no matter how prudent its provisions, could guarantee.

But no, of course not! He clasped Lisa, almost wanting to wake her, afraid of his thought.

Of course not! He was alive and happy, intensely alive and happy. Then he had the thought that though he'd drafted his last testament it was not in any real sense a testament, it was not even *his* testament. It was only a testament about the minor matter of his possessions and what should become of them when he was no more. But it was not the real testament of his life, its stuff, its story. It was not a testament at all to how he was feeling *now*.

How strange that people solemnly drew up and signed these crucial documents that were really about their non-existence, and didn't draw up anything—there wasn't even a word for such a thing—that testified to their existence.

Then he realised that in all his time of knowing her he'd never written a love letter to this woman, Lisa, who was sleeping in his arms. Though he loved her completely, more than words could say—which was perhaps the simple reason why he'd never written such a thing. Love letters were classically composed to woo and to win, they were a means of getting what you didn't have. What didn't he have? Perhaps they were just silly wordy exercises anyway. He hardly wrote letters at all, let alone love letters, he hardly *wrote* anything. He wouldn't be any good at it.

And yet. And yet the need to write his wife a love letter assailed him. Not just a random letter that might, in theory, be one among many, but *the* letter, the letter that would declare to her once and for all how much he loved her and why. So it would be there always for her, as enduring as a will. The testament of his love, and thus of his life. The testament of how his heart had been full one rainy night in May when he was twenty-five. He would not need to write any other.

So overpowering was this thought that eventually he disengaged his arms gently from Lisa and got out of bed. He put on his bathrobe and went into the kitchen. There was the lingering smell of toasted cheese and there was the unfinished bottle of wine. They possessed no good-quality notepaper, unless Lisa had a private stash, but there was a box of A4 by the computer in the spare room and he went in and took a couple of sheets and found a blue roller-ball pen. He'd never had a fountain pen or used real ink, but he felt quite sure that this thing had to be handwritten, it would not be the thing it should be otherwise. He'd noticed that Mr. Reeves had a very handsome fountain pen. Black and gold. No doubt a gift from Sylvia.

He returned to the kitchen, poured a little wine and very quickly wrote, so it seemed like a direct release of the thickness in his chest:

My darling Lisa,

One day you walked into my life and I never thought something so wonderful could ever happen to me. You are the love of my life . . .

The words came so quickly and readily that, not being a writer of any kind, he was surprised by his sudden ability. They were so right and complete and he didn't want to alter any of them. Though they were just the beginning.

But no more words came. Or it seemed that there were a number of directions he might take, in each of which certain words might follow, but he didn't know which one to choose, and didn't want, by choosing, to exclude the others. He wanted to go in all directions, he wanted a totality. He wanted to set down every single thing he loved about his wife, every moment he'd loved sharing with her—which was almost *every* moment— including of course every moment of this day that had passed:

the walk across the common, the rain, her red blouse, her black skirt, the small slithery sounds she made sitting in a solicitor's office, which of course were the sounds any woman might make shifting position in a tight skirt, but the important thing was that *she* was making them. She was making them even as she made her will, or rather as they made *their* wills, which were really only wills to each other.

But he realised that if he went into such detail the letter would need many pages. Perhaps it would be better simply to say, "I love everything about you. I love all of you. I love every moment spent with you." But these phrases, on the other hand, though true, seemed bland. They might be said of anyone by anyone.

Then again, if he embarked on the route of detail, the letter could hardly all be written now. It would need to be a thing of stages—stages!—reflecting their continuing life together and incorporating all the new things he found to commemorate. That would mean that it would be all right if he wrote no more now, he could pick it up later. And he'd written the most important thing, the beginning. But then if he picked it up later, it might become an immense labour—if truly a labour of love—a labour of years. There'd be the question: When would he stop, when would he bring it to its conclusion and deliver it?

A love letter was useless unless it was delivered.

He'd hardly begun and already he saw these snags and complications, these reasons why this passionate undertaking might fail. And he couldn't even think of the next thing to say. Then the words that he'd said to himself silently in his head, even as he held Lisa in his arms, rushed to him, as the very words he should write to her now and the best way of continuing:

I never thought something so wonderful could happen to me. You are the love of my life. Remember this always. Whatever comes, remember this . . .

Adding those words, in this way, made his chest tighten again and his eyes go prickly. And he wondered if that in itself was enough. It was entirely true to his feelings and to this moment. He should just put the date on it and sign it in some way and give it to Lisa the next morning. Yes, that was all he needed to do.

But though emotion was almost choking him, it suddenly seemed out of place—so big, if brief, a statement looking back at him from a kitchen table, with the smell of toasted cheese all around him. Suppose the mood tomorrow morning was quite different, suppose he faltered. Then again, that "whatever comes" seemed ominous, it seemed like tempting fate, it seemed when you followed it through even to be about catastrophe and death. It shouldn't be there at all perhaps. And yet it seemed the essence of the thing. "Whatever comes, remember this." That was the essence.

Then he reflected that the essence of love letters was that they were about separation. It was why they were needed in the first place. They were about yearning and longing and distance. But he wasn't separated from Lisa—unless being the other side of a wall counted as separation. He could be with her whenever he liked, as close to her as possible, he'd made love to her twice today. Though as he'd written those additional words, "whatever comes," he'd had the strange sensation of being a long way away from her, like a man in exile or on the eve of battle. It was what had brought the tears to his eyes.

In any case there it was. It was written. And what was he supposed to do with it? Just keep it? Keep it, but slip it in with the copy of his will—the "executed" copy—so that after his death Lisa would read it? Read what he'd written on the night after they'd made their wills. Is that what he intended?

And how did he know he would die *first*? He'd simply had that thought so it would enable Lisa to read the letter. But how did he know she wouldn't die first? And he didn't want to think about either of them dying, he didn't want to think of dying at all.

And even supposing Lisa read these words—these very words on this bit of paper!—after his death, wouldn't they in one undeniable and inescapable sense be too late? Though wouldn't that moment, after his death, be in another sense precisely the right moment?

Love letters are written out of separation.

He didn't know what to do. He'd written a love letter and it had only brought on this paralysis. But he couldn't cancel what he'd written. He folded the sheet of A4 and, returning to the spare room, found an envelope, on which he wrote Lisa's name, simply her name: Lisa. Without sealing the envelope, he put the letter in a safe and fairly secret place. There were no really secret places in the flat and he would have been glad to declare that he and Lisa had no secrets. Had the opportunity arisen, he might have done so to Mr. Reeves. But now—it was almost like some misdeed—there was this secret.

But he couldn't cancel it. Some things you can't cancel, they stare back at you. There was nothing experimental or feeble or lacking about those words. His heart had spilled over in them.

He went back to bed. He fitted himself against Lisa's body. She'd turned now onto her other side, away from his side of the bed, but she was fast asleep. He kissed the nape of her neck. He wanted to cradle her and protect her. Thoughts came to him that he might add to the letter, if he added to it. But the letter was surely already complete.

His penis stiffened, contentedly and undemandingly, against his wife. She knew nothing about it, or about his midnight session with pen and paper. He thought again about Mr. Reeves and about last wills and testaments. Pen. Penis. It was funny to think about the word penis and the word testament in the same breath, as it were. Words were strange things. He thought about the word "testicle."

The rain was still gurgling outside and whether it stopped before he fell asleep or he fell asleep first he didn't remember.

The truth is he did nothing with the letter the next morning. He might have propped it conspicuously, after sealing the envelope, on the kitchen table, but he didn't want to disturb the tender atmosphere that still lingered from yesterday, even though that same tenderness gave him his licence. Wouldn't the letter only endorse it? He felt a little cowardly, though why? For what he'd put in writing?

He looked adoringly, perhaps even rather pleadingly, at Lisa, as if she might have helped him in his dilemma. She looked slightly puzzled, but she also looked happy. She was hardly going to say, "Go on, give me the letter."

His line of thought to himself was still that the letter wasn't finished. Yes, he'd add to it later. It would be premature, at this point, to hand it over. Though he also knew there was no better point. And the moment was passing.

It was a Saturday morning. Outside, the rain had stopped, but a misty breath hung in the air, and over them hung still the curiously palpable, anointing fact that they were people who'd made their wills.

The truth is he could neither keep nor deliver, nor destroy, nor even resume the letter. It was simply there. Though he did keep it, by default. His hesitation over delivering it, a thing at first of just minutes and hours, became a prolonged, perennial reality, a thing of years, like his excuse that he'd continue it.

And one day, one bad day, he did, nearly, destroy it. It was a long time later, but the letter was still there, still as it was on that wet night in May, still in the envelope with the single word "Lisa" on it, but now like a piece of history.

And his will, now, would certainly need altering. But not yet. Not yet. He thought of destroying the letter. It had suddenly and almost accusingly come into his mind—that letter! But the thought of destroying a love letter seemed almost as melodramatic and sentimental as writing one.

How did you destroy a love letter? The only way was to burn it. The smell of Welsh rarebit reinvaded his nostrils. You found some ceremonial-looking dish and set light to the letter and watched it burn. Though the *real* way to burn a love letter was to fling it into a blazing fire and for good measure thrust a poker through it. And to do this you should really be sitting at a hearthside, rain at the window, in a long finely quilted silk dressing gown . . .

Then his chest filled and his eyes melted just as they'd done when he first penned the letter.

The truth is they separated. Then they needed lawyers, in duplicate, to decide on the settlement and on how the two children would be provided for. And, in due course, to draw up new wills. He didn't destroy the letter, and he didn't send it on finally to its intended recipient, as some last-ditch attempt to resolve matters and bring back the past, or even as some desperate act of guilt-inducement, of warped revenge. This would have betrayed its original impulse, and how hopeless anyway either gesture would have been. She might have thought it was all a fabrication, that he hadn't really written the letter on the 10th of May all those years ago—if so, why the hell hadn't he delivered it?—that he'd concocted it only yesterday. It was another, rather glaring, example of his general instability.

He didn't destroy it, he kept it. But not in the way he'd waveringly and wonderingly kept it for so many years. He kept it now only for himself. Who else was going to look at it?

Occasionally, he took it out and read it. He knew the words, of course, by heart, but it was important now and then, even on every 10th of May, to see them sitting on the paper. And when he looked at them it was like looking at his own face in the mirror, but not at a face that would obligingly and comfortingly replicate whatever he might do—wrinkle his nose, bare his teeth. It was a face that had found the separate power to smirk back at him when he wasn't smirking himself, and to have an expression in its eyes, which his own eyes could never have mustered, that said, "You fool, you poor sad fool."

The Best Days

⌒

Sean and Andy found themselves standing to one side of the steps up to the church, on the edge of the broad sweep of driveway. Now it seemed all right to do so, Sean took a pack of cigarettes from his jacket, took one out, then offered the pack in his usual abrupt way to Andy. They'd been together at Holmgate School just six years ago, then together at Wainwright's till it closed.

The hearse and a couple of following limousines had driven off, leaving the lingering, spreading spillage of a surprisingly large congregation—a "good turnout," as their former headmaster, Clive Davenport, had been apt to say about various other occasions. He was now in the hearse on his way to be cremated.

"She looks a right little whore," Andy said.

Sean said nothing. Then he said, breathing out smoke, "How many whores have you seen lately?"

They were referring to Karen Shield, who'd been at Holmgate with them, in the same year. Neither had seen her for some time, but she was recognisable and certainly noticeable.

It was a grey mild blustery afternoon in April and it had rained recently. There'd been a general standing solemnly and silently as the hearse departed, then one or two people had waved. Someone had called out, "Bye, Daffy!" and the atmosphere had broken. The new atmosphere was almost like gaiety. Everyone was freshly aware of being alive in the world and not dead in it and that they'd been involved in something dutiful but oddly animating. There were now many more waves, of recognition, much milling, hand-shaking, smiling and embracing and a good deal of sudden laughter. No one seemed to want to leave immediately.

As if to share the mood, the sun broke through a gap in the clouds and made the surface of the driveway gleam. To one side of the church, the big cedar, stirred by the breeze and with a sudden sparkle, shrugged off its burden of drops.

The news about Clive Davenport—felled by a heart attack only three years after retiring—had circulated quickly, along with tributes to the fact that he'd been head of Holmgate almost since it had opened. This accounted for the impressive gathering, which in turn had reassured many members of it who'd been uncertain about coming in the first place. Several generations of former staff and pupils were involved. Some present had few fond memories of Holmgate and had even once wished old Daffy dead, but the passage of time and the needs of the occasion had instilled an infectious makeshift nostalgia. Perhaps Daffy hadn't been such a bad headmaster. Perhaps life itself at Holmgate hadn't been so bad. Life after Holmgate hadn't always been so great.

Many had turned up simply to see who else would be there and how they were looking now. It was a way of satisfying that curiosity without having to sign up to any grim "reunion." But undoubtedly another motive for attending was having nothing better to do on a Thursday afternoon. It was unemployment.

St. Luke's, a big stone barn of a place, stood on a hillside, within a railed enclosure large enough to feel like a small public park. Below, a good portion of the town was visible, its rooftops wetly glinting. You could even make out, appropriately enough, the playing fields at Holmgate.

"Has she seen us?" Andy said. "Has she recognised us?"

"Doesn't look like it," Sean said. "Not yet."

Though in fact, inside the church, when he'd craned his head round, Sean had received a definite look of recognition, though it hadn't come from the woman (woman was now the word) Andy was speaking of. For a fraction of a second he'd wondered *who* it had come from.

"Well, shall we say hello?" Andy said, taking a drag. He had the stance he'd many times adopted, pint glass in hand, in bars on Friday nights. When Andy said "right little whore" he didn't necessarily mean it as a term of abuse or of rejection.

"If you want," Sean said, but made no move.

Andy had the bravado, Sean had the actual command, it was how it had always been. But—despite the description just given her—their record with Karen Shield at Holmgate was much the same. Neither had got very far.

Andy said, "Christ, is *that* her mother? Talking of whores."

Sean said softly, "Andy!" It was almost, strangely, a rebuke, as if he might have added, "You're in church." Except they weren't any more. And he could see Andy's point.

They were both dressed in cheap suits—their "interview suits." Many around them were similarly dressed, but there were also definite outbreaks, especially among the women, of something showy, even provocative. It was as if many of the former pupils of Mr. Davenport, in wishing to pay their respects, wanted also to demonstrate that they weren't at school any more, they hadn't turned into obedient little adults. Or else they wanted to prove to their peers, not seen for years, that they were still alive and kicking, they hadn't turned drab and sad.

Misery and grief had anyway driven off in the two family cars behind the hearse.

The group of four, less than thirty yards away, that Sean and Andy were eyeing consisted of Karen, her mother (it was her mother), her father and some chattering friend, of the parents' age, who'd intercepted them and was preventing them looking round, back towards the church. Sean was rather glad of this.

Karen wore nothing that wasn't in theory appropriate—it

couldn't be faulted on its colour—but what she was actually got up in was a pair of black ankle boots, dark tights, with a seam up the back, a tight shiny-black waist-length jacket, a black nonsense of a hat with some black gauze attached to it, and a short flouncy charcoal skirt with which the wind was now playing mischievously.

The extraordinary thing was that the mother was wearing an outfit that was almost identical—the boots, the seamed tights, the short skirt and flimsy headpiece. Her top was a little different, but if anything more tarty.

It was hard not to conclude that they'd conspired over it, even gone shopping together. If not, who had started the competition, who had copied whom? There might have been something fetching about it, if it had worked. But the big difference between them was that while the daughter got away with it—it was fancy dress, but she had the looks anyway—the mother, the other side of forty, was a sight. The daughter's hair was dark and glossy, the wind toying pleasingly with it too. The mother's hair was a brownish frizz, the face rounded, puffy and fairly smothered in make-up.

Strangely, neither woman at this moment seemed aware of the effect. They were both laughing at something the fourth person was saying. They now and then with exactly the same action curled their knuckles cutely round the hems of their skirts. They might have been two happy perky twin sisters.

The father was something else altogether. Beside the two women, he was an unredeemed scruff. No tie, not even a white shirt. His excuse might have been a blunt, "I don't dress up for funerals." Or, on this occasion, "He wasn't *my* headmaster." But his face, never mind the clothes, was a mess. It was podgy and red, the sun struck it harshly.

But he too was now laughing, as if experiencing some rush of joy or of cocky pride in his womenfolk. It was the face—both Sean and Andy could spot this even at a distance—of a man who'd been drunk when he arrived and who did his best to be drunk as often as he could.

"She looks a right old baggage," Andy said.

Sean didn't answer this at first. Then he chose to agree. "You can say that again."

"And is that her dad?"

"I suppose so."

"He looks shit-faced."

In any case the main attraction was Karen. Sean looked at her without voicing any opinion. Tart's clothes or not, the only right word was lovely. She'd been lovely at Holmgate too, in the last couple of years, though "lovely" wasn't in the vocabulary then. It wasn't in the vocabulary now, not with Andy Sykes around, but it was the right word.

And he was wishing Karen had worn something plainer—to curb her mum. He was also wishing that fourth person would stay there with them, so he and Andy (though Andy was clearly getting other ideas) could just slip away. They'd decided to turn up, for whatever mad reason. For a laugh? To do their duty by Daffy? What had he done for them? They'd come anyway, and now they could just clear off.

He'd tried it on, of course, with Karen at Holmgate. He wasn't the only one. How many had succeeded? Depending, of course, on what was meant by success. But he wasn't the only one to try. It seemed an age ago now, being fifteen or sixteen. It hadn't helped that he hadn't lost it yet, or not in the true sense, the big V. He didn't know if *she* had, for all the tease. The more she teased, in fact, the more he thought she hadn't. Then he'd think what would be better, for his chances? If she had, but he hadn't? If he had (theoretically), but she hadn't? If they both had? If they both hadn't?

He remembered it now, standing outside St. Luke's, all those possibilities running through his head. Had old Daffy been aware of it all—all going on like a sizzling pan under his nose?

One day he'd gone to Karen Shield's house in Derwent Road, carrying the school bag she'd left on the bus. It wasn't until he'd got up to get off himself, two stops later, that he'd noticed the bag lying on the seat up ahead. Otherwise, when she'd brushed past him (and she liked to brush) with Cheryl Hudson and Amina Khan he'd have grabbed her wrist and when she tugged back, said, "You've forgotten something."

But there it was, and he knew it was hers because it was a plastic imitation leopard-skin. How could anyone forget such a bag?

He never would.

So he'd got off at Thorpe Avenue, his stop, carrying two bags. Then everything had happened. It was all a gift. It was a gift that she'd left her bag. It was a gift that he'd been sitting on his own on the bus and not sitting with handy-Andy here. He hadn't known, yet, what kind of gift.

He could still see himself walking down Thorpe Avenue, coming to a decision, with two bags, one a somewhat embarrassing pretend leopard-skin. He could still see the October sun coming out from behind the clouds and smiling at him.

The proper thing would have been to phone Karen up and say, "I've got your bag. I can bring it round if you like." It would have earned him points and might have led to something. But it was just a bit too goody-goody and he didn't have her number. Though that might be in the bag. As might her *phone!*

Or: he might have taken the bag with him to school the next morning and said coolly, "Here's your bag." And then perhaps said, "I had a good look inside." He decided that this option had less going for it.

Though he did look inside, right there in Thorpe Avenue. Or rather he opened the flap and saw a label underneath saying "Karen Shield, Holmgate School." Then her home address. Well he'd known it was Derwent Road, on the Braithwaite Estate, and now he knew the number. But something about the label made him not delve any further. An odd primness came over him. It was like the label for some little girl much younger than and quite different from Karen Shield, and he didn't want to know about her.

His feet made the decision for him anyway. He turned and walked in the direction of the Braithwaite Estate. Two stops on the bus, but not so far on foot if you cut through the back streets.

Points from Karen, he calculated, and points from her mother, if she was there. If Karen's mother was there, then Karen couldn't be anything but nice and grateful to him, her mother would ensure it. But perhaps he was only thinking of Karen's mother being there to control his excitement about the possibility he really hoped for, of Karen being there all by herself, worrying about the bag she must have stupidly left on the bus.

He rang the bell at number fifteen and, after a pause, Karen's mother stood before him, blinking at him. Perhaps his disappointment was written on his face. But he had to go ahead.

"Mrs. Shield? I've got Karen's bag." He held it up like a piece of evidence. "She left it on the bus."

He noticed how she blinked and he noticed her red fingernails on the edge of the half-opened door. She stopped blinking and looked at him sternly.

"Who are you?" she said slowly, as if she might have just woken up.

"I'm a friend of Karen's. At Holmgate. Is Karen here?"

He'd peered in, towards a tiny hallway and the foot of a staircase. There was no sign or sound of anyone else.

But Karen's mother was undoubtedly Karen's mother. She was like a bigger version of Karen. She was wearing a smoky-coloured dress of a close-fitting but fluffy material. It went somehow with the red nails. The dress wasn't very long, and what he mostly noticed, as he tried to look beyond her, was her hip. As she stood holding the door one hip was hidden, but the other was pushed out. It was oddly alert. The idea of a hip, even the word "hip," seemed new to him. Strangely, it had never entered his mind when he thought of Karen.

"She's not here," Mrs. Shield said, still looking at him sternly. "Karen's not here." She said it so deliberately it almost sounded like a lie, but he felt sure himself now that Mrs. Shield was alone.

Karen had got off the bus less than half an hour ago, to go home. It was a mystery. And he was somehow now under suspicion, for his good deed.

"She goes round to Cheryl Hudson's most afternoons before she comes home," Mrs. Shield said. "God knows what they do there."

She looked at him as if this were something he should have known already, as if he should have gone himself to Cheryl Hudson's. (What went on there?) He felt put on the spot. It was like being called out to the front by a teacher. But Mrs. Shield didn't look like a teacher. And, though she was Karen's mother, she didn't really look like a mother.

"Have you got a name?"

"Sean."

"Sean who?"

"Sean Wheatley."

"And that's Karen's bag?"

It seemed a strange question, and even before he could answer she said, "I can see it's Karen's bag."

She looked at him searchingly. Her hands were still holding or rather fingering the edge of the door.

"Tell me something, Sean Wheatley. Did you come round here now to hand over Karen's bag, or did you come round here because you were really hoping to see Karen?"

It was a big question and he knew there was no ducking it.

He knew that Mrs. Shield would have spotted a false answer better than any teacher.

"Both, Mrs. Shield. Mainly to see Karen." She looked at him again for a long while.

"Well, you'd better come in and wait for her."

This was confusing. If Karen was round at Cheryl Hudson's, then how long was he going to have to wait? Did he want to wait? But he also somehow knew that just to have handed over the bag and left would have been a big mistake.

She shut the door behind him. There was the vague smell of what he thought of as "other people's house." It was different in every house and you could never work out exactly what it was made of. Part of it must be Mrs. Shield. Part of it must be Karen.

But, now the door was shut, Karen seemed suddenly far away, even though he was for the first time inside her home and he was holding her leopard-skin bag.

"Through here," Mrs. Shield said.

There was a small cluttered living room, like any living room, with a glass coffee table. He knew that quite often in other people's houses (sometimes in his own) there'd be a bottle of something, opened, on the coffee table, even in the afternoon. But he couldn't see any bottle. The telly was on with the sound down. She must have turned it down when she answered the door. The picture on the telly was weak because of the sunshine now streaming through the window. Outside, the clouds had completely dispersed.

He stood by the coffee table, politeness enveloping him, along with dazzling sunshine. He knew that you weren't supposed to sit in other people's houses till they asked you to.

"So, Sean—" she said, taking a breath. Then she stopped. "God, it's blinding in here, isn't it?"

She turned. It was the first time she'd moved suddenly and spontaneously, almost girlishly. She drew the curtains. They were a pale yellow and still let through a buttery glow. To close them, she put one knee on the sofa and reached up behind it. He saw an exposed heel and again, dominantly, her hips. Both this time.

As she turned back there was a flustered smile on her face at her own agility. It made her look younger and even less like a mother, certainly not the thirty-five or more she must have been.

She came right up close to where he still stood compliantly. The scent and breath of Mrs. Shield were suddenly all over him. There was no trace of drink that he could detect.

"So, Sean, how long have you been friends with Karen? I mean, friends, not just at school with her?"

But once again she didn't wait for him to answer. With one hand she pulled down his fly zip, then slipped the other hand inside, like a pickpocket stealing a wallet.

"Have you got an erection, Sean? Do you have one all the time?"

Then he was, in all senses, in her hands.

Silent seconds passed. There was the technical consideration: suppose Karen were to come home any moment now. But that seemed somehow irrelevant, or dealt with. Mrs. Shield plainly knew what she was doing, even as she deferentially asked him, "So what do you think we should do now, Sean? What do you think we should do? Perhaps you should put those bags down."

She kept her hand where it was while he did what she suggested.

"I think we should do the whole thing, don't you? The whole thing. Can you hang on?"

Hang on!

She took her hand away and, as nimbly as she'd managed the curtains, she left the room, then returned with a large white bath towel. She spread it on the sofa.

It was all done quickly. How could it not have been? Hang on!

But afterwards she'd had the goodness—if that was the right word—just to lie with him for a while, her arms round him, or perhaps it was more that his were round her. He'd felt his own slightness and her bigness—if that too was the right word. She was a fully formed complete woman, like no schoolgirl could ever be. He'd wanted to tell her this, but didn't know how, or if it would be wise. He'd wanted to thank her, to praise her, to express all his grateful amazement, but hadn't a clue how to do it. What he should have said—he knew it now, standing outside St. Luke's—was that she was lovely.

In the glow from the window he tried absurdly to work out his bearings. Which was east, which was west? Which way did the window face? Where was Craig Road, where he lived? Where was Holmgate School, the Town Hall, Tesco's, Skelby Moor? Minutes ago he'd been standing on a front doorstep, holding a leopard-skin bag. Less than an hour ago he'd been sitting on a number six bus.

Finally, as if a timer had registered the appropriate interval, she moved, loosened their mutual grip, kissed him, just a peck, on the cheek and made it clear they should tidy themselves up.

Had she done this before? Was she in the habit of doing it? It was certain that she knew he'd never done anything like it before, just as it was certain that he'd never do, at least in one sense, anything like it again.

"Now," she said before he left, her stern face back again, "you don't breathe a word of this." And while he gravely nodded and she looked into his depths, she added, "More than your life's worth if you do."

Then she said, "Don't forget *your* bag. The name's Deborah, by the way. Since you ask."

He realised later that she'd effectively vetoed his going any further with Karen. She'd simultaneously equipped and unequipped him. He looked at Karen now with something like pity.

.   .   .

The sun shone on the wet driveway. That fourth person, who-ever he was, seemed to be moving on. The remaining three now turned to look around and a hand suddenly went to cover the daughter's mouth in a show of recognition and surprise. Her eyes widened. She took away the hand and, at that distance, they half heard, half lip-read her words.

"Well, well, look who's here!"

She was making such a thing of it that he didn't notice the look on the mother's face. Or he didn't want to look at the mother's face, daubed with all that slap. Or at the father's. Karen's face was the only one you wanted to look at.

The mother. He knew her name.

And now all three of them were walking directly towards them and Andy was saying, flicking at his cigarette, "Well, I don't like yours much."

He didn't want to look at her, but he wished there were some secret sign he might nonetheless make, without the need to catch her eye, to indicate that he'd never told anyone, not at Holmgate, not at Wainwright's. Other blokes might have done, sooner or later. "I banged her mother." He'd never breathed a word. Least of all to his best mate Andy Sykes here, goggling like a prat.

Some sign. So at least she wouldn't feel humiliated on that score. Only on the score of looking a mess—a dressed-up, painted-over mess, which made it worse. But maybe she really didn't know that. Maybe she thought she looked the image of her daughter.

He wasn't sure at all how he was going to manage this. It was cowardice not to look at her. Were they going to have to do all that hand-shaking stuff, the hugging and kissing, the strange grown-up but childish lovey-dovey stuff that was going on all around them?

"She looks a right dog, doesn't she?"

"Shut up, Andy, they'll hear." Just for a moment he hated Andy.

"Where-as!" Andy was preening himself, wriggling his shoulders. "And she's not *with* anyone, is she?"

He looked at the father. *He* can't ever have known, or he'd have known, himself, big-time. And Karen can't ever have known, he was sure of that. Or she wouldn't be acting so full-on now.

Just for a moment, as she drew close, he hated Karen Shield too. Intensely. For looking fantastic and making a fool of her mum.

"Ooo-ooo!" Andy was saying, clearly about Karen. Then he said, "Is that really her mother?"

"Yes," he replied with an authority he didn't like. He dropped his cigarette end and trod on it. "So, Andy boy," he said, "let it be a lesson to you."

He had to say it quickly, under his breath, with no time to explain what he meant—if he knew what he meant. Though he thought, rapidly and cruelly, of what he might have gone on to say.

Karen was upon them, in her silly irresistible hat.

"Sean Wheatley and Andy Sykes! Still together after all these years!"

He'd always been a jump or two ahead of Andy; now he felt he might be twice Andy's age. He almost felt he might be like old Daffy, up there on the stage at morning assembly, telling them all what was good for them, telling them what the future held.

"Have you got an erection, Sean?" He'd hear those words on his dying day.

Karen was opening her arms as if she meant to enfold them both like lost sons.

"You run after them, Andy boy"—this is what he might have said—"you get the hots for them and you have your wicked way with them and then you end up marrying them. And then years down the road, look what you get. So—let it be a lesson to you."

Half a Loaf

Half a loaf. Not even that.

She has gone again. She's stayed the night and she's gone again. But part of "my time," as I think of it—I don't ever dare think of it as "our time"—is the time it takes for her to walk from the front step to the street corner, no more than a minute, the time in which I watch her, getting smaller, from the angle of the bay window. She never looks back. Perhaps she guesses that I watch her. I've never told her. To tell her would be to give her ammunition—for my eventual destruction. It's coming one day. Of course it is.

Don't give her ammunition. But then if you make out you're calm, you're equable, you will only give her the excuse she needs.

Her name is Tanya. Even to watch her walking away is something. And it's a kind of training—but I don't dwell on that. You've drunk the glass, I tell myself, till it's filled next time, but there's still this last drop. Don't waste it.

I stand at the window. It's a quiet street. She crosses it at a long, oblique, efficient angle, between the parked cars, then at the main road she disappears, but I stand perhaps for a minute more, as if I can see through walls. Just to imagine her walking along a pavement, descending into the Tube is something. Just to imagine her being in the world is something, and may be all I'll have one day, any day now.

She disappears, but I don't move. In my head already is a picture of a woman in a red coat, sitting in a Tube train. She's the woman you notice as soon as you get in, and you can't keep your eyes off her. This is true for all the men in the carriage, but I don't think of the other men. She sits as if she's entirely unaware of this swamp of attention, as if she'd be surprised, embarrassed if you put even the possibility to her. She sits as if she's also completely, nonchalantly aware of it, as if it goes with being alive. I want to reach out and touch her, but not as a young man would. I want to put my hand on the crown of her head and say, "Stay as you are, always. May no harm ever come to you." How absurd, when she has the power to destroy me.

Half a loaf? But isn't this life, the whole of it? Shouldn't I be thanking, praising heaven?

My mother used to say, "All good things come to an end." Perhaps all mothers say it. As if the worst harm she foresaw for me was the tragedy of good stuff not being constantly on tap. Lucky little brat. But she must have seen the look of abject misery on my face whenever some seaside holiday or just some happy sunny day approached its end.

There it is, there it isn't. Now you see it, now you don't. But now I know it's not as simple as that. Thank heaven.

My father was a churchman, a man of God. In the war he was an RAF padre. It wasn't a get-out card, he flew on missions too. But when others broke down, he couldn't. He had to be their comfort. He never talked about it much, but once he said, "Believe me, Eric, a lot of praying went on, and it had nothing to do with me."

When I grew up, because of my father, I used to think a lot of good things were bad things—or rather I secretly thought a lot of bad things were good. At any rate I thought: One day God will punish me, he'll surely punish me. And he'll surely punish me for not believing in him.

But he never did punish me. And meanwhile my mother

dispensed her regular balm: "All good things come to an end." I sometimes wondered if she too really believed in God.

But look at me now, looking at someone who's no longer there, and rehearsing a silent prayer: Please, God, let there be another time, another week. And what would my dead father think if—as God is supposed to do—he could see my every action and could see me, as I may do very soon, go up to the bedroom to touch the still-wrinkled, faintly warm sheets. To pick up a pillow and press it to my face.

I'm an osteopath. It's my business to lay hands on people, to manipulate them, both men and women. But never, ever. Until now. There are walks of life—university lecturers, osteopaths— that must arouse the particular fears of wives, but my wife, Anthea, never had reason, nor, having Anthea, did I. I'm not unaware—this is only alertness, not vanity—that there are certain female patients, perhaps male ones too, who come to me not exactly for their back problems. But I'm saved by the clock, by the session. Time's up—till the next time. And of course it's in my power to say (all good things) there won't be any next time.

But my wife died. Nearly three years ago. It was neurological. My field can border on the neurological, but I'm not a neurologist and there was nothing I could do for her. Nor, as it turned out, anything that neurologists could do for her either.

I wanted to die. I won't pretend. I wanted to die even before she died—to be spared the fact of her death. I prayed. And after her death I wanted to die, and prayed that I might, even more.

My life was over, I went through the motions. One, two years. To steady myself, I thought of my parents, I thought of them getting through the war. All bad things. No one ever says that. My father died fifteen years ago, and my mother barely six months afterwards. There were medical reasons, but I think she died simply of my father's death. And I wanted something similar for myself. I waited for it, willed it to happen, but I'm of sound health.

I came close to making it happen, but I'm also a coward.

Then there was Tanya. Or put it another way: I had a mental breakdown. Certainly a professional breakdown.

Lower-back pain. There's so much of it about. I bless her lower-back pain. I bless her lower back. I bless the fact that in one so young it was something readily curable, and I could cure it. I could be her magician. *Her* magician!

"There," I said, "that seems to have done it."

And then suddenly there were tears running down my face because of the sheer delight on her face at having been so simply, quickly cured—there'd even been a little click—and at having been spared, or so I'd vouched, only more pain and interminable waiting on the NHS.

And because she was the most beautiful creature I'd ever seen and in a moment, if I wasn't careful, I might say so. And because I was having a mental breakdown . . .

And because if Anthea was watching me, as God is supposed to watch, I thought she might not wish to punish me, or even reproach me. She might even be thinking: About time, Eric, about time something like this happened. I'm even glad for you that it's happening. Go on, Eric, seize what you can.

The truth is I didn't even *think* this. I'm sure that I heard Anthea actually saying in my ear, "Now I won't have to worry, Eric, and grieve for you so much. But for God's sake stop blubbering, stop making a complete spectacle of yourself. It's life, it's happening. And you're not a complete spectacle, you're still a good-looking man. I'm frankly surprised, Eric—but I'm glad too—that nothing like this ever happened when I was alive. But you're a free man now. I'm dead, you're not. Go on, don't be a bloody coward."

All this as if she were at my shoulder, while in fact cowardly tears were rolling down my face and a partially unclad woman of extraordinary health and beauty and less than half my age was still perched on my couch, and I was saying, "I'm sorry, I'm terribly sorry. I was thinking of my wife—my late wife. I'm most terribly sorry. But your problem is cured. You really don't have to see me again, but—but would you, could you do me the honour" (and where did I get that phrase from?) "of having dinner with me tonight?"

I didn't delude myself that she really thought—in spite of that click—that I was Mr. Magic. With a face full of tears? Perhaps for some women charm, if I have any, is well mixed with a little vulnerability. But this was hardly vulnerability, or a little of it.

Was it naked bribery? A performance I'd somehow mustered? I don't care. Was I about to say (some men must do this sort of thing all the time), "If you'll have dinner with me I'll forget the fee?" Or was I, before she could answer, about to cut my own legs from under me by saying, "I'm most frightfully sorry, but please forget all this, forget it ever happened?"

The fact is she said with a simple, quick, uncomplicated smile, "I'd be happy to." The fact is she took the box of Kleenex that I keep ready for the occasional upset patient (I'm not unfamiliar with the psychosomatic) and held a bunch of them out to me. "Here," she said.

The fact is we had dinner that evening at Zeppo's, the very place where I used to go with Anthea and where I still had the thought: Anthea is willing me on, this is all under her aegis. And it was Anthea who'd surely warned me in the hours beforehand: Don't go for somewhere you think is *her* kind of place, a *young* place, don't be an idiot. Stick to what you know.

And the plain fact is that she—that is, Tanya—left my bedroom (my bedroom!) early the following morning, to return home, then to go to work. It was not yet seven. Breakfast wasn't wanted. And I thought: Of course—she's leaving, she's going, that's that. But as she made her exit, urging me not to get up, I asked the ridiculous and doomed question, "Will I see you again?" And she said, with that same uncloudy voice, "Why not?"

I never thought to see it. A pale young body slipping through the dimness of my bedroom, like some creature glimpsed in a forest.

And of course I got up. Of course I went down, in my dressing gown, and stood, as I'm standing now, at the window. If only to tell myself that this was my home and this had really happened.

Half a loaf? So it has continued now for nearly two months. I'm not blind. I'm not, actually, foolish. It can't last. Two months is already beyond any due allowance—whatever that might be. Is it pity? Charity? Amusement? Curiosity? I don't mind. I don't ask. So long as she comes. She has the power to destroy me at any moment, and maybe that in itself is the reason why she comes: the thrill of having another human soul dangling from her fingertips—a thrill that in one so young (she's twenty-six) isn't hampered by conscience, but a thrill that can only be consummated once, then it's gone. One day she will open her fingers. There! Like the click of a bone in her back.

I don't dare believe that she comes because of something I give her. What could that possibly be? Something that she takes from me and can't find elsewhere, and is worth at least one stray, but now almost routine, night out of seven? I know she has a boyfriend—a regular boyfriend. His name is Nathan. I don't ask, I don't picture. But she talks about him freely and unprompted, which makes me think she must talk in the same way to him about me. There have been no repercussions, no phone calls, no dramas. I don't know how it works with Nathan, this piece of her life with me, a man over twice her age. Maybe he thinks: If that's the deal . . . don't rock the boat. I'd think the same perhaps, if I were him. Maybe he thinks: Half a loaf. Or, in his case, just the one slice that's missing.

Tanya.

Only she knows. Or perhaps she doesn't. She looks at me sometimes with a clear, clean gaze as if she wouldn't know how to question, to examine anything. She looks at objects in my house, pictures on the wall, as if she wouldn't know how such things, such collections are assembled. I long ago began to accept, though I was young once, that the young are a mystery, a different species. But people are a mystery, period. You can understand, even correct their bone structure—everyone comes with a skeleton—but where does that begin to get you?

It can't be because she's still grateful for her back. Her back! It will be the last thing, standing like this one day, I'll see of her.

I don't talk to her about Anthea. I don't tell her the stories behind those objects she so vacantly inspects. I'm like my father not talking about the war. You don't want to know. She doesn't ask.

And so I don't tell her this very strangest thing, that's been true now for nearly two months (and how would it help me to tell it?): that when she's present, so too is my wife. That it's only been since all this began that I've felt my wife come back to me, after three years, as if (it sometimes really seems like this) she'd never gone.

It's all right, Eric, it's all right that this is happening. I feel her at my shoulder right now, by the window. I hear her even saying, "I hope she comes back."

Half a loaf? But surely it's the whole thing, it's everything. And I wouldn't mind if it were only a crust. I'd be as joyous, as terrified, as grateful. Some men in my bereft situation might eventually resort to prostitutes, doing so perhaps with much agony and shame, and wanting less to perform or have performed upon them certain acts than to have the simple proximity of warm female flesh. They come perhaps to some sad weekly addictive arrangement.

It's not like that with me, though I can see it has a semblance. I don't pay her, I don't offer her anything, except dinner. Nonetheless, if it were needed—a crust!—I'd empty my wallet every time.

From where I stand right now I can see the brass plate on the white stucco by the front porch (Anthea used to say it made us look like an embassy) that tells me who I am and what I do. I sometimes make bad things come to an end. It's sometimes been my professional pleasure and privilege to watch people leave me, who I'll never see again, who suddenly feel alive again "in their very bones."

She sits in a Tube train, no longer having to sit with care because of the pain in her back. But that's a thing of the past now, she can't even remember perhaps what it was like. Twenty-six is less than half my age, but not so young that she can afford to follow any strange, diverting path indefinitely. Not so young that, wanting to end it, she might lack the courage or heartlessness to do so.

I know it will end, of course it will end. The day will come. And when it comes I know one other terrible thing for certain. This sense that Anthea is with me and is glad for me, even egging me on, this sense that I'm wrapped in her generosity and that she no longer has to mourn for me, locked out here in the cold zone of life—that too will be gone. I won't feel her presence, won't hear her voice in my ear. I'll be just another lost, dutiful man going once a week to mutter words to a stone and getting no words back.

Saving Grace

⌒

Dr. Shah had never ceased to tell the story. "I'm as British as you are," he might begin. "I was born in Battersea." Or, more challengingly: "My mother is as white as you. You don't believe me?"

In his early days in medicine, even though by then the National Health had become awash (it was his own word) with black and brown faces, it was not uncommon for patients to cut up rough at being treated by an Asian, or an Asian-looking, doctor. Such a thing could still happen, but now his seniority, his reputation as a top consultant and his winning smile usually banished any trouble. But the story was still there, the chapter and verse of it, or just his satisfaction at relating it once again.

He tended to tell it these days, since it really required time and leisure, during follow-up sessions when the patient might be well on the mend, and in the half-hour slot there'd be little else to discuss. He'd even come to regard it as simply his way of bidding patients farewell. A final prescription. Though it had nothing to do in any clinical sense with cardiology.

"No, I've never been to India. Perhaps I never shall. But my father was born in India . . ."

It had lost none of its force, especially now his father was dead and he and his mother were sharing their mourning. Less than a year ago he'd embraced his father, so far as that was possible given his pitiful condition, for the last time. He'd held him close and had the fleeting bizarre thought that he was also holding India. He'd said to his mother, "They're making him comfortable, making him ready, he won't feel any pain."

His father wasn't his patient, but of course Dr. Shah knew about such things. For a moment he'd quite forgotten that his mother (it was very much part of the story) had once long ago been a nurse.

As a medical man he should have been protected against grief, but he wasn't surprised by how much now it overtook him, by how much he still felt, even after several months, the non-medical mystery of his father's absence.

"My father was born in India," he'd say, "in Poona, in 1925. All this will seem like ancient history, I'm sure. In those days of course the British ruled. *We* ruled." Dr. Shah would smile his smile. "He was born into one of those families who revered the British. He had an education that was better than that of many boys born at the same time in Birmingham or Bradford. Or Battersea. And spoke better English too."

The smile would only widen.

"Yes, I know, there were many Indians who didn't revere the British. Quite the opposite. But when the war broke out in 1939 there was no question that my father, when he came of age, would sign up with the Indian Army to fight for the British in their war. There were many Indians who felt differently. There were many Indians who wanted to fight against the British. But of course I had no say in these things, I wasn't even around. My father's name was Ranjit. As you know, that's my name too.

"So one day he found himself on a troopship bound for Italy, which was where most of the Indian soldiers who came to Europe went. The fact is I might have been Italian, I might be telling you this in Naples or Rome. Think of that.

"But because of some mishap of war—they had to switch ships—my father's unit ended up in England, in the spring of 1944, and it was decided that instead of shipping them all the way back to Italy they should be trained up for the invasion of France."

Dr. Shah would seem to wait a moment, as if to let his story catch up with him.

"England. A camp in Dorset to be precise, not far from Sturminster Newton. The truth is my father couldn't believe his luck. He'd grown up worshipping everything English. He spoke English, good English, not Italian. And there he was in the English countryside, in spring—thatched cottages, primroses, bluebells, everything he'd only read about in books. He even got himself a bicycle and whizzed round the lanes."

Dr. Shah would give a sympathetic shrug.

"No, I don't quite fully believe it either. I don't believe it can have been all fun for a bunch of Indian soldiers in Dorset in 1944. Just think about it. But I'm only telling you what my father told me. He called it luck.

"It wasn't the only piece of luck either, though you might think this next piece of luck wasn't any kind of luck at all. He took part in D-Day. He was one of very few Indian soldiers who did so. He served the British in their war. To the utmost, you might say. He was on that big fleet of ships. But he was very soon on a ship coming back, and very soon after that he was in a ward in a hospital here in London, commandeered by the Army, where all the patients had serious wounds to the leg, or legs.

"I don't know the details. It was somewhere in Normandy, not far from the beaches. I'm not sure he knew himself. All he'd say was, 'I was blown up.' Once he said, 'I was blown up and I thought I was dead.' And he went a little further still. 'I thought I'd been blown to pieces,' he said, 'and had come back together again as somebody else.' That's not physiologically possible, of course. I can't comment on that as a medical man. But then—we transplant hearts."

Dr. Shah would smile.

"He was in the leg unit, or more plainly the amputation

unit, though no one, I suppose, would have called it that. The only saving grace was that it might have been better to have a leg removed there than back in the thick of things in France. Though sometimes, I believe, it's important to amputate a leg fast. But the crucial fact is that he was the only Indian man, the only brown man, occupying any of the beds. Not a saving grace you might think, but wait.

"I've never amputated a leg. It's not my field, as you know. But anyone knows it's an extreme procedure, if sometimes the only way of saving life. And I'm talking about over sixty years ago and about patients who might have had other complicated injuries too. In short, not every amputee would have survived and every man on that ward would have known the risks.

"My father once showed me a photograph when I was a boy. It was of three men in pyjamas, in wheelchairs, all of them missing a leg. But all of them smiling, as if they were pleased with their stumps. It was a rather scary photograph to show a small boy, but my father wanted me to see it. He told me the men were some of his 'old pals.' Then he told me that if ever I should feel disadvantaged in life I should remember his old pals. 'Disadvantaged.' That was his actual word. It was a big word for a small boy, but I remember it clearly."

Dr. Shah's smile would broaden again and his listener might think—as he or she was perhaps meant to think—that "disadvantaged" sat strangely on the lips of a senior consultant in an expensive pinstriped suit.

"I used to think that the smiles on the faces of those amputees were a bit like my father saying he'd had the time of his life in Dorset. Anyway there was another photograph of him and his bicycle, and he's smiling in that. You need two legs to ride a bicycle.

"Working on the leg unit there were of course doctors, surgeons, nurses. One of the nurses was called Nurse Watts, but my father would get to know her as Rosie. And I would get to know her as my mother. One day, apparently, my father asked her if her family had kept a newspaper announcing the news of D-Day. Many families kept such a thing. Could she bring it in to show him? He wanted proof that he'd been part of history. But it was the start of something else.

"Working on the leg unit too was a doctor, a doctor and assistant surgeon—only a junior, not the top man at all—who discreetly let it be known to a few of the men that if they let him 'do' them he could save their leg. Also of course, by implication, their life.

"Quite an offer, you might think. But so far not a single patient had signed up to it. It wasn't that he was only a junior. The simple reason was that the man's name was Chaudhry and he was a brown-skinned doctor. From Bombay. From Mumbai. He too had come from India to serve the British, in a medical capacity. And they—the other patients, I mean—didn't want his brown fingers meddling with them. In fact there was even a sort of soldiers' pact among them that the brown doctor's offer should be refused.

"Silly fools."

Dr. Shah would leave a well-rehearsed pause at this point.

"But you can imagine that the position and response of my father was rather different."

There'd be another pause, almost as if he had come to the end.

"I hardly need to tell you, do I? The others underwent their amputations, successfully or not, but my father's leg was saved. After a while he was even able to walk again, almost as easily as he'd always done. He had a very slight limp and—or so he liked to say—perhaps a few tiny grains of metal still inside him, courtesy of Krupp's. But that's not all. His relations with Nurse Watts—with Rosie, my mother—had meanwhile reached a point where they both clearly wanted to take things further. Against all the odds. To take them further, in fact, for the rest of their lives.

"You can imagine it, can't you? All those men with their

stumps. It wasn't just their legs they'd lost, was it? They'd lost out on something else. And there were Ranjit and Rosie, like two turtle doves. As my father put it, he got his leg and he got the girl too. Now do you see why he talked about his luck?"

Dr. Shah would sometimes leave things there. It was the simple version and it was enough. He'd only add, "And that's how I came to be born in Battersea, in 1948." He'd leave a pause and look closely but disclaimingly at his patient. "No, my field isn't genetics either, and I can't explain it, but it's how I came out."

But if he wished to tell the longer and fuller version, he'd go on.

"Imagine it. London, Battersea. At the end of a war. Against all the odds. But my mother always said there were no two ways about it. Ranjit was the one. And if she could fall in love with a man with his body all smashed up and the possibility that he'd lose a leg, then wasn't that a pretty good test of love? Setting aside the other matter that had nothing to do with the war.

"Let me tell you something else. For nearly ten years my father was a hospital porter. You won't catch me talking down to a hospital porter. Then he rose to the dizzy heights of hospital administration. I mean he was a clerk, lowest grade. With his education. Having fought at D-Day. And all of that because it was all he could get. And that only because of some string-pulling from his nurse wife—and no doubt from Dr. Chaudhry too.

"But he accepted it and stuck with it. Because, I have no doubt, he thought it was worth it, because he thought it was a small price. And for the same reason he began gradually to realise that he'd never go back to India. It was how it was. His home was in England now. His family, his mother and father in Poona—he'd probably never see them again.

"He once told me that he looked at it like this: he might never have gone back anyway. He might have been killed in France. Or in Italy. And hadn't he done a fine thing anyway, even in the eyes of his family? Married a British lady. Perhaps he was right. He'd been blown up and he'd become somebody else.

"And this of course was the time—just before I was born—that India got home rule. Home rule and partition. We cleared out—the British cleared out. India was divided and terrible things happened, and all this while there was this other division my father had made between India and himself. It can't have been easy. He got his leg and he got the girl, but he lost something else. They say that amputees never stop feeling the 'ghosts' of their limbs.

"But of all of this, too, you could say it was a pretty good test.

"And do I have to tell you the rest? Do I have to tell you that the man who saved my father's leg, Dr. Chaudhry, became a sort of second father to my father? And like an uncle to me. He became a friend of the family. And do I have to tell you that it was because of Dr. Chaudhry—his name was Sunil—and with his encouragement that I set my sights on taking up medicine too? I was born in 1948. I was born along with the National Health. I was fated to spend my days in hospitals."

Dr. Shah's smile, now more like a triumphant beam, would indicate that his story was over. He'd look distinctly young, even though he was over sixty and was even mourning his father.

"But you are free to go," he'd announce—if he were speaking to one of his recovered patients. He'd hold out his hand, his brown hand with its fine dexterous fingers.

"At this point I always like to say I hope I never see you again. Please don't take it the wrong way. Take it the right way. Remember my father and his leg."

There were things he might have added, but didn't, things only to be inferred. He didn't say that, though he'd been born into the Welfare State, he'd certainly known, once upon a time in Battersea, the "disadvantages" of which his father spoke. He didn't enlarge on the fact that, though he'd been encouraged by

Dr. Chaudhry, he hadn't gone into orthopaedics, but cardiology. And he didn't say that in becoming a doctor himself, not to say eventually a senior consultant, he'd become, too, like a sort of second father to his own father and—there was really no other phrase for it—had gladdened his father's heart.

Cardiology, back in his days at medical school, had certainly become the glamour field. Everyone wanted to be a heart surgeon, in spite of the fact that the heart is only an organ like any other. No one gets worked up about a liver or a lung or a lower intestine. Or even perhaps a leg.

He'd held his father very gently, but wanting to hold him as tightly and inseparably as possible. His father had become as puny and as nearly weightless as a boy. He'd seen for a moment that photo, the men with their stumps. And for a moment he'd seen too the map of India as it had once appeared in old school atlases, in the 1950s, blush-red and plumply dangling, not unlike some other familiar shape.

Tragedy, Tragedy

"Tragedy, tragedy," Mick says. "Ever feel there's too much tragedy about?"

We're in the canteen. Morning break. Mick has the paper spread, as usual, over the table. He peers at it through his half-rims. Two damp rings where our mugs have been.

I thought: Now what?

"Tragedy," he says. "When bad stuff happens, when people die. It's always a tragedy, it's tragic. That's what the papers say. Tragic."

"Well, isn't it?" I say.

He looks up at me, over the half-rims, and takes his usual pause.

"When Ronnie Meadows had his heart attack on the forklift, was that tragic?"

I have to take a little pause too.

"Well—no," I say, wondering whether it's the right answer. Whether it's fair to Ronnie to say it wasn't tragic.

"Exactly," Mick says. "It was just Ronnie Meadows having a heart attack. But if Ronnie had died in, I don't know, a train crash and it had been in the papers, they'd have called it tragic. See what I mean?"

True. But it's not as if they'd have mentioned Ronnie at all. I could see the word printed in the paper. I could see the headline:

"Rail Crash Tragedy." Not just "Rail Crash." I couldn't see the headline: "Ronnie Meadows Dies in Rail Crash Tragedy."

I was drumming on the edge of the table with my fingers.

"So?" I say.

"Or if Ronnie hadn't been a fork-lift driver, if he'd been, I don't know, a Member of Parliament or someone on TV, and he'd died doing something just as boring—pushing a lawnmower—they'd have called that tragic."

"So?" I say again.

I thought: Drink your tea, Micky, I'm gasping.

"So. So it's just a word. It's just a word they use in the papers about things that get into the papers. It's just a word they use because they can't think of what else to say. It has to be tragic."

Mick likes to do this. He likes to read the paper—I mean not just look at it, but read it—and he likes to mouth off about whatever he's reading to anyone he's with. Which is me, Bob Lewis. But he likes to do it now specially, to make me suffer, now he's trying to quit. I wanted him to finish his tea and fold up his paper so we could go outside for a smoke.

"So it has no meaning?" I say.

I thought: Idiot, why encourage him?

But I also thought it's not true that no one called Ronnie's death tragic. Mick wasn't as close as I was, when the ambulance came. Ronnie's wife had come too. She had to come. I've forgotten her name. Sandra? Sarah? And Mercer was there, in his white shirt, he had to be. He said, "It's tragic, Mrs. Meadows. Tragic . . . tragic." He said it several times. He looked like he didn't know what else to say, and Ronnie's wife looked like she wasn't listening.

Ronnie was still lying under a pallet cover, because it was technically an industrial accident and he couldn't be moved yet. There was a pointy bit of the pallet cover that was Ronnie Meadows' nose.

Did Mick hear what Mercer said? As I remember it, he was

hanging back a bit. It was over three months ago. Ronnie had to go and drop dead right in the middle of the yard where everyone crosses to get to the gate. Even for a smoke at break time. I saw people skirting round for days, weeks afterwards. I skirted round myself. Then one day I realised, same as everyone else: I've just walked over the spot where Ronnie Meadows died and never thought about it.

But now I remembered Mercer saying "tragic" to Ronnie's wife.

"Yes it has a meaning," Mick says. He takes a breath. I thought: Here we go. He could see me drumming my fingers.

He started wearing the half-rims a couple of months ago. Because of them everyone began calling him "Prof." But I think the glasses only brought out something already there. It was like his face had been waiting for the glasses to complete it. Mick himself had been waiting. Mick Hammond, the man who likes to let you know he thinks.

"It has a meaning . . ."

He was all shy at first about wearing them, but now he fancies himself in them, he likes the business of looking over the top of them. And I quite like Mick in his reading glasses. Because they make him look serious, and that makes me want to laugh.

"It has a meaning . . ."

I could see he really was doing some thinking now, but he was also in a bit of a fix. I thought: You started this, Micky mate.

But mainly I thought: I'm gasping. And I thought: He's only dawdling over his tea because he's trying to quit the fags. He doesn't want to cross the yard with me and slip out the gate to what we used to call Death Row. Till Ronnie Meadows died.

Mick's a mate, but this whole giving-up thing's a bastard. It doesn't seem right for Mick to stop me nipping off for a drag. But it doesn't seem right for me to nip off anyway without Mick. Even if he's not going to smoke himself, he should come outside with me and stand beside me while I do. But that's daft too.

"If . . ." he says, "if . . . a famous mountaineer dies while trying to climb a new way up the north face of the Eiger, the papers
would call that tragic, but it wouldn't be."

That seems a long way from Macintyre's warehouse, but I
let it go. I can see Mick is getting all important with himself. I
thought: Stay calm.

"What would it be?"

"It would be . . . well, heroic maybe."

"Or mad," I say.

"No, no, it would be the right sort of death for a mountaineer, wouldn't it? It would be how a mountaineer might even *want*
to die."

I don't say, "Who *wants* to die?" And I don't say, "Why are we
talking about mountaineering?"

"So?" I say.

He shifts the half-rims on his nose a little, lifts them up with
one finger, lets them drop again. Any moment now he'll take
them off and wipe them. He didn't just get new glasses, he got a
whole new act, a whole new bloody Mick Hammond, or the one
that had only been waiting.

Maybe because of Mick and his glasses, I thought: Tragedy's
about acting too. It's about stuff that happens on stage. Shake-
speare and stuff. That's the thing about it. It's not real life. And
Mercer can't have been thinking that Ronnie Meadows dropping
off his fork-lift was—well, like *Hamlet*.

Micky Hamlet, I thought. Mickey Mouse.

"If, on the other hand . . ." he says.

I thought: Here we go.

". . . if a famous mountaineer dies not on the north face of
the Eiger, but climbing up some easy-peasy little mountain in, I
don't know, the Lake District, then that's tragic."

I didn't know what to say to this. Mick must have done some
thinking, I'll give him that, to come up with this. I sort of got
what he was getting at, but then again I didn't, I didn't at all.

I thought: I never knew Mick had a secret hankering to be a mountaineer. And I thought: We're nowhere near the Lake District, Micky, we're in Stevenage.

So I said, "Why?"

Which is always the killer question. When I said it I couldn't help thinking of when Gavin, our first, started up with his "Why? Why? Why?" It often sounded more like "Wha! Wha! Wha!" but, God, he knew it was the killer question.

Gavin's nearly eighteen now.

"Well, don't you see?" Mick says. "It's got something about it. It's not how a mountaineer would want to die, or should die. It's—"

"Just stupid," I say.

"Tragic," he says.

Mick Hammond's totally different from me. But, yes, he's my mate, has been for years. Search me.

"If you say so, Mick."

And those glasses sometimes make Mick look like a grand-dad, twice my age, though there's only a year in it.

I didn't say, "If you say so, Prof." I thought: How did we get to this? The newspaper. Ronnie Meadows. The Lake District. But it was the newspaper first. I thought: I'm gasping.

And then I thought: If I get up and leave Mick here and go out across the yard to the gate to have a smoke and if I keel over while I'm doing it, would that be tragic? Smoking kills. It says so on the packet. Or would it be more tragic if Mick comes with me, is standing right beside me when it happens, and if he's smoking too? Or if he isn't, because he's trying to give up and he's just keeping me company?

Or would it be more tragic still if I go and have a smoke all by myself and feel all the better for it and meanwhile Mick here slumps forward and croaks. Slumps forward, with his tea unfinished, onto his newspaper with the word "tragic" dotted all over it.

"If you say so," I say.

Mick thinks quitting smoking is wise. It goes with the glasses, maybe. But I know he only started trying to quit because of Ronnie. It wasn't because he's wise. It was because he was scared.

When Ronnie dropped off the fork-lift onto the yard floor he was still in a sitting-down position. It must have been a zonker of a heart attack.

I thought: Mick's wrong. He's talking cobblers. None of those deaths would be tragic.

I'm not a newspaper reader, I'm not any kind of reader, but when I was at primary school and it rained and we couldn't go out to the playground, there'd be this big box of old *Beanos* and *Dandys* brought out for us to read. I used to love reading them— because it wasn't reading at all. How they used to make me laugh. Biff! Bam! Kerrchow! I never thought then I'd end up being a warehouseman at Macintyre's, dying for a smoke in my break.

Mick did his nose-shift thing again. He looked very pleased with having won his argument, if that's what it was, or with me not understanding and just giving up. Or with him getting away—we'd run out of time now—with not having a smoke. If that's what this was really all about. His little score on that.

Not exactly mountain climbing, Micky.

I thought: Okay, Mick, you're my mate, if you're really giving up, then that's up to you, but next time I'm going out by myself, I'm leaving you here, matey. And don't you ever start preaching to me, with your new glasses, about how I should give up myself. Don't you ever start that.

Then I saw, in my head, Mick slumped forward over his spread newspaper, dead as a sack of cement.

And of course I understood. Of course I understood that tragic was a word people used when they didn't know what else to say—about people dropping dead. But I thought: It's not because they don't know what to say. It's not that at all. It's because they can't say the other thing, they can't ever say it. The thing that goes with tragedy and happens on the stage too, and doesn't have much to do with Macintyre's warehouse either.

Biff! Bam! Kerrzang! How I laughed. How I'd love to get out a copy of the *Beano* in the canteen. Though I'd look a bloody idiot, wouldn't I? The word you ought to use about that mountaineer in the Lake District, or about Ronnie dropping off the fork-lift still sitting down, or even about Mick here, slumped over his newspaper with his neat little new half-rims all scrunched up against his face, is comic.

Comic. That's what you ought to say. But you can't.

As Much Love as Possible

He'd been early and Sue had still been upstairs, getting ready, as Alec ushered him in. Her voice had floated down, through a half-opened door, from above. "Hello, Bill." Then a hurried and apologetic, "I'm not decent."

"You're always decent," he'd called back.

What did that mean? And the word stuck with him: decent.

Alec had phoned days before and said that Sue was having a night out with the girls, so he'd be all on his own. Why didn't Bill come over?

"I've got a bottle of Macallan. Fifteen-year-old. It fell off the back of a lorry."

Alec didn't say that he knew Bill would be on his own too—Sophie and the boys being away for half-term at Sophie's parents while he soldiered on at the office. Bill reckoned that it was Sue who knew this, not Alec, so this was really Sue's idea, Sue's invitation. But Alec was Bill's oldest friend.

"Come over. I haven't seen you for ages. Don't bring anything, just yersel." Alec could get all Scots when he wanted.

So there he'd been, a little early, and Alec was giving him a cardiganed hug and there was the smell of the shepherd's pie in the oven that Sue had cooked for them. He'd driven, which was easiest, but also stupid—given the bottle of Macallan. But he'd told himself that if he drove then he'd have to go carefully on the whisky, and if he had his car outside then he'd avoid any pressure as things got late to stay the night, which was all false upside-down logic. It wasn't that he didn't like being with Alec and Sue, quite the opposite.

Alec had flicked his eyes upward and said, "Making herself beautiful." Then said, "How dastardly of me, there's no making about it." And Bill had smiled and thought nonetheless how women made themselves beautiful for nights out with other women. For a boys' night out, or in, men hardly bothered. Witness the pair of them, like two adverts for woollens.

They'd hardly settled when Sue had come down and appeared in the doorway. Many years ago Bill had thought that Sue was just the sort of dumb and ditzy blonde Alec would end up marrying, then find the novelty wearing off. It had been his own reason for not marrying her, or rather for not making any move at all, though he might have done. He'd given precedence to his friend and felt he'd been shrewd.

He'd been best man, naturally, at Alec and Sue's wedding, but by then he'd met Sophie and she and he had been the first pair to get hitched. And to have kids, pretty quickly, one after the other. Alec and Sue had waited several years. Perhaps there was a difficulty, but they hadn't seemed unhappy at the time. So much for shrewdness. Maybe they'd waited simply because of that: because they were happy and wanted to have time just with each other. Then they'd gone and had twins. A boy and girl.

They'd be upstairs right now, still only four years old. Or was it five? He ought to know, he was their godfather.

Bill had said to Sue as she appeared in the doorway, "Sue, you look fantastic." He should have allowed Alec to say something first, perhaps. Anyway it was true. She was wearing a dress that wasn't quite a party dress, but it had a shimmer. Or it was more that *she* had a shimmer, a kind of ready, default-mode excitement.

It was only a girls' night out, he'd thought, it wasn't a ball.

She said, "You look pretty good yourself, Bill." He said, "Rubbish," and had got up to meet her embrace which was always full-on and generous, as if she had arms for everyone. She'd been holding a black coat and a cream scarf but had slung them momentarily over the banister at the foot of the stairs, on top of his own undistinguished Puffa thing.

She picked up the coat again and looked at her watch.

"Alec, you did ring for the taxi, didn't you?"

Alec was already fetching two whisky tumblers. He thumped his forehead with his free hand.

"Oh shit! Shit! I'm sorry, sweetheart. Let me drive you."

Sue had said, "No, you have to look after Bill." There wasn't any hint of anger or dramatics, just the small practical quandary. So, while Alec had done more breast-beating, he'd said, "I'll drive you, Sue." It seemed a neat and diplomatic solution. His car was still warm. Alec would have to get his out of the garage. And he didn't want Sue to be late.

"Where are you going?"

"Hathaway's. Park Street."

"I know it. Good choice. No problem."

Sue had protested, then finally said, "You're an angel, Bill." And Alec had said, "The man puts me to eternal shame."

Alec had put the tumblers down and helped Sue on with her coat. There was no reproachfulness. She said, "Don't forget about the shepherd's pie. And the twins are sparko. I looked in."

Alec had draped the scarf round his wife's neck then kissed her tenderly by the ear. "Sorry, precious," he said. "You better give this man here a decent tip." That word once more. Then, to him, he'd said, "I'll see you later, buster. I'll try not to open the bottle."

So now here he was—it was only a ten-minute drive—sitting beside Sue in the car opposite Hathaway's, and Sue, though she was several minutes late, didn't seem in a rush. All through the short journey he'd felt inevitably that they were like some couple going out on a date themselves—particularly at the start as they got into the car, he holding the door open for her, chauffeur-fashion, she swinging her legs in and gathering up her coat, and Alec watching contritely from the front porch, like some stoical father.

Sue had spent the few minutes saying how sweet it was of him and he'd spent it establishing that the "girls" were Christine and Anita and that all three of them had been at the hair academy together and now they each had salons of their own.

He wondered what a hair academy was and had his bizarre mental pictures, but didn't ask. He'd long since stopped thinking it obvious that a fluffy blonde whose principal feature was her hair would go into hairdressing. Nothing was obvious any more.

He knew Sue's salon was called Locks and that it had been set up—funded—by Alec. For all Bill knew, Alec might have among his many business interests a small chain of hair salons which involved funding Christine and Anita as well.

Bill had often passed Locks but never entered. He'd sometimes wondered how it would be if he were to walk in and ask to have his hair cut—by Sue herself of course. It seemed the most innocent yet intimate of requests.

Salon. Hair academy. These were easily scoffed at, bogus expressions. But he no longer thought like that.

Sue said, as if she hadn't thanked him enough, "Why don't you come in for a moment? I could introduce you to the girls." It was a strange impetuous suggestion and was perhaps only meant jokingly.

"It's a bit late in the day for that sort of thing, isn't it?" He smiled. He hadn't meant to sound rueful.

She said, "All okay, with you and Sophie?"

"Yes. Fine."

"And the kids?"

He snorted. "I hardly think of them as kids any more. They're eleven and twelve."

There was a little weighty pause. She could just get out. It didn't need a speech.

"You know, Bill, all I've ever wanted, all that's ever made me happy, is to do something for other people that makes them feel nicer. That's all, nothing special, nothing more than that. They come into my salon, they walk out again a little later—feeling nicer."

His hands still held the steering wheel. He hadn't had a drink yet. He thought of Alec, waiting for him, staring at a (still virgin?) bottle of Macallan. He thought how many months since he last saw Sue? When would he see her again? And when would he again, if ever at all, sit beside her like this, just the two of them, in the convenient bubble of a car?

Across the road, Hathaway's was lit up, but curtained. If Christine and Anita were inside waiting, they couldn't be seen.

He said, "I love you, Sue. I love you. I could say something like 'I'm very fond of you,' but I love you. I don't mean I don't love Sophie. I don't mean I don't love lots of people. But I love you. Don't you think there should be as much love as possible?"

There. He held the steering wheel. He held it, looking straight ahead as if he were still driving.

He heard, eventually, the slow punctilious creep of a woman's clothing as she moves deliberately to kiss a man. It was barely a touch against the side of his face, by his ear, as if she wished to say something that could only be whispered, but he felt just the brush of her lips and a small expulsion of warm breath.

"Well," she said, drawing away, "I better not ask you in then. You better not meet the girls."

She could never have been so suave years ago.

She opened her door and got out, but then lingered on the pavement, despite the cold, one hand on the open door, her coat unbuttoned, leaning in while he leant across, constrained by his seat belt.

What was there to say? It was as if it was late and he was dropping her off.

"Enjoy your evening," he said like some polite stranger. Like a cab driver.

"And you. Don't get sloshed."

"Nor you. I'll see you later."

"Yes. But—"

"But what?"

"Don't wait up."

What did that mean?

"Go on," he said. "It's cold. The girls are waiting." To puncture the mood and effect a disengagement he added, "I can see down your top when you lean like that."

It was a fifteen-year-old bottle, to be treated with respect, so they sipped slowly, both acknowledging how they couldn't cane it like they'd used to. And there was the shepherd's pie to mop it up. It was a very good shepherd's pie. Perhaps he praised it too much, but Alec had simply said, waxing Caledonian, that short of a decent haggis there was no finer accompaniment to a good whisky. Decent haggis. That word again.

All the same, after a certain point—he could recognise the symptoms—he knew he should start to put his hand over his glass or ask for a coffee. And he really didn't want, now, to have that moment when Alec would say, "There's a spare bed upstairs, mon. No problem." He didn't even want, now, to be around when Sue returned. Don't wait up.

The point should come, before Alec launched off on some other topic, when he should say, "Look, if you don't mind, I'll head back now." And make whatever feeble excuses. He'd already told Alec that, strictly speaking, he was under doctor's orders.

It wasn't true, though he'd had a fairly schoolmasterly doctor's warning.

On the coffee table were two abandoned plates and the dish, with an encrusted serving spoon, that had contained the shepherd's pie. They'd eaten like slobs, on their laps. He wondered how the table was looking at Hathaway's with Christine and Anita.

He should make a move before he lost his power of decision—he was near that—and, yes, definitely before Sue returned. He needed a pee, so he went upstairs, resolving that when he came down and while still on his feet he'd mouth his garbled adieus. It had gone eleven. No, he was okay to drive. He had work to do tomorrow.

But he made the mistake, when he came out of the bathroom, of peeping into the room with the just-open door along the landing. Why did all kids want to sleep with the door just open? Had he once? He peered in, even crept in a little, and stood inside the doorway. There was that barely-lit atmosphere of utter peace, utter immersion in sleep—sleep like no grown-ups have. There were the two little concentrated forms beneath blankets, each in their own small bed. A guarding clutter of inert toys.

He knew about this from his own experience. It was a primal parental joy. But here there was an extra magic, an extra harmony and rapture: twins. He stood and looked, as if these were his own children. His heart turned over.

He stood there long enough, if it was only seconds, to hear the noise of a car creeping up the quiet cul-de-sac outside. He felt sure it was a taxi bringing Sue home. So she, at least, had kept her power of decision and made her departure before things got late and disorderly. Or—they all had their salons to think about—there'd been a general sensible dispersal.

He hurried downstairs, if only to get to the living room before Sue could reach the front door and to avoid the awkwardness—was it an awkwardness?—of coming face to face with her as she let herself in. And of course as he re-entered the living room Alec poured him another slug, even as they both heard a car door close outside, and Alec said, "That must be Sue. Rather early. The good wee lassies."

Half past eleven wasn't exactly early and there was a tiny touch of tension in his voice. Was he still smarting from his earlier blunder? He went through to be at the front door.

"Hello, precious," Bill heard, holding his topped-up glass and feeling the edge of the waft of February air that Sue brought in with her. He knew now he had no control over how things would proceed. He saw himself in the spare room—further along the landing—in solitary inebriated confinement in a house of couples.

She appeared in the doorway, just as before, Alec behind her now, removing her coat. Yes, the shimmer was all hers. There was a light inside her. It was only a girls' night out, he thought again, it wasn't a ball. Life wasn't a ball.

"All well here?" she said, quickly stooping to release her high-heeled shoes. One hand on the door frame, leaning in.

"Yes," Alec said over her shoulder. "Look how much whisky we haven't drunk."

Alec slipped back into the living room, touching Sue's bottom with his palm as he did so.

Bill said, "And how was your evening?" It sounded, again, absurdly polite.

She smiled. She drew herself up, smoothed her skirt, shook her hair a little, then took a deep and, so it seemed, utterly thrilled and pure breath, like someone on a mountain top.

"Oh, I've had the most wonderful evening."

Yorkshire

Nobody spoke, nobody said anything. They spoke about the dead who couldn't speak back, they stood around with poppies, but the ones still alive, they shut up and got on with it. Wasn't that the best way, anyway, of being grateful to the dead? It's what you did, it's what everyone did.

And what did she know or care, a schoolgirl, a teenager on a bicycle whizzing down Denmark Hill, flashing her underwear? It had all been over before she was born, it had all been over for nearly twenty years. Her mother called her "flighty," as if it was her new name, though her real name was Daisy. Daisy Leigh. She said, "You'll end up in trouble, Daisy, one of these days." But her father said nothing, he shut up and got on with it. He coughed.

She quite liked "Daisy," she liked being a daisy, but she liked "flighty" too. She told Larry it was her middle name, it was what her mum called her. He said, "Flighty? Well, that settles it then, doesn't it?"

And now Larry was sleeping in the spare room. What did it mean? They'd been married for over fifty years. Her name wasn't Leigh, it was Baker. What was flighty about that? But Larry was sleeping in the spare room.

Her hair flying and her skirt too. Well if they saw it wouldn't be for long, would it? Sometimes she'd let go of the handlebars, just because she knew she could do it, and hold out her arms like wings. Wheeee! She must have been saved up for Flight Sergeant Baker.

Trouble?

All over for nearly twenty years, but it hadn't been so long since they'd told her, or rather since her mum had told her, as if it was something to be whispered between women about the man in the next room. But it must have been agreed between them. You tell her, Gracie.

"Your daddy was gassed at Wipers."

And what was that supposed to mean? She said the word "gassed" as if it was a bad word that shouldn't be repeated. She said it in the way she'd hear people later say the word cancer. And she said Wipers as if it was a real name you might find on a map.

And how, at nine or ten or whenever it was, should she, Daisy Leigh, have known otherwise? All she knew was that her daddy had a "chest," a "funny chest," it went with him just as surely as he wore trousers. And he was still, so far as she was concerned, her same daddy with his same funny chest.

But the fact that she'd been told this thing like a secret not to be passed on had something to do, though she couldn't have said what, with her becoming the sort of girl who didn't mind too much if her skirt blew up and who got to be called flighty, not Daisy. It was a bit like the word "Wipers."

Then along came another war anyway to take your mind off the old one, to wipe it away. Just come home, Larry. Just come home to your Flighty. She might be in or out of her nightie.

And now Larry was sleeping—or not sleeping—in the next room, but it was just like one of those black nights when he might never have come home. What did it mean? Tomorrow there was going to be a police investigation. He was going, voluntarily, to the police station, to "clear all this up." He was going *voluntarily*. No one was being arrested. So there was still this night, it could wait till the morning. And what was he going to do anyway, run off somewhere? At seventy-two?

He was going to the police station, voluntarily, to help with inquiries. He was cooperating. But then? All hell let loose, she was sure of that. All hell, either way, whatever the outcome, whatever the decision. Never mind the voluntarily. All hell, she was sure, if this wasn't hell already.

Which was what they'd all said when they didn't want to say—or couldn't think of how to say—anything. All hell. You don't want to know.

But there was still this night, this black interval, and she wished it could be truly lastingly black. She wished when she opened her eyes—what was the point of shutting them if it didn't make things go away?—there'd not be that glow, from the streetlights, round the edge of the curtains. My God, she wished she had blackout curtains. She saw them again as if it were yesterday, the dusty black brutal things they'd had to get used to, instead of the swirls of flowers or the Regency stripes. The curtains in her old bedroom in Camberwell had daisies. Of course.

What did it mean? Voluntarily. "Clear all this up."

And what did this mean, right now, him being in the other room? That he didn't want to be near her, touching her, let alone talking to her? Or that he thought that *she* wouldn't want him there, not now, next to her? That she wouldn't want to be touching him or, my God, for him to be touching her?

She told herself it was his confession, his way of saying it. She told herself it was just the disgrace, the sheer disgrace at the very idea of it, the very suggestion. Imagine. Either way, he was contaminated, not to be touched. Either way it was all hell.

And how could you ever tell anyway when things themselves went right back into blackness? It was what Addy herself had said, it was her trump card.

"We're talking here, Mum, about earliest memories. No,

not even that. We're talking about when you shouldn't have any memories at all. But you have them, don't you, if they're strong enough, if they're bad enough? You just suppress them, don't you, submerge them? You pretend to forget."

Suppress? Submerge? It had gone through her head to say, "You're not in one of your classes now, my girl, you're not in front of a blackboard." And she'd seen for a moment (something she'd never ever actually seen) her daughter facing rows of young faces. Why had Addy chosen to be a teacher? The thought of her becoming one had once vaguely scared her. She'd seen herself back at school, a target for her own teachers.

Pretend to forget?

What *could* you say about that time where memory vanishes into darkness? You could say nothing. Or you could say anything, you could say what the hell you liked, it was anyone's guess, and no one could prove you wrong.

My girl. Addy—little Addy—was forty-eight.

"You tell me what your earliest memories are, Mum. Go on, try it on me."

She actually said that, to her own mother, as if she was accusing *her*, or as if she was saying, "Come on, join me."

And now here she was *doing* it, at three in the morning, trying to go back in her memory as far as possible, to where memory slips down a black hole. And she couldn't tell if it was because she was searching for something—and why the hell should she be?—or because she just wanted to slip, herself, down that black hole and never come out again . . .

She could remember being held against her father's chest, when she was small enough for most of her to fit against it. She had a blue cotton dress, it was her first dress. She could remember him hugging her to his chest and her hugging him back. What was wrong with that? She could remember having her ear against her father's chest and hearing the strange sounds it made, like rocks or pebbles shifting inside a cave—a cave by the sea with waves washing into it. She could remember it being as though he was letting her listen to the sounds, just her specially. What was wrong with that?

She could remember being in the paddling pool in the children's playground in Ruskin Park, though she couldn't say how old she'd have been, and a man had popped out from behind a big tree with his trousers undone and all his stuff showing. He'd done it very quickly and cleverly, just as she'd looked up and when no one else was looking, because she'd turned round and everyone was looking the other way. And when she'd looked back the man had gone as if he'd never been there. But she could remember his stuff showing, his red bobbing thing. She couldn't have invented that. She could remember thinking what was wrong with him, what sort of—disfigurement—was that? Though she didn't know then the word "disfigurement."

Anyway she'd got over it and never said a word. And it wasn't her daddy.

Her face was wet. Addy was making her do this. The bitch.

And if it had been all right to hug her father still, her father who'd been gassed, and for him to hug her since he was still her same daddy, then it was all right to hug Larry now, no matter what, to hold him and hug him against her own sad chest, against her own flat breasts, and say, "It's all right, Larry, I'm here. You're still the same Larry."

Except he wouldn't let her. He'd gone to the spare room. What did it mean? It could mean that he thought that *she* must think that he'd really—

The bitch, the evil bitch. She was making them lie like this in separate rooms, both in their own separate blackness.

And he was lying, for God's sake, in Addy's old room. It wasn't, at least, in her old single bed. That had gone ages ago, it had been the spare room for ages with a new double bed from Debenham's. But it was the bed where Addy and Brian had slept enough times when they'd visited, and they'd visited enough times in nearly twenty years. Brian had said once it had "tickled" him to sleep in Addy's old room. He'd said that. And then they'd brought their kids, Mark and Judy, first one then the other, in their carry-cots, to sleep with them in that same room.

And if all this, now, was true, then how could they have done that, come here, kept visiting, with their kids too? Though it had been a while, it was true, since any of them had visited, and the kids weren't kids any more. She should have said, perhaps, like some interfering mother, "Is everything okay?"

Which was just the point Addy was making. Years went by and people never talked, did they? She, Adele Hughes, born Baker, hadn't talked for over forty years, but she was talking now. She'd kept it to herself, she'd "struggled," but now she had to "speak out." And she was talking face to face, notice, she wasn't flinching. She was looking at her own mother, hard in the eye, as if her own mother might have known all along what all this was about and covered it up. And she wouldn't be the only one to speak out, would she, not by a long way? The world knew that by now. It was others speaking out that had given her the courage.

Courage?

She said she'd been "traumatised." All her life she'd struggled. But it had to stop now. She had to have her "release." At forty-eight? And had she talked to Brian first about it all? "Tickled." Had she had *him* sleeping in another bed?

Or was he doing that anyway?

She said that when she was very small, almost too far back for memory—there she went again—Larry, her own father, had done things to her, had interfered with her. He'd molested her. He'd traumatised her.

"He what? He did *what*? Where? When? *What*?"

She'd exploded into questions—which seemed to be all she had now. She was lying in this bed, under a rubble of questions.

"You better have some facts, my girl! You better know what the hell you're talking about!"

It had surprised her, the fierceness and quickness of her answer. She hadn't been lost for words exactly, or for a way to say them. She'd spoken in a certain voice and with a certain look. She knew she had a certain look, because Addy had actually stepped back. She'd flinched—for all her being unflinching. And whatever else that look was saying, it was saying, "I'm not your mother any more, my girl. I've just become your deadly enemy."

And whatever Addy had thought that talking to her mum would achieve—she'd wanted comforting? To be told she had guts?—she knew now she'd been seriously mistaken. And anyway she'd crossed a line for ever and there was no going back. But she must have thought of that—she should have thought of that—long before she opened her mouth.

Then her own mouth had opened again and she'd said to her own daughter, her own child of forty-eight years, "You lying evil bitch."

He was stationed in Yorkshire. Flight Sergeant Baker, wireless-op Baker. As it turned out they were from barely a mile apart, he was from Streatham, but he was stationed in Yorkshire. It might as well have been another country. He said on the phone, "I'm safer here than where you are, I have it cushy here." But she knew it was a lie, or a daytime truth and a night-time lie, since any night he could be killed. That was the truth, that was the deal now. It wasn't hanky-panky any more in the back of the stalls, though there was some of that, it began with that, but it went beyond.

Night-time, bedtime. How everything was turned round. How could she sleep when he might be over Hamburg or Berlin? But she never knew where, or even if, he'd be flying that night—so she might be scaring herself stiff for nothing. She'd actually preferred it when she had to be in the shelter. At least she could think: Well he's dropping bombs on them. She didn't care about Germans at all. That was their hell.

But the nights when she just lay in bed were terrible. They were like this night now. She didn't even know where in Yorkshire, just Yorkshire. "Believe me, Flighty, you wouldn't know where, even if I told you." But because she didn't know anything, which nights or where, Yorkshire itself became like the place, the word for all things terrible. Yorkshire terriers. Like the word for terror itself.

That's where he was now. Or she was.

And that's where you came from, my girl.

He never talked either. He shut up and got on with it too. The fact is he came back, he always came back, but she never knew, nor did he, that that was how it would be, till it was all over. He came back and he never talked. "I'd rather talk about this, Flighty." His hand you know where. In the Air Force they called it Lack of Moral Fibre if you didn't shut up and get on with it. Larry never had Lack of Moral Fibre.

He had nightmares, of course, for a long time afterwards—so yes he talked, even screamed a bit, in his sleep. But that was something she could deal with simply, easily, gladly. "You were dreaming, Larry, only dreaming. Look, you're here beside me, you're alive, these are my breasts. Put your head in my breasts."

If only she could say that now. "You're here, Larry, you're not in Yorkshire."

And then, in 1947, Adele was born. Little sweet Adele. And wasn't that the universal cure? Everyone was doing it. Little babies galore. And didn't that help to wipe things away?

And if Addy had been waiting all this time to talk—if there were any reason to—then she might have waited till the two of them were dead. If she'd waited anyway till she was *forty-eight*. Or she might have waited till they'd lost their marbles, gone doolally, so they wouldn't know a thing anyway. Same difference.

But to say it now when they were seventy-two and seventy-one, though still going strong, in their "sunset years" and trying to make the most of them. Having passed their Golden and hoping to make it to their Diamond (what was flighty about that?). Not to mention to the year 2000, to a new millennium. Think of that, Larry, we've lived through a millennium.

But Addy had actually given *that* as her reason. If she'd waited till they were dead, till *he* was dead, then there wouldn't have been any justice, would there?

Justice?

She actually said it was the thought of them reaching the end of their lives that had "forced her" to it, the thought of them being dead and the thing just disappearing into the past, then her having no "redress" and just having to carry on living with it till she was dead herself.

She actually said that. All her life she'd protected them, but enough was enough.

Protected them?

Well, she'd made the sun set now sure enough. There was only this night, which she wished would go on for ever.

No matter how tightly she closed her eyes, she couldn't make it black enough. To *want* night, to want blackness! Yet to be made to feel at the same time that you had to shine some nasty poking torch into it, like a policeman at a murky window. And there could be no stopping it, could there, no end to it, once you got into that area where memory itself stopped and no one could say what was true or false? Beneath everything a great web of— disfigurement. It must be there because no one talked about it.

How she'd dreaded it, once, sunset—the thought of the sun setting over Yorkshire. Now she wanted only darkness. She couldn't say what Larry wanted.

She saw herself on a bicycle, arms outspread. She saw again her little room in Camberwell, bands of light from the street. Her daisy curtains. Her father's cough across the landing.

Though she'd never felt it before and never imagined she might feel it, she felt it now like some black swelling creature inside her. The wish not to have been born. Or was it the wish not to have given birth? She felt it, decades on, but as if it were happening all over again, the exact, insistent, living feeling of carrying Adele inside her. Though was this Adele? At four months, at six months, at eight, at—

Then she woke up and felt sure she'd been screaming, screaming out loud. She felt sure she'd screamed—so loud that Larry, in the next room, must have heard, even if he'd been sleeping. Yes, he was in the next room, but it was only the next room, so he must have heard, a scream like that. And she wanted this to end it, she wanted it to be the thing that would make him snap out of it and leap up and come back to her and hold her and soothe her and crush her against his chest and say, "It's all right, Flighty, you were only dreaming."

Holly and Polly

Holly likes to say—and Holly likes to say everything—that we're in the introduction business. We can't make anything happen, but we can bring the parties together. She'll say this to men in bars when they home in on us. It's a wonderful thing to watch a pair of them edge our way and to see the light in their eyes before they get the full picture.

"So, don't tell us," one of them says, "the two of you work in a dating agency?"

"No, but you're close," Holly says. "Sure, getting the date right can be an important part of it."

"You wouldn't be Irish by any chance?"

"By every chance. But that's not what you're guessing."

Isn't it a wonderful thing—isn't it *the* most wonderful thing—how things come together in this world, how they can even be meant for each other? But you can't tell, you can't guess it in advance.

"So—you've got one more guess. Yes, we work together. It's not an office. And it's not a dating agency. You two wouldn't be after a date now, would you? Without the agency?"

"We're thinking," the other one says. "Don't talk, we're thinking."

Then the first one says, "No, you'll have to tell us. We give up, you'll have to say. I'm Matt, this is Jamie."

"I'm Holly and this is Polly. Yes, we know. But look now, we're doing what Polly and me do all day, we're making introductions. We're clinical embryologists. Have you heard of those people? We spend all day looking at sperms. We're experts on the little fellers. We pick out the good ones, the best from the rest, and then we introduce them to eggs. We say to them, 'There now, say hello, youse two, and on you get with it.'"

And then the lights go off, or they go brighter. A turn-off or a turn-on. They might want to get mucky. And Holly can do mucky.

And they haven't even seen the full picture.

You can't make it happen. You can bring the parties together. But tell me, please, how does *that* happen? How does it happen that there was Holly Nolan, raised in a convent (though you might not think it) somewhere in Ireland and there was me, Polly Miller, meek and mild, but raised in a comprehensive in Bolton, both of us fired by the same thing ("Sure, isn't it the only subject now, the science of life?"), both of us getting, in different places, our B.Sc.'s and our certificates, so that she should cross the sea (it not being a field that Ireland's big in) and we should meet in a brand-new clinic, in a clean white room with clean white counters and white expensive instruments, like two specimens ourselves in some sort of clinical trial, both of us in the pea-green scrubs we were provided with.

So that we would be introduced to each other.

"I'm Holly."

"I'm Polly."

"Would you believe it? Hello, Polly. We're to work together."

"Yes."

"In these things! Have I come all the way from County Kildare just to wear green?"

Both of us only twenty-three (*junior* clinical embryologists), but both of us qualified and trained for a job that some people say is the job of playing God.

"Well I like that now! Are we not a pair of goddesses?"

So that we would come together, so that it would happen. So that my life would at last begin.

When I'm out with Holly in a bar, teasing men, I sometimes see the touch of red in her black hair—what she calls her "burn." I see her tarty brashness, what they think is her being up for it. I hear her unstoppable voice. I think: Not my type, not my type at all.

How wrong can you be?

"Well now, Polly dear, there's such a thing as the attraction of opposites."

When she first arrived here she used to say things about her Catholic upbringing that could make me blush. Or blush inside. That could make me think: Hold on, that's wrong, that's blasphemous. She said that she and her convent-school friends used to sing a plainsong rendering of the sexual act, in Latin. And she sang it for me—intoned it for me—in her purest priestly voice:

Penem in vaginam intro-duxit.

To which the response was, as from a choir of monks:

Et semen e-mi-sit.

With a long sustaining of the *"mi."*

It was hardly filth, and it was Latin. And it had me in stitches. The stitches maybe hid the blushes. But it was the very idea of it, I suppose, the idea of singing such a thing as if it were a prayer. It was the feeling of a wickedness unavailable to such as me. Me with my godless (but chaste) upbringing. My only shred of religion was that I'd worshipped once my biology teacher, Sandra Rhys.

Which is only to say I felt jealous. Why should that be? Jealous of Holly and of her convent schooling and of her chorus of profaning schoolfriends.

"I haven't shocked you now, have I, Polly? In our line of business."

And how many jobs are there—tell me one other—in which just along a corridor men go into little rooms and, well, as Holly would say, they engage in private devotion and offer themselves up into little jars, and the jars are passed discreetly our way for us to examine closely.

For a while we couldn't mark the arrival of such a tribute without actually singing, softly, in unison, or wanting to sing:

Et semen e-mi-sit . . .

I was even jealous of her familiarity with Latin. If you're a biologist you need to know a little, but for her it had really once been a sort of second secret language.

"*Introduxit*"—from *introducere,* to lead into or towards. The introduction business.

And it's a serious one. We're not God. We're not playing either. Though sometimes you have to laugh. We're the girls in the lab, the girls in the back room. It's Dr. Mortimer and his nurses who do the meeting and greeting and perform the intimate procedures, but we sometimes get to see the clients, to say hello to—Mr. and Mrs. Desperate. And Dr. Mortimer, as *he* makes the introductions, will inevitably call us his behind-the-scenes angels, the ones who perform the real miracles. The smoothie. Or the buck passer, as Holly would say.

You have to laugh.

And we'll sometimes see in the faces of Mr. and Mrs. Desperate the surprise, or sheer alarm, at knowing that their chances depend on such a pair of youngsters. Two girls in green. Or else see them thinking: Well it's all right for them, it must be a lark for them, hardly out of school and with all their bits inside just as they should be, but not even thinking about it yet, not even caring about it. Though getting in plenty of practice, no doubt, on the preliminary activity.

If only they knew, if only they knew the real cause of our clinical detachment.

We don't often think about it, but sometimes we do. We know that one day in a living room somewhere, because of something we've done in our clean white lab, and because the moment has come, Mr. and Mrs. Desperate will squeeze each other's hand, and she will go to the bathroom where there's the testing kit our clinic has provided. And he will wait, perhaps saying a small prayer. And a little while later they'll squeeze hands again while they cry tears of joy. Or just cry.

What is it that makes things happen?

I thought, with all her mouth—a cherry-lipsticked gash of a mouth—and all the language spilling from it, she can't be a virgin. But why should I have had that thought at all? She was twenty-three, and had crossed the sea. They grow up, don't they, Catholics, with the Holy Virgin, they worship their Holy Virgin? Though hardly this one. But there wasn't the mention or even the hint about her of any man. Despite all the mouth. Despite the way she could twist Dr. Mortimer round her little finger. And that despite the fact that Dr. Mortimer, good and caring gyno though he is, likes everyone to know that *he* does the charming round here.

Is she a virgin? Why should I even have thought it? In our line of business.

For the simplest plainest reason.

She said, "Are you doing anything tonight?" Not of itself a remarkable question. But she said it in a certain way, with a certain tilt. She said it even, I like to think now, with a little toss of her hair. Except she couldn't have done that in her scrub cap. And of course she was a virgin. For the same reason and in the same sense that I was. It takes one to know another perhaps, but there's still the attraction of opposites.

The plain truth of it was that we ourselves were two Miss Desperates. There had never been, in all our years, for me or her, a *"penem in vaginam"* situation. Oh the handiness of Latin. Though there had been some false introductions.

It takes some less time, it takes some perhaps, poor souls, much longer, but it had taken each of us all our lives to discover and acknowledge, then to nurse and hide, in our different ways, our secret. Both wondering all along, like good little girls intent on being pure even till their wedding nights, if there might be someone, the right one, one day, with whom we could share it.

Was there ever such a strange way, among our sperms and eggs—and, goodness knows, they have their difficulties—for the likes of us to come together?

"Was there ever, Polly angel darling, such a sweet and charming thing?"

That couple in the living room, with the tears running down their faces, they can't have anything to do with the likes of us, can they? And yet they have everything to do with us. And we might as well have been, that night, that couple in the living room, tears of joy—this was how the test had gone—running down our faces. How magical, how all-confessing, how all-absolving, are the little words "Me too." How all-embracing.

We went for a drink in the Radcliffe Arms. Then we went for a Chinese in the Blue Pagoda. And then. And then. Like the beginnings of all things everywhere. She said the province of Northern Ireland with its bloody Union Jack had been shoved up against the Republic of Ireland for nearly a century. But it hadn't taken us very long, had it?

Not my type at all. Oh how I love her. And oh how happy I am to be with her, to wear green with her, two peas in a pod, to work with her among our sperms and eggs, to have found among them the one I am and the one I should be with, so far as I'm concerned, for ever.

And if we should ever want to be what the likes of us can't be, to have the thing the likes of us can't have, then we're in the right place, aren't we? We know how it can be arranged, don't we?

We walked into the clinic that next morning as a couple. That's to say, we made sure we didn't walk in together, but a good half-minute apart. The nicety of lovers. It was Holly who went ahead. Naturally. And so bumped straight into Dr. Mortimer, fresh from his silver BMW and his drive in from Wilmslow. How much did he see straight away? How much had he guessed already?

But it's common knowledge now anyway. I mean it's common knowledge in this place. And truly this place is a place where there's precious little to be coy and canny about, with pots of sperm being passed around all day.

But Dr. Mortimer looked at Holly and said, "You're looking particularly glowing this morning, Holly. Is there something I don't know?"

And Holly said—because I was near enough by then to hear, near enough to see and to know how much I love her—"Sure, if you're not God around here, Dr. Mortimer, if you're not Our Lord Father Almighty. Don't you know everything?"

Keys

He drove Clare to the station. The traffic was unexpectedly heavy and they just made it in time. Their goodbyes were rushed and clumsy, but this spared him. He had no idea what to say. "Call me," he said. Then, "Quick!" Then he said, "I love you." He hadn't planned on saying it. It just happened. He watched her blink and scan his face even as she hurried.

"Quick!" he said again, and she turned, wheeling her small case into the station entrance. He loitered in the forecourt as her train arrived. He should be going with her, of course, but she'd brushed aside the need for this. They both knew he'd never got on with her brother, couldn't stand him in fact. And now her brother was suddenly, perhaps dangerously, ill.

It spared him. It would have been false. But as he watched her train pull out he felt a pang. He thought of her sitting there like some newly made orphan or refugee. She had to cross London, then take another train from Euston, some four or five hours in all. Plenty of time to be alone with her thoughts, plenty of time before she'd have any reason to call. But he somehow knew she'd only call him if things looked not too bad. If they looked really bad she'd be immersed in it all and in her family and she'd forget him. He'd be peripheral. He was just a husband.

Being an only child himself, who'd lost his parents years ago, he hated the stifling stuff of families, and sometimes couldn't hide it. It didn't sound good at all for Adam, and Adam was only forty-two.

He asked himself why he'd never been able to bear him. There was nothing rational about it. Simply because he was Clare's older brother? No, it was because he was weak. That was the truth. He hated weak men. He could spot them. And the truth about weak men was that they got ill, and even died.

He remained parked for some time after the train disappeared, as if he were now waiting for someone to arrive. It was a leaden August afternoon and thick sparse spots of rain began to fall. He thought about his affair with Vicki. It hadn't lasted long and it was the only time. He thought of how he'd hidden it from Clare—whether she'd had her inklings or not—and of how his hiding it from her had come to seem like a kindness, even a virtue.

Then he drove back home, only to discover that, in the unusual circumstances, he'd forgotten his keys.

He knew at once where they were, in the pocket of his zip-up jacket, slung over the back of his chair by his desk. He'd decided hastily not to wear it after all. Then, while he'd carried out Clare's case and put it in the boot, Clare had locked the front door. And now of course he didn't have the remedy that Clare, with her keys, could come to his rescue.

Rain started to fall in earnest as he sat outside his own home, staring at it like some riddle.

The normal thing in such a situation was to seek the help of a neighbour. He'd done it before. The houses were terraced. At the back of theirs was a window on the first floor with a broken catch. It had been possible that previous time to raise the lower sash from outside, then crawl in. Thanks to his negligence in getting the catch repaired, it might be possible to do the same again. But first he'd have to be let in by his next-door neighbour, explain himself, make embarrassed apologies, borrow a ladder and climb over the garden fence, somehow manhandling the ladder over too.

And now it was August and both the Wheelers on one side and the Mitchells on the other were on holiday. Last time, it had been the Mitchells. He knew they had a ladder. But the Mitchells would be in their place in France.

And the irony was that the window—the window that was by no means guaranteed to save him—was the window to his study and only a few feet from his abandoned jacket, with his keys in it, over the chair. Last time, he'd squirmed through the window, then found himself swimming on his desk.

He could of course call a locksmith. He'd forgotten his keys, but he had his phone. How long would it take for a locksmith to arrive?

At least he was sheltered from this rain in the car.

For a moment he did nothing, immobilised by the fact of being excluded from his own home, his own life. There it was, but he simply couldn't get to it. There was his desk, with his zip-up jacket over the chair, his drawing board where he'd resolved just to get on with the work he'd brought home from the office—having taken today, Friday, off—right through the weekend if need be while Clare was away.

He had to revise all the drawings on the Neale Road project. It was the stupid developer's fault, but it was a significant job and they had to swallow it. There was a bit of a panic and he'd said he'd see to it by Monday. He vaguely knew it wasn't so tricky. The future residents of Neale Road would have a little less space than they might have done, that's all. But they'd never know about it.

He said he'd tackle it anyway over the weekend, and felt this piece of noble volunteering already scoring him points. Clare would have to put up with it, but he'd say he couldn't wriggle out, and she was used to work coming home with him. Then the situation had changed dramatically. His weekend commitment became another, secondary reason why he couldn't accompany her. It also became his own self-sacrificing task to counterbalance, at least a little, her more demanding mission.

Except now he had this other problem.

He realised that in confronting this minor catastrophe of being locked out he'd for some minutes suspended all thought of his wife's much more grievous situation—or her brother's. He saw her again sitting on the train, the window streaked with rain, not thinking of him. Her keys in her handbag.

The truth was he didn't think Neale Road should take more than half a day, though he could make out it had taken longer. He saw himself handing in the results to Vicki on Monday and in doing so scoring personal points with her that he couldn't precisely analyse. "There we are," he'd say, as if really saying in a certain victorious way (victorious—ha!), "No hard feelings."

He looked at the unremitting frontage of his own home, briefly seeing the immured but none-the-wiser residents of Neale Road.

It was so strange: his life there, himself here, but the sensation was not entirely foreign, or unwelcome.

The rain grew suddenly heavier, a real downpour. Then he saw a light go on, on the first floor, in number twenty, the Mitchells' place—at 4:30 in the afternoon.

He was surprised how rapidly he solved the mystery. It would be their cleaner. He was sure of it. She came once a week, on Fridays. The Mitchells were away, till Sunday, but they'd no doubt asked her to look in and do a few chores, water the plants and so on, before their return. He remembered now—but he'd hardly forgotten—coming home once from the office early and just as he was reaching for his keys (his keys!) seeing her emerge from the adjacent front door.

She'd been visibly startled to see him standing there so close.

"I'm John. I live here," he said reassuringly, then held up his keys by way of proof. She held up her own keys—or the set of keys the Mitchells had given her. For a moment they'd done a flustered mutual jingling with their two sets of keys, a hand dance, as if this was more effective than speech.

"Olga," she eventually said. "I clean." She was blonde, indeterminately foreign, no more than twenty-five.

She'd lowered her eyes automatically, at first, from his gaze. Now she suddenly gave him a quick direct stare, half smiling, half something else. He felt the feral punch of it, even as he knew his own stare was stripping away the thinnish dress she was wearing. This mutual jolt was something he hadn't really felt (except with Vicki) since before he married Clare, though he'd felt it often enough back in those days, and he felt its submerged familiarity now.

Olga. He'd always thought it was an ugly name, implying ugly women. Olga, Friday afternoons. Perhaps he'd noted it even then. So: that light going on next door—it was in the Mitchells' bedroom—must be her. And Olga could be his legitimate means of getting into his house.

She was perhaps stranded herself, he thought. This sudden torrential rain. No umbrella. We forget things. And if it was that same thinnish dress. And this same bucketing rain, he also thought, might make rather tricky, or at least postponable, the business with the ladder and the fence-hopping and the unsecured window.

He got out and scrambled to the porch of number twenty. Even these few paces left him wet. He rang, then for good measure rattled on the letter box and rang again. It might be her policy not to answer the bell when doing the Mitchells' cleaning. But, after a moment, more lights came on and she half opened the front door.

"Remember me?" he said. "John? And my keys? Well now I haven't got any."

It was the same dress. A mix of washed-out pinks and greys. Maybe it was the only dress she did the cleaning in.

"I'm locked out," he said, wondering if this was an expression a foreign woman with limited English would understand. He couldn't hold up a missing key. Was she Russian, Polish, Romanian? It turned out she was Moldovan. He wasn't quite sure where Moldova was.

But she understood the situation and what he needed to do. She even met his apologetic laugh at the comedy of it all with a cautious laugh of her own. If this was all some ruse on his part, then it was peculiarly inventive.

But it was she who made the first move. That is, the move to say that he—they—shouldn't attempt his breaking-and-entering plan, or at least not straight away. With this rain he'd get soaked. And suppose the ladder slipped. It could be dangerous.

And suppose, he might have said, the rain continued for hours still. Suppose it continued all night.

Which it did. In fact the rain, gushing down incessantly, was like some conspiring screen (had anyone seen him enter not his own house but number twenty?). More than that, there was something insistent about it, the very noise of it like a rush of blood.

He'd been here before. And she knew it. She'd been here before. Though he'd never been before, like this, inside the Mitchells' house. But he'd been in this place, or in a place like it, many times before, before Clare. He recognised it as his element.

Many years ago he'd discovered his power—a simple power that was also so like a mere proneness, a gravitation, that he wondered why other men didn't simply, naturally have it too. Why for other men it could sometimes seem so damn difficult. It was just weakness perhaps, other men were just plain weak. Or they just didn't know how to pick up a scent.

Years ago he could have said to another man, though of course it was unthinkable actually to say it, that in a little while, just a little while, he'd have that one there. That one over there. And in a little while after that, probably, he'd make her cry.

So sure was he of this repeated cycle, so familiar, even faintly fatigued by it, that he'd wanted relief and sanctuary. He'd wanted marriage, a wife, a house and all the other things that go with them. And he was an architect by choice and qualification—he fashioned domestic spaces. But he knew there was still this stray animal inside him. And now he was locked out of it all anyway.

There it was, just the other side of a wall: his life. It even seemed for a moment that he and Clare might actually *be* there. He had turned into someone else. There they were. He felt tenderly, protectively towards them. And of course if they were there, then Clare couldn't be travelling somewhere northwards on a train to where her brother was gravely ill, perhaps even dying. And he couldn't be here.

It was a weird thing to be occupying the Mitchells' house, even—as it proved—their bed. Weird and undeniably wrong, but undeniably thrilling and enveloping, like the rain, which didn't let up. It wasn't his house, it wasn't hers. They had that in common. They were both displaced people, though in his case all it took was a wall. Weird and undeniably violating. It made the Mitchells seem the imposters.

At some stage of the evening, or night, he managed to ask her where she was from and why and how she'd come to England. He couldn't get from her much more than the hint of some gaping separation, or loss, that even in his comforting arms (or he thought they might be comforting) she didn't want, or know how, to explain. Where was Moldova? She seemed to retreat behind her poor English. He didn't press or insist. No more than she did about his mysteriously absent wife.

So he just held her, as she seemed to want him to do, as if just being held was his side of a bargain that she'd secured from him.

He thought, as he held her, of how Clare hadn't called. It was really dark now, it might be the middle of the night. She could have arrived and had news, but she hadn't called. And how would he have spoken to her if she had? He hadn't switched off his mobile—as if that might have been an admission of something. But of course she would call on their home phone, the land line. He strained his ears as if to hear it ringing through the wall: an unanswered phone in an empty house. But heard nothing.

She hadn't called, so no problem. Or that is, according to his earlier logic, things must be bad for her brother.

He thought of when, if at all now, but it somehow didn't seem to matter, he'd perform that farcical act with the ladder, his legs poking from the window. He thought of himself breast-stroking on his desk. He thought of himself, earlier, driving Clare diligently to the station and saying unexpectedly "I love you" and returning, truly meaning to knuckle down to work and not knowing at all then how this sudden chain of events would overtake him. He thought of his jacket, with the keys in the pocket, hanging over the chair.

Of course Clare had her inklings.

As he held her, she began to shudder uncontrollably, then to sob and to cry out loud. He'd somehow known this would happen, without knowing why, and knew he must hold her, it was all he could do. He held her and she cried. Then after a while, a long while it seemed, the crying and sobbing ceased and she fell asleep, but he continued to hold her, alert and alone in the dark with just the hiss of the rain.

Lawrence of Arabia

I never thought this would happen to me, Hettie, though I always knew it could. But I never thought I'd be lying here like this in your spare room, looking at your picture of the "Old Harry Rocks at Studland" on the wall. Death's a funny thing, Het. Can you say that?

Have I told you about Lawrence of Arabia?

There's supposed to be a family that rallies round. But it was just me and Roy, like it was just you and Dennis. We were the two Mrs. Underwoods, but there was something tricky with the Underwood genes. Never mind. Carry on. Now it's just you and me, and it feels like we're a couple of real sisters, not sisters-in-law, and you're the older one, though you're not, because you went through all this ahead of me with Dennis. Not the right order, but what bloody order is there?

And when Dennis went you had Roy and me. Or rather we both had Roy. We both had Roy being an older brother like he'd never been before, taking charge like he'd never taken charge before. Well, he stopped taking charge just over a week ago, and it was all I could do, in the time before he went, to make him understand he didn't have to take charge any more.

I know, Het, of course I do. Studland. It was where you and Dennis went for your honeymoon. It was a joke once, wasn't it? In a different world. Honeymoon. Studland. And Roy and I went to the Scilly Isles. There was a joke there too.

A couple of sisters, a couple of widows. It makes me think of a couple of crows. Or do I mean crones? Who'd have thought it, years ago, when it was Roy the Boy and Dennis the Menace, that one day we'd become like those pairs of crumple-faced women you used to see in pubs, nursing their glasses of black Guinness.

No, all right, that's not exactly us. Nursing our glasses of white wine.

I'm so grateful to you for taking me in. You had other plans. You were going somewhere warm. I've forgotten where already. Not Studland anyhow. You said, "I've cancelled everything, Peg. You're staying with me." You said, "It's Christmas, but it can be whatever you want, it can be not Christmas if you like. I don't have a bit of tinsel in the house. Don't argue, Peg, you're staying with me."

Did I say "taking charge?"

And why should Roy have hung on for Christmas? So he could spend it in a hospital bed? So I could come in with a cracker for us to pull, if he had the strength? So he could wear a funny hat?

They say however much you prepare, nothing prepares you. They say it doesn't hit you till after the funeral. Well, that was yesterday, the day before Christmas Eve. You can't choose your date, can you? Or the weather. A howling gale, umbrellas blowing inside-out. And you'd been going somewhere warm.

They say—who are these they with their big mouths?—that you're in a state of shock. I don't know about that. Do you know what I thought, Het, when I left that hospital, after he'd gone? I thought: This can't be happening, I can't just be sitting here on a number nine bus. I thought: He's with me still, of course he is, it's up to me now to make him be with me. I felt in a state of importance, that's what I felt. Never mind shock. Nothing so important had ever happened to me before. Except of course the importance of meeting Roy in the first place.

The Scilly Isles, 1965. Us and Harold Wilson.

A state of importance. Does that sound silly? I'm not an important person. Nor was Roy. All he did, before he retired, was get to the top of the Parks Department and run five public parks and nine other sites of horticultural amenity. And how he took charge of them.

There I was on that bus, wanting only to be with him, wanting only to make him be with me. But do you know who else was on that bus too?

Peter O'Toole.

Maybe I'd already heard it at the hospital. Maybe I'd heard one nurse say to another, "Have you heard—Peter O'Toole has died?" And if I did hear it maybe I'd thought: No, I didn't hear that. I don't want to hear it anyway. Not now.

But the bus was full of people going to work, holding newspapers with Peter O'Toole on the front. I couldn't not know about it. And only days before it had been Nelson Mandela. Deaths don't come much bigger, do they? And I hadn't wanted to know about that either. But even Roy, lying there with his tubes and drips, had to be aware that Nelson Mandela had died. Nelson Mandela who took charge of South Africa. And you know what he said? "Well perhaps it's all right for me then." And perhaps in some way it was. And you know what else he said? "All these black nurses, Peg. It matters for them, doesn't it?"

There I was on that bus, at seven in the morning, with the Christmas lights floating by outside, just two hours after Roy had died, looking at the face of Peter O'Toole. Except it wasn't even Peter O'Toole. It was Lawrence of Arabia. On every newspaper. It was as if Lawrence of Arabia had died all over again. As if Lawrence of Arabia had got on the bus.

How unfair to Peter O'Toole. How unfair to Roy.

But the truth is I couldn't help thinking, just like everyone else: Those blue eyes, that golden hair, that man in the white robes, striding along the roof of a train. How old were we when Peter O'Toole suddenly came along? And what girl wouldn't? In her dreams.

Two hours after Roy had gone and I was thinking about Peter O'Toole. Or thinking about Lawrence of Arabia. Or not thinking about either of them, since I was thinking about that man in the fluttering white robes, who only ever existed in a film, didn't he? I've seen pictures of the real Lawrence of Arabia and he looks like a little squinty man you wouldn't want to spend any time with.

But he was important, wasn't he? He'd done something important. So had Peter O'Toole, if only to turn into Lawrence of Arabia. And so of course had Nelson Mandela. A state of importance, don't we all want just a bit of it?

It must be Christmas morning already, Het, no longer Christmas Eve. I'm so grateful to you. A couple of sisters, in our separate rooms, waiting for Father Christmas, in his red robes, who never existed either.

All those crazy Englishmen—and Peter O'Toole wasn't even English, was he?—who went off to foreign parts, to do crazy things, wear Arab costume or whatever, to make their mark on the world, take charge. All those crazy Englishmen in the midday sun.

There I was on that bus, riding along Fairfax Street with Lawrence of Arabia. Now here I am in your spare bedroom, with the light on because I don't want to lie in the dark, wondering who the hell was Old Harry.

Well, I'm a lucky girl. Most widows get a few flowers, I get five parks.

Roy never had blue eyes or golden hair or wore white robes, like some bloody angel. He died in one of those hospital nightie things, all peek-a-boo up the back. He had brown eyes and black hair, most of which had gone anyway. His little brother went before him. So did Nelson Mandela. And now he's gone too, Hettie, he's gone too, like his hair.

Ajax

When I was a small boy we had a neighbour called Mr. Wilkinson, who was a weirdo. He must be long gone now, but I've often wondered what became of him. I was his undoing.

Let me stress that I never thought he was a weirdo, it wasn't my word. It was an opinion I was made to have of him. I was too young to have opinions of my own, or so it was thought. I was just a small boy going to primary school. But I didn't think Mr. Wilkinson was weird. I thought he was interesting, I even admired him. I was driven into taking an opposite view.

When I was with my mother and we met him in the street he'd always be well mannered. He'd doff his hat. He'd always wear a hat and be well dressed, often in a suit, even if the suit had seen better days. He'd ask courteously after my father—"Mr. Simmonds"—and he used words with a feeling for them, as if they were things you should treat appreciatively, not just mechanically, employing standard phrases. Maybe it was his enthusiastic use of language that first made my parents think he was weird.

He looked entirely respectable. The dearest wish of all the grown-ups in our street was to be respectable and, by being respectable, to better themselves. So you'd think they might have regarded Mr. Wilkinson as a model. It was obvious even to me that he was in some ways a cut above our street, he'd come down in the world to it. It was also obvious that he was what people called "educated."

I'd had it drummed into me by my parents from the earliest age that education was the most important thing in life and the key to everything, and I believed them. "Education" was one of the first long words I learnt, and learning it was—rather magically—an example of the thing it proclaimed. At school I had no problem with teachers. I revered them. They were the purveyors of this most important thing. It struck me that Mr. Wilkinson had the qualities of a teacher and perhaps had been one once. He seemed, in fact, even more educated than any of the teachers at my primary school, and for this reason too I couldn't see why the whole street didn't look up to him, instead of thinking he was weird.

But Mr. Wilkinson lived alone. That was one mark against him. And though he'd always be respectably dressed when you met him in the street, he was in the habit of engaging in physical exercises in his back garden in just his underpants. In all weathers, even in mid-January. Just his underpants.

It wasn't only exercising. There seemed to be a whole ritual medley of things that sometimes involved simply breathing—a vigorous expanding and deflating of his lungs—and sometimes involved not doing anything in particular except chanting. Chanting was the best word for it. You might sometimes have called it humming or even singing, but chanting was the word that got used. In his underpants.

Anyone can do what they like in the privacy of their own home. This was something my parents would have firmly and fairly asserted. But they also said, about many things, that there were limits.

Our street was like thousands of others built in the outer suburbs on vacant land just after the war, but for some reason it had been decided to erect a pair of semis, then a bungalow, then another pair of semis and so on. If you had a bungalow you only had the one floor, but you had the privilege of being detached. There wasn't a great deal of space, but you could walk all the way round your own home. Even in your underpants.

On the other side of us, in the adjoining semi, were the Hislops. They'd been there, as had my parents, since the houses were built, but were a slightly older generation. Their two boys—I never thought of them as "boys"—were old enough for one of them to have done National Service. I remember him in a beret, with an unexpected moustache and a kit bag. Their father ran a small printer's. The boys had girlfriends, tinkered around with cars and got married. There was nothing particularly educated about the Hislops, they were even slightly rough-edged, but they were a family and normal.

On the other side was Mr. Wilkinson.

There was a high wooden fence, with a bit of trellis on top, between ourselves and Mr. Wilkinson, so the only way you could see him in his underpants was from our spare bedroom or my parents' bedroom, both at the back upstairs. This put us in the position of spies, while all Mr. Wilkinson was doing was— minding his own business. Nonetheless, my parents and particularly my mother didn't want to live next door to someone who was even known to stand around in his underpants and chant. And you could hear the chanting sometimes without needing to look.

Mr. Wilkinson, I should say, was quite old. By that I mean that he seemed old to me. He must have been in his fifties. He had thinning, whitish hair, but had none of the stoopingness or vulnerability of old people. He was well built, even quite muscular (as could be seen) and, plainly, he kept himself fit. He was a good advert for physical education too.

I only remember him as "Mr. Wilkinson." I can't recall ever knowing his first name, perhaps it was considered wrong to know it. Mr. Hislop was also Tony. My parents christened me

James, and gradually gave up the battle against "Jimmy." When I was first introduced to Mr. Wilkinson (before we knew anything of his habits) it was as James, but he immediately and perhaps only in a spirit of friendship called me Jimmy. I saw that this set my mother against him.

Not only was there the fence and the trellis, but because the street was on a hill and Mr. Wilkinson was above us, it was virtually impossible at ground level to see the back of his bungalow or into his garden. In the months when the trellis wasn't overgrown you might just glimpse his white-haired but imposing head moving past, or even a pale pink shoulder. Which could make you wonder if he was wearing underpants this time or nothing at all.

On warm days I used to like playing by the flower bed at the foot of the fence, near the back of the house. Playing really meant re-landscaping the flower bed according to my infant purposes, which naturally displeased my parents. But I remained so set upon this activity that they eventually allowed a (strictly limited) part of the bed to be used for it. Perhaps they thought it was good for my development and that I might one day become a civil engineer. In fact, though they didn't know it, I was rearranging, in miniature, our street. I was in charge of every household in it.

Imagine a region of pebble-dashing and occasional bursts of mock-Tudor, of rowans, laburnums, trim hedges, trim lawns and clumps of purple aubrietia. You have the picture. I think of it now with an odd fondness, but with an abiding, far-off sense of its own weirdness.

One day, engaged in my flower-bed projects, I caught Mr. Wilkinson watching me intently through the trellis and the tendrils of clematis. He must have been doing it for some time before I looked up, but, if I was surprised, I wasn't frightened. He wasn't spying on me (as we spied on him) so much as waiting to speak to me.

He asked me if I was interested in agriculture and if I was a vegetarian.

These were two long words I didn't know—I found them even difficult to remember—and I must have disappointed Mr. Wilkinson with my answer. But he seemed eager that I should *be* a vegetarian. I told my parents (I was at heart a truthful, conscientious boy) and I must have repeated the words accurately enough. They said agriculture was farming and vegetarians were people who didn't eat meat.

Then my mother said, and my father backed her up, that I should never speak to Mr. Wilkinson through the fence, or anywhere else, if I was by myself, even if he spoke to me. This had probably been the first conversation—or one-to-one encounter— I'd had with him anyway.

He stood around in his back garden in his underpants and he was a vegetarian. This settled the question of his being a weirdo. Every Sunday, without fail, the whole street smelt of roasting meat.

If the underpants and the vegetarianism didn't clinch it, there was the matter of the visitors. Mr. Wilkinson didn't go out at regular times as people did who had jobs, but he had visitors. They came just now and then, not in a steady flow, and didn't stay for very long. They were all sorts, but it's true that among them were a number of what my mother called "young girls."

There was nothing intrinsically improper about this and, again, you had to keep watch on Mr. Wilkinson's bungalow even to notice it. The simple explanation—that went with his teacherly demeanour—was that Mr. Wilkinson gave some kind of lessons. He taught music perhaps. Given the chanting, perhaps he taught singing. But no one arrived, it's true, with a musical instrument and we never heard, though we heard the chanting, the muffled sounds from within the bungalow of a piano or a poorly sung scale.

He taught something anyway, for which people were prepared to come for an hour or so and pay him. I actually had the misplaced fantasy that I might go round to Mr. Wilkinson's myself and be taught whatever it was he taught. Since the key to life was education. But I was glad I kept this thought from my parents.

The teaching theory never held much water, even if it was plausible and I wanted to subscribe to it. My mother—in over-heard conversations with my father—kept coming back to the young girls, as if that in itself disproved it. But I could easily imagine Mr. Wilkinson teaching young girls something. Elocu-tion, deportment. I'd discovered that even very small girls at my primary school could be subjected by their parents to bouts of extra-curricular improvement. And if Mr. Wilkinson had some dubious interest in young girls that was simply to do with their being young girls (and which I knew nothing of), why didn't he restrict his visitors to young girls only? But I never voiced this argument either.

The teaching theory was scotched anyway by what, it became known, Mr. Wilkinson had himself disclosed about his occupa-tion and livelihood. Some other neighbour, bolder or more pry-ing than my parents, had pinned him down on the matter and been obligingly told that he practised his own form of "alterna-tive medicine." It was something he'd evolved over the years through study and application. He advertised professionally and had many satisfied patients. He had even asked the inquisitive neighbour (I think it was Mrs. Fox at number seven) if there was anything he might do for her.

My mother said, "Alternative medicine?" Then said, "What's that when it's at home?"—a favourite phrase of hers which I much later thought was particularly apt in this case. Then she added, "In his underpants?"

These were remarks put to my father that, again, weren't for my ears, though I overheard them. My father said (and, think-ing about it much later too, I thought it pretty near the mark),

"Alternative medicine? If you ask me, I think he might once have practised ordinary medicine. But now—if you see what I mean—he has no alternative."

I retained those words because, though I didn't understand them, I could tell my father thought he'd said something clever. The cleverness had even taken him by surprise. And though I didn't know what the cleverness consisted of, I felt pleased for him because for a moment at least he seemed to possess the artful and inventive way with language that was characteristic of Mr. Wilkinson.

I couldn't, myself, picture Mr. Wilkinson as a doctor. My childhood experience of doctors was that they were gruff, chilly people who could do nasty things to you. I continued to see him as a teacher, an educator, and perhaps alternative medicine (if it wasn't just something bad-tasting in a bottle) was really a form of teaching. Perhaps Mr. Wilkinson had some special wisdom to impart. He wasn't a weirdo at all. The visitors who turned up now and then to ring his doorbell were his followers.

One day I had another "conversation" with Mr. Wilkinson which proved to be rather more than a conversation. I did the thing I wasn't supposed to do, and I exceeded even that. It was in the school holidays. My father was at work, my mother was going to see her mother for the afternoon. I was to be dispatched, while she was gone, to play with my friend Roger West at number ten, and thus be under the watchful eye of Mrs. West. But some minor crisis in the West household prevented this, and my mother, for whatever reason, couldn't suddenly disappoint my grandmother.

For perhaps the first time in my life I was told that I'd have to be alone in the house for a whole afternoon, though it wouldn't be so long really and I was old enough for it. But I was, strictly, to stay in the house or in the back garden and not to answer the door to anyone.

It was a warm summer's day, so I was happy to keep to the back garden, doing more reconstruction of "my" section of the flower bed. I don't think Mr. Wilkinson can have been aware of my exact situation, because of the question he asked me. But there he was again suddenly, peering through the clematis, and there was no one to witness that I was breaking my solemn oath not to speak to him.

He said, "Excuse me, Jimmy. Does your mother—does Mrs. Simmonds—have anything for clearing drains? I'm awfully sorry to trouble her, but I've a spot of bother with my one at the back here. Nothing drastic, but in this hot weather, you know . . ."

I could see that Mr. Wilkinson was sporting a shirt collar. He wasn't just in his underpants.

I had the child's instinct not to say that my mother was out, the child's alertness to the possibility of adventure—at least to the possibility of getting to know Mr. Wilkinson better. Not to mention the child's excitement at the forbidden. I didn't know about clearing drains, but I knew there was a cupboard in the kitchen where the sort of thing that might clear them would be.

I said to Mr. Wilkinson, "I'll go and ask her."

Did I say truthful and conscientious?

In the cupboard there were various jars and bottles, but there was a big tall tin labelled "Ajax." I vaguely knew it had a variety of uses (my father sometimes used it for something in the garden) and that it was my mother's answer to anything unpleasant. There was another tin of the stuff in the lavatory upstairs. Drains? Why not?

I picked it up and decided that, instead of trying to pass it over the fence—impossible for a small boy anyway—I should take it round to Mr. Wilkinson directly. It was only a matter of opening the side door, which fastened with just a latch, then walking up his front path. The truth was that I was impelled by a sly curiosity: I would be just like one of those mysterious visitors, of whom there might already have been one or two that morning.

Mr. Wilkinson opened his door. He looked at me and smiled. He was wearing clothes. His strong arms projected from rolled-up sleeves. "Oh that's good of you, Jimmy. And so kind of your mother." He studied the Ajax tin, perhaps frowning a little even as he continued to smile. He could hardly reject my offering. "Well, perhaps it might do the trick."

He looked at me again, the frown deepening, and seemed to hesitate. I can see now that he was coming to a significant decision: whether to take the tin, say he'd return it later, and send me away, or whether, since I was there and it was our tin, to make me a party to his drain-clearing operation. Perhaps he thought I was just a small boy and there was no danger—that is, to him. Or perhaps he was just infected with the same impetuous rush towards the hazardous that had overcome me.

"Well," he said, "we may as well go straight round the side."

This disappointed me. I wasn't going to be allowed to pass through the house. On the other hand, I could see (or could see later with hindsight) that he'd decided, wrongly, to trust me. If trust even came into it.

He liked me, I think. He thought he'd found a friend.

We walked along by the flank wall of the bungalow. There I was on the other side of the fence over which he'd peered at me and over which he could sometimes be seen standing near-naked and ululating.

He'd taken the tin from me and, raising it now like an exhibit or something in a lesson, he said, "Isn't it a sad thing, Jimmy, that one of the great heroes of the Greek myths, one of the most glorious of those who fought in the Trojan War, should be reduced to being a tin of scouring powder?"

I hadn't the faintest idea what he was talking about, but these words made a great impression on me and have stayed with me ever since. I still hear them being spoken in the eloquent, playful yet lamenting way Mr. Wilkinson uttered them.

The fact is that it is to this unintelligible but memorable

remark I owe all my later discovery and enthralled exploration of the Greek myths. I owe a whole world of narrative and magic and meaning. I owe a whole education.

When my parents asked me later that year what I wanted for Christmas I said at once (having done some precocious research at my primary school) that I wanted a book that would tell me all the stories of the Greek myths, the Trojan War included. This request rather surprised my parents, but they found me such a book. It was a little beyond me at first, but I grew into it. I have it still.

But more than this. Much more. I owe to Mr. Wilkinson's remark all my lasting fascination not just with how a great Greek hero gets turned into a tin of scouring powder, but with all the strange turns and twists and evolutions this world can take, all the bizarre changes of fortune, for good and bad, it can offer. And I should know about them.

I owe to it an education. And an education.

"When we say scouring powder, Jimmy, we really mean lavatory cleaner, don't we? No doubt at your age you have your lavatorial interests. Did you know, Jimmy, that in Elizabethan times a lavatory was called a jakes? A jakes. Ajax. Do you see the connection?"

Again, I hadn't the foggiest what he was on about, but I found it all beguiling, tantalising.

He took me round to the back of the bungalow where an outflow pipe from his kitchen led into a little gully with a drain hole and a grille. We had something similar beneath our own kitchen. I could see he was now hesitating again, that he wasn't sure he should be doing this in my company, but I could also sense his mood of wilful risk-taking, that he wanted to let me, even, into his secret. I could see that he'd removed the grille and had been poking about with a stick.

"Ajax," he said. "Will it—will he—do the trick?"

Whatever it was that was clogging his drain it was deep down, or else there was some uncooperative bend in the pipe. The hole was abnormally full, almost to overflowing, of dirty water. But it wasn't just water, it was water with a distinctly reddish colour. It made me think at once of the slop bucket that would be some-times visible in our local butcher's, where I'd go with my mother and where there'd be sawdust on the floor and halves of pigs hanging on huge hooks and dripping.

A little bobbing shred of something, a mere gobbet of scum, floated in the water.

Let me say that everything was so much more primitive in those days, even if gentlemen doffed hats. It was so much nearer the Middle Ages. There'd been a war and there'd been rationing. My mother was perfectly capable of skinning and cooking a rab-bit, but there came a point when she wouldn't have liked to admit to this, or even to eat rabbit. When my parents developed their desire for respectability and advancement they really wanted to move into the clean modern age and leave behind them all traces of the ancient gutter. They weren't squeamish and they weren't innocent, but they wanted to live tidy lives, and they didn't like weirdness.

I could see that in theory our street didn't mind Mr. Wilkin-son's being weird, but they minded his being weird in our street. They hoped that somehow something would be done about it. But, short of some superior agent's stepping in, they believed that by the sheer force of their adverse opinion Mr. Wilkinson might be compelled to leave and take his weirdness elsewhere. They wanted him flushed out. In this situation was the whole history of the world.

I could see that the mucky water in Mr. Wilkinson's drain was composed partly of blood and I could see that for some inscrutable and perilous reason Mr. Wilkinson wanted me to see it, and not to say anything.

But, yes, I was at heart a conscientious, a truthful boy. I hon-oured my father and mother. I had a sense of moral responsibility. I'd told my parents about the vegetarianism when I might have said nothing. Now I'd have to tell them about breaking the edict that had followed from that first honesty and—worse—about taking the Ajax tin and going round to Mr. Wilkinson's when I should have stayed within clearly prescribed bounds.

But all this was capped by the greater and more glaring obligation to truth I had: to let it be known that Mr. Wilkinson clearly wasn't a vegetarian—a slander of my own unwitting instigation—and was even, though I hadn't been able to see into his kitchen, a fairly zealous eater of meat. And, by implication, he was at least in that respect so much less of the weirdo than he'd been unfairly made out to be.

I can never be sure whether it was this action on my part, with all its complexity and for which I was punished by not being allowed out, even into the garden, for most of the next day, which led directly to Mr. Wilkinson's leaving us, which led to his being, as I was to discover later, taken into custody while a search warrant was issued and (discreetly) acted upon for his bungalow.

Having been so roundly punished, I was soon being, confusingly, asked questions by a kindly and patient policeman while my mother tenderly held my hand.

There were things you couldn't do in those days, the law didn't allow it, which you can do now. It was all very primitive, and perhaps the changes which have occurred since then are further evidence of the importance of education. For example, Mr. Wilkinson lived alone, he might have been a homosexual, but he wouldn't have been allowed by law to be one in any practical sense.

I say this because I'm a homosexual myself, though I didn't know it then, I discovered it later. You might say I had to be educated into it. There's a whole other story I might tell, involving me and my parents, which is even more painful in some ways than the story of Mr. Wilkinson. But this is not the time, and perhaps you can imagine it. There are plenty of stories, but this is not the time.

But I think about Mr. Wilkinson and about what I did to him.

He disappeared anyway. It was what the whole street wanted, but I missed him, I even felt a little bereft. I wish I'd known his first name. A nice couple, the Fletchers, who soon had their first baby, a little girl called Jilly—I remember *her* name—whom my mother unashamedly adored, moved in. And that was what the whole street wanted too.

There are some people who might say or think of me, now, that I'm a little weird, or at least odd. But then if you're a professor of Greek you're allowed to be that, the world even rather expects it of you, especially if your hair has become a snowy fleece and you wear tweed suits and affect white-spotted red bow ties.

I have never, so far, walked across the court here to the senior common room—across the grass on which only a few are permitted to walk—in just my underpants. Or, for extra brio, with my Fellow's gown on too. But I'm sure if I did this (and frankly I'm tempted) it would be forgiven me, at least once, since I'm the Morley-Edwards Professor of Greek. And I'm sure that far more scandalous acts have occurred in Oxford colleges and yet been permitted, or at least smoothed over—acts that would never be countenanced in suburban streets.

All my life I've taken seriously—pursued and furthered—my parents' creed that education is the most important thing, education that leads us on an ameliorating journey through life. I am their exemplar, their vindication. What could better have answered and glorified their tenet than that I should have become a professor at an Oxford college?

If you want weirdness, real weirdness, the weirdness we're all made of, if you want the primitive that never goes away, then go to the Greek myths and to what the Greeks made out of them. Though don't forget your Ajax tin.

Ajax, son of Telamon and mighty warrior, second only to Achilles, but ousted by the brain of Odysseus, went mad in the end, mistaking sheep for people. I know this now.

Was She the Only One?

Was she the only one? Was it all her fault?

Was she the only one not to wash her husband's shirt? It hung in the wardrobe with all its creases and wrinkles, his best white shirt, his Sunday shirt, the last shirt he'd worn before putting on a uniform. She took it down and pressed it to her nose. When the letters arrived she crushed it to her face and, as she read, breathed deeply. It was the best that could be done. Was she the only one?

In those days a man's white shirt was quite an item, with its long tails, double cuffs, its round neck with the stud holes. It was more like a sort of starchy nightdress, and it served her as such often enough. So the wrinkles multiplied, so there was her smell mingling with his. But that was only right. They were husband and wife. It became a superstition. If she didn't wash it, so long as she didn't wash it. Not until. Was she the only one?

Months went by. The letters came less frequently. She had to be sparing in her use of the shirt, or her smell would take away his. It was getting rather ripe, it's true. His first leave was cancelled. He couldn't say why. It was a blow that made her weep, but it wasn't like a message to say he was dead. And she hadn't washed the shirt.

.   .   .

This was her short marriage to Albert. Most of it was separation, most of it wasn't a marriage at all, most of it was marriage to a shirt. He was a railway clerk from Slough, but he had his notions. One day he'd be a station master. He was fussy about his shirts. He only liked to be called Albert, never Bert.

She was Lily Hobbs from Staines. She was eighteen and didn't mind: either Lily or Lil.

I'm Bert, Bert, I haven't a shirt . . .

Months went by. Then he came home. Because his previous leave had been cancelled he now had two weeks. Was it true, two whole weeks? And he was untouched—not a scratch, or so he wrote. Was it true? Was he being brave? Still she didn't wash the shirt. Seeing was believing. She'd heard stories of telegrams arriving before men due home on leave. She had two choices anyway: to wash it, specially, for his arrival, or not to wash it— until. She chose the latter. Her big mistake.

If she'd washed the shirt, would everything have been all right?

I'm Bert . . .

But there he was on the doorstep. So, it had been just as well. There he was. Or there he wasn't. Albert Tanner. He said, "Hello, Lily. Can I come in?" Which was just like him, but not. She rather wished he'd said "Lil." She rather wished he'd clapped a hand quickly to her behind, but he hadn't.

He'd never mentioned the shell shock. That was news to her. Did it explain everything, and what was it anyway? Shell shock. Had he invented it? He said that he had it, like something catching, like measles. Was that why he hardly touched her? He said it was why he had the two weeks. He said he'd have to report every other day to a doctor, an MO, in London, who'd assess him to see if he was fit to return. Which was like saying—was he saying this?—that his two weeks, depending, might go on indefinitely.

In which case, God bless shell shock. In which case, Albert, be as shell-shocked as you can.

Was it all lies? Was he preparing for his desertion? Did he really have two weeks? There was something about him, standing there in his uniform. He didn't look like a soldier, or even a railway clerk. He looked like a crafty door-to-door salesman. He looked like the sort of man women left at home had to watch out for. He looked up to no good. He looked—was this really the word?—like a criminal. Albert? A criminal?

Then he saw the shirt.

He wanted to know, he *demanded* to know why it was hanging there like that, his best white shirt, "in that filthy condition." And before she could explain to him the several reasons (but couldn't he guess?) he was explaining to her, he was shouting in her face that the reason why it was hanging there in that filthy condition was that she'd lent it to another man, she'd been letting another man wear it. And to prove the point he thrust his nostrils into the fabric, pushing it to his face, then let out a disgusted "Pah!"

None of this had she imagined. None of this in her wildest anticipations had she allowed for. He wouldn't be untouched, he'd have a bit missing. An ear or something.

I'm Bert, Bert, I haven't a . . .

Now that this was happening the sheer absurdity of it couldn't smother her terror. Was he going to hit her? Albert? Hit her? For a moment she actually looked at the shirt and saw it, perhaps as he was seeing it, like some other man skulking there in the wardrobe, just as they were supposed to do in naughty stage plays.

She knew she had to stand her ground, keep steady, be reasonable. Yes, of course, of course: over there (but she'd never thought of this before) it would be the constant talk, what their women got up to back home. They'd tease and torture each other with it, they'd tease and torture themselves.

It was June, 1918. No one knew the war had only five months to run. If he hadn't been a railway clerk but a railwayman—a signalman say—he might have been permanently excused, but he'd joined up anyway.

Yes, of course. She was eighteen. She walked down streets on her own, her skirt swung. But.

"It's your smell, Albert, no one but yours."

Which was a lie, a half-lie, because the smell by then was mostly hers. But she could explain that, and wouldn't the explanation, surely, please him? Wouldn't it even be the clearest sign—it seemed ridiculous to have to grope for a word—of her loyalty?

But she never did explain. She saw his rage boil over. Was he really going to hit her?

"Wash it!" he said. "Wash it, right now!"

He'd barely got home. It was like an order, a bellowed military order. "Wash it!" He was a corporal now, with a stripe on his shoulder. He'd gone away a private and come back a corporal. What had he done to become a corporal so quickly? She didn't like the word "corporal," she liked the word private. He'd gone away Albert too.

"Wash it!"

She couldn't disobey. He would have struck her. She washed it while he stood over her and watched her wash it. She put it through the mangle. Then later she ironed it while he stood over her too and watched her. She hadn't imagined this. But she foolishly supposed that when this task was finished all might be restored. This was her punishment—her penalty, her humiliation—all thoroughly undeserved, but so be it, she would undergo it, if it would bring Albert back again. Perhaps, when the shirt was fully laundered, he'd break down, see the obvious truth, beg her forgiveness.

But it was she who had to face the less obvious truth that, yes, she really was washing away another man's smell, and that other man was Albert.

"There's your shirt, Albert. All clean. Now, wear it. Please. Wear it for me."

She foolishly imagined, only extending her delusions, that once he wore it, that would do the trick. It would mean, of course, having to remove his uniform. He didn't seem to want to remove it, it was like his skin. It would mean having to have a good scrub in the tub. And among her many anticipations had been seeing herself assist him in doing just that.

What she really meant by "wear your shirt" was make love. She didn't have the way to say it directly, but might he not see that it was what she meant? Might he not see that "wear your shirt for me, Albert" actually meant don't wear it—yet. She would have gladly washed it for him anyway, having explained to him first those reasons—as if they were needed—and having, first of all . . .

If she could only get round now to saying that she'd gone to bed with it, she'd worn it in bed—wasn't it obvious?—then wouldn't the other thing follow? And she didn't really mind, now, how it was done—gently, roughly, fumblingly, slowly, all too rushed and quickly. So long as.

But he stared at the clean shirt she held out to him and all that happened (though it was something) was that his anger seemed to leave him, even turn for a while into something like its opposite, into complete bewilderment, even panic, as if she were offering him something terrible. A white shirt, he was staring at a white shirt.

"Please, Albert." What could she do that wasn't wrong?

If he were to wear it, if they were to be to each other like man and wife. It was all ifs. It took nearly a week before he wore the shirt. As for the other thing, as for her own desires, she understood that what Duncan, her second husband, would one day call her "appetites" had not only been thwarted, but neutralised, chilled.

How could she do it with Albert if Albert wasn't Albert?

"You have appetites, Lily." So Duncan had said, barely a fortnight before the Armistice. She couldn't tell if he was confused or impressed. For all his fine words, he was just a boy, like Albert.

.   .   .

It took nearly a week before he wore the shirt, including the days when he had to report to the MO. If that's what he did. Need it have taken so much time? Had he invented the MO just so, when he'd hardly got home, he could disappear every other day? How absurd, how humiliating—and somehow just as agonising—having waited for him all those months, to have to wait for him now to come home on a train from Paddington. Or wherever. Would he come home at all?

"Hello, Albert."

"Hello, Lily. Can I come in?"

What was happening? He'd be in his uniform again, for the MO presumably. She had the first flicker of the thought that she wanted him back where he'd come from. Not Paddington, or wherever. Where he'd come from. Did he see it in her face?

"I want you to wear your shirt, Albert."

She didn't give up. She had a plan. If he'd made her do what she'd done, then she'd make him do this, if it was the last thing she'd ask of him.

"Listen, Albert, listen. I want you to wear your shirt. I want you to wear your shirt and to go with me this Sunday to Marlow. The weather will be fine. I want you to take me out on a boat on the river. Remember?"

To her surprise (she was ready for more coaxing) he said, "All right, Lil."

"Lil." Was it something the MO had said?

He wore the shirt. He submitted. He became so woodenly docile that this, too, alarmed her. It was tit for tat, it was his punishment? But it was hardly that, an outing on the river. He was preparing to say he was sorry? I'm sorry, Lil, I'm so sorry for everything—his eyes, Albert's pale brown eyes, trying to express the measure of what he was sorry for.

Or it was nothing of the sort, and he knew better? Yes, if she wanted, yes, if it meant so much to her. Yes, he'd fit into this foolish picture of hers. At least he didn't explode and say: So this is what she'd done all this while, gone to Marlow, on the river, with other men.

They went to Marlow. They took the train. They changed at Maidenhead. She didn't know if he still kept in his head the timetables he'd once so diligently kept there. Cookham, Bourne End . . . She didn't know any more what he had in his head. He was wearing the shirt. She was wearing her long narrow skirt and carrying the little parasol that had once been her grandmother's.

When one day she was a grandmother herself she'd find it impossible to explain to her teenage granddaughters, who wore next to nothing, that she'd once thought it the height of *sexiness* (though the word hadn't existed) to loll back in a creaking boat, water lapping at its undersides, in a long white skirt, twirling a parasol, while a man—but the man was Albert—removed his jacket, rolled up his white sleeves and rowed you rhythmically upriver.

As impossible as to explain to them about Albert anyway, though that was her firm decision. Just the name and that he'd died in the war—the first one that is. She'd had this other husband once, before Grandpa Duncan. But what should they care? He hadn't been their grandfather. Even her own daughters, Joyce and Margaret: he hadn't been their father. No logic in saying that he might have been.

"Albert," she would say, with a fragile smile. "He never liked to be called Bert."

They took a boat. The water sparkled. Willows and swans. But she saw at once (if she didn't know already), from the put-upon way he shoved off from the little jetty, that this journey by river was going nowhere, certainly not back into the past. He took it out on the oars, whatever it was he had in his head. He worked it out on the oars. She could loll and twiddle her parasol as much as she liked.

When they returned to the jetty she suddenly pictured Channel steamers, packed with reeking men. She hadn't thought of it: a train, a boat. What could she do that wasn't wrong? It was as if this brief Sunday excursion was like the whole brief non-event of his leave. An hour, two weeks, what was the difference? He wanted to go back. She saw this. Did he see her tears? He wanted to go back and be really dead.

His leave was actually truncated. Was it all his invention again, the invention of an invention? The doctor had said now, apparently, that his shell shock was all an act, he should snap out of it and return. But which was the act? He said, in a flat voice more appalling than rage, that there was nothing he could do about it. He'd been "found out." Found out?

I'm Bert, Bert . . .

And—this was the worst part—she was actually glad. Had it shown in her face, like that other flicker? Would it have mattered? They were both glad.

And there was another level to her gladness. His too? She was glad—no chance of it in those last few days—that they'd never conceived a child.

"Goodbye then, Lily. I'll be seeing you."

"Goodbye, Albert."

There was only the shirt again, hanging in the wardrobe, smelling now of a sweat worked up on the River Thames. But it wasn't Albert's sweat. It had no magic. It was a general dreadful now commonly manufactured sweat and, yes, it was like an infectious disease, it was like the measles, she seemed to feel it spreading from the wardrobe all through the house. She couldn't stand the thing hanging there like that. On the other hand, she wasn't going to wash it. Not now.

It took a week, a week of contending with the shirt. It was like a miniature war. Then she could bear it no longer. She lit a fire—in June—and flung it on. She knew what she was doing. She didn't thrust it into the kitchen stove. She wanted to watch it burn.

It was the 25th of June. Two days later she got the telegram. "25th June. Of wounds." But it came as no surprise.

So she was a widow now. Was she the only one?

Three months later she met Duncan. Duncan Ross. Of all places, it was on Slough station. The train was late. They exchanged shy words. Then he actually paid for her to travel first class, as if it was his sudden flustered duty. He had to, you see, in his uniform. They sat together to Reading, where he had to change for Aldershot, and where she was going for an interview, as a maid.

He was in intelligence, which meant he couldn't talk about it. So, how did she know? She didn't say that, of course. She looked at him, at his brown moustache, perfectly demurely. She didn't say, "So, it was a bit like shell shock then."

And her own private joke to herself—something else she'd never say—was that he was in intelligence, but the intelligence was all hers. In intelligence, and based at home. Neither of them knew the war had just two months left. An officer, a newly made lieutenant, an educated child. And clearly—but never mind that, she'd cope with that—above her station.

But my people are well off, you know . . .

Dear Duncan. In thirty years' time they'd have lived through another war and he'd have been safely in intelligence again—rising to major. And they'd have had Joyce and Margaret, their darling girls, who not only lived through that war too, but cut a fine swathe through it, having a high old time. Girls! You could have said this was part of her intelligence too. Though she could hardly have insisted on it from Duncan. Only girls, please. But perhaps because she wanted it so much, it was what she got. Duncan obliged. And girls for grandchildren too.

It was agreed, on the platform at Reading, that they'd meet again. Going for the interview, she'd thought, was a little like Albert going to see the MO. Duncan and Lily . . . It had a ring, like the name of a superior grocer's. They managed in due course to scrape a whole day together, in Maidenhead, by the river. It was meeting halfway.

Maidenhead! Well, it was where her new life began, her second one, her real one.

"You have appetites, Lily."

But she'd never tell even Duncan, who had the good sense—the intelligence—not to probe for details. Not even the date. Often there wasn't any date. Often there wasn't anything.

The 25th of June: she'd have to live through it every year.

Just the bare facts: she'd been married before, then widowed. She wasn't the only one. It had all taken less than a year. His name was Albert. Just the little extra morsel, the gently smiling decoy: "Always Albert. He never liked to be called Bert."

Knife

He stood by the opened kitchen drawer. It was a warm April afternoon. He'd come home from school meaning to take the knife at some point before the following morning and hadn't thought that his best chance might be straight away. The clock on the microwave said 4:25. His mother was in her bedroom with her boyfriend Wes. He could hear them, they were loud enough. Boyfriend wasn't really the right word, but it was a word that would do. Either they hadn't heard him and didn't know he was there, or they'd heard him and didn't care. By the sink were the scattered cartons they'd been eating from. They'd been eating KFCs and fries with ketchup, just like kids who'd come home from school themselves.

They could do it without making a noise, possibly. But he understood that the noises went with doing it. He'd been in this situation before, of having to be around and just listen, but not in the situation of taking the knife.

The brothers had told him that he should get a knife. He knew what they were saying. If you want to move on to the next stage, if you want to stay with us. So he'd thought at once of the kitchen drawer. It was the easiest way, the simplest way. "Here is a knife." He wasn't going to say that it was really his mum's knife. It didn't matter, it was a knife.

But perhaps it did matter. Perhaps it mattered very much that it was his mum's knife.

The noises from the other room only made it easier to take it. They were almost like a permission. So why should he hesitate? Why shouldn't he just go ahead? He understood that at this moment, though he was only twelve, he had about as much power in the world as he would ever have. He understood it almost painfully now. At twelve you could not be held responsible, even if you were. To everything you could say: So? So what are you going to do about it? And at twelve you were still small enough not to be picked on. People would think twice.

The brothers knew this. That's why it was worth their while to take on twelve-year-olds, to string them along and train them up, like dogs. But then there'd come the moment when they'd say, "Do you really want to be one of us?"

He knew—he knew it especially now—that this place wasn't his home. If he belonged anywhere now it was with the brothers. Only with them could he have any respect. If you had nothing else, then you had to have respect.

His mother might have said to Wes, "No, not now. Danny will be back from school any second." But then just caved in and not cared.

He'd meant to take the knife—it wasn't even stealing, to take a knife from your own kitchen drawer—but he hadn't thought he'd be pushed into doing it as soon as he got home. And he hadn't thought of all the other thoughts that would rush into his head—almost, so it seemed, into his hand—just before he did so. What it means to hold a knife, in a certain way, in your hand.

At twelve years old he knew he was fearless, or just about. He knew he could look anyone, or almost anyone, in the eyes and they'd give in first. So? So what are you going to do? The brothers perhaps recognised this quality in him.

So: a knife in your hand ought to make you even more fearless. But if you could be fearless without it, why have it? This was

the real point. At twelve years old he understood that his fearless-
ness, rapidly acquired, might soon be over. He would not have
the untouchability of being twelve.

He'd been in this same situation before—without the issue
of the knife. In a little while Wes would emerge, perhaps buck-
ling his belt. Wes had a belt with a big shiny buckle, part of which
was shaped like a skull. But he wasn't afraid of Wes. Wes wasn't
his enemy, he wasn't his friend, and he'd just want to clear off
anyway, but first they'd have to look at each other. Each time
they'd done this before Wes had lost. At twelve years old he was
good at looking, even looking at people like Wes who were more
than twice his size and twice his age. There'd be a point when
Wes's eyes would flicker, as if to say, "So what are you looking
at?" Once Wes had actually said that. Now he didn't say anything.
There'd be just the flicker, then he'd clear off.

Wes was afraid of him. He was twelve, but Wes was afraid of
him. Wes had a skull on the buckle of his belt and shoulders that
bulged through his T-shirt, but Wes was afraid of him.

And now when Wes emerged he could go a step further.
What was a knife for? He might not only look at Wes, but as he
did so he might be holding a knife, pointing a knife. He'd never
thought about this till moments ago. He'd never thought about
it as he was coming home from school. Then there'd be an even
bigger flicker in Wes's eyes, not just a flicker, and he'd clear off
even more quickly. And not come back.

Or he could go a step further still. This thought made his
hand sweat. He could take the knife and just go into the other
room and stick it in Wes's back. Wes's back might very probably
be turned and bare. This is what a knife enabled you to do. The
thought made him freeze.

Wes wasn't his enemy. In some deep-down way he didn't
even mind his mum having Wes. He was something she needed.
Maybe she got money from Wes. In any case she got something
she needed. He didn't even mind them being at it right now like

animals and making their noises, even as he was standing here in the kitchen. It was just how it was. He understood very clearly now that it might also have been just how it was with his father, twelve years and more ago. So if he stabbed Wes it would be like stabbing his father. Which might have been the best and the right thing to do. Except he wasn't around then to do it. If he'd stabbed his father then he'd never have been around at all. Which didn't make any sense.

His father's name was Winston. That was all he knew. Winston. Wes. Maybe his mother had invented the name Winston. She had to have a name, at least, to give him. His father had cleared off twelve years ago. Just like Wes would. And had never come back.

Outside, there were noises too, the noises of kids playing. Just kids playing, kids younger than him, cackling and screeching. Both the noises inside and the noises outside were like the sounds of animals.

Wes would emerge and look, and flicker, and clear off. Then there'd be quite a long gap, and then his mother would emerge. Then they'd look at each other too. It would be like him and Wes, but his mother would always win. When she emerged she'd have a deliberately lazy way about her, which he hated, as if she wasn't going to hurry for anyone, and once when they'd looked at each other she'd thrown up her chin and said, "So what are you looking at?" The very same words Wes had used once and failed. But his mother would always win. She was the only one who could.

And she was the only one he was really afraid of. In all the world. He was afraid of her even now. Once, his mother had needed to come and collect him from the police station. At twelve years old, or less, you could laugh at the police. He wasn't afraid of the police. But when his mother had come to the police station she'd spoken to them all very obediently and softly, as if she were a child herself.

Then on the way home she'd changed, she'd kept trying to

say things, but she couldn't, her mouth had seemed not to know how to work. Then when they'd got home her mouth had tried again, but not worked either, and then she'd beaten him—hard, with the full swing of her arm and the full whack of her hand. It was an attack. It hurt. But he'd known she was only hitting him because she was incapable of finding the right words, she might as well have been hitting herself. She was hitting him because in some way *she* was afraid. He understood this. And yet he was afraid of her. His own mum.

Even now he was afraid of her.

Fear was a strange thing. Even right now, with these noises that were like a permission, he was afraid of the simplest thing. To take a knife from a drawer.

His mother might not even notice it was missing. Since when had she taken stock of what there was in the kitchen drawer? And even if his mother were to say later, "Where's my knife? Where's that knife?" he might simply say he didn't know, and shrug. It wasn't his knife. Or he'd say it must have got chucked in the waste bin by mistake. Plenty of things did, including once one of her big orange bangles. Or he could say that it was another of the things Wes must have walked off with.

He could simply say that. "Wes took it."

And if it really came to it, if his mother looked at him, not saying anything, but with a look that said, "You took it, didn't you, Daniel?" then he could look back at her with a look that said, "Well? So? So? What did you ever do to prevent me? What did you ever do to stop me going down this road? What did you ever do that was so right and good that you could tell me that taking a knife from a drawer was wrong?"

But he wondered if he could actually do that—and win.

It was the easiest thing. What was the simplest way of getting a knife? But he knew it wasn't simple, since he knew there was the question: Why did it have to be her knife? Why did he *want* it to be her knife? He knew this wasn't so much a question now as a question that would come later. A question that might even be his excuse. And even now it seemed he could hear people, people in the future, asking him the question.

Because . . . But couldn't they see? Wasn't it obvious? Because if it was her knife then anything he did with it—if he did anything—would have to have been done too by her. And if they didn't see it (who were these people?) *she* would.

Because . . . Because she could talk about *her* father. She could talk about him and she could even talk about *his* father, her father's father. And when you got back to him, to his mother's grandfather—he even knew that *his* name was Daniel—then you were talking about someone who'd stepped off the boat. You were talking about fucking Bridgetown, Barbados. She had all that, she belonged to all that, and if she didn't know what to do with it then that was her problem.

He belonged with the brothers.

It was a line, she had a sort of line. But he didn't have it or want it, no fucking thanks. And everyone knows what you can do with a line. Everyone knows that when you're born there's this cord, but it doesn't stay there for long.

Where is the knife, Daniel? What did you do with the knife? (Who was saying this to him?) What did you do with the knife?

Where is my knife, Daniel?

It was only something she'd have bought in a shop once. In Hanif's Handy Store. A cheap kitchen knife. He couldn't remember when he'd last seen her use it for what it was meant for. Slicing a piece of chicken.

He heard the kids outside and the thought came to him that one day he'd remember this moment, he'd remember it very clearly and precisely as if he were twelve years old all over again. Standing here like this, hand over the drawer, not yet holding the knife. The smeared cartons. The kids outside. In his white school shirt with his tie insolently knotted so that just a few striped inches of it dangled from his neck.

He heard the noise his mother would start to make when things were getting near their finish. It was a rough gasping repetition of a single word, so rough and gasping you could hardly make out it was a word. It was like when she couldn't find the words before she beat him. But it was a word, and it wasn't a word that said don't.

He put in his hand and took out the knife. It was the simplest, easiest, most ordinary thing, to take a knife from a drawer.

Mrs. Kaminski

"Mrs. Kaminski?"

"That's me, dear."

"I'm Dr. Somerfield. I need to take some blood."

"Take as much as you like. It's no good to me."

"We need to do some tests. Are you feeling more comfortable?"

"You should work in an English hospital, dear, a nice girl like you. The National Health Service, it's the best in the world."

"This is an English hospital. It's St. George's, Tooting."

"It's the way to Poland."

"Are you Polish, Mrs. Kaminski?"

"No, but I'm on my way to Poland."

"I need to ask you a few questions. Do you know how old you are?"

"Ninety-one."

"Date of birth?"

"March the 4th, 1923."

"And your first name?"

"Nora."

"Can I call you Nora?"

"Please yourself. How old are you, dear?"

"Twenty-five. Do you know where you were born, Nora?"

"Carshalton, Surrey."

"Do you know what month it is?"

"Why?"

"You had an accident. A funny turn. A fall, in the street. You were brought here. We're trying to find out what caused it all. Do you know where you live?"

"Flat four, Romsey Court, Neville Gardens, Mitcham."

"You just said you were on the way to Poland."

"That's right. Haven't you noticed all the Polish people? They do the plumbing, the cleaning, the central heating. They mow the lawns. They do it all for us."

"Do you live alone there, at the address you just gave me?"

"I don't live there any more, do I?"

"Do you have a husband, Nora?"

"Yes."

"Where is he?"

"He went to Poland."

"When did he go there?"

"1944."

"1944?"

"June the 18th, 1944."

"That's a long time ago. You said you were going there too."

"That's right. I'll soon be seeing him, won't I? I just have to find him. Or he'll have to find me. Perhaps you can help us, dear."

"Do you have any sons or daughters, Nora? Brothers, sisters?"

"Relatives, you mean?"

"Yes, relatives."

"I have a son. Ted."

"Where does he live?"

"He went to Poland. He'll be with his father. He'll be there too."

"We should let your son know that you're here."

"Of course you should. And his father. They'll both want to know I'm here. You should go and find them for me, dear."

"I mean we should let your son know that you're here, in hospital, that you've had a funny turn. If he's your next of kin."

"Kinski. People sometimes just called us the Kinskis. He went to Poland. 1964."

"You mean he's really living in Poland?"

"He got a job as a boilerman. In a hospital. He had to keep the boilers going that kept the hospital warm. They gave him a boiler suit."

"This is a hospital, Mrs. Kinski. Sorry, Kaminski."

"It's the way to Poland."

"You're confused. You've had a nasty turn."

"He hung himself in the boiler room. He hung himself by the legs of his boiler suit. He went to Poland. He went to join his father."

"I'm getting confused, Mrs. Kaminski."

"You said I was confused, dear."

"What did your husband do?"

"He was a pilot. He went to Poland. 1944."

"He flew there?"

"He flew into the English Channel. Haven't you heard of all the Polish pilots? There were lots of them. They came over here. They shot down Germans for us."

"So your husband was from Poland."

"Lodz."

"Lots?"

"The white cliffs."

"The white cliffs?"

"The white cliffs of Dover. The English Channel. They never found him. Little Teddy was born after. He never knew his dad. But he'll know him now, he'll have known him for a long time. They'll be getting ready to see me. You must tell them where I am. It's been such a long time. It will be so lovely."

"I'll take that blood now. It won't hurt. I'll just dab your arm."

"Pour it down the sink, dear, when you've finished. Down the sinkski."

"What was your husband's name?"

"Ted. He was Teddy too. I had to call little Teddy by his dad's name, didn't I? But his real name was Tadeusz. It's a Polish name."

"Tadeusz."

"Tadeusz. Ted's easier. Ted Kaminski. My two Teds, they'll be here somewhere. Do you speak Polish?"

"So you have no relatives, Nora? No living relatives we can inform?"

"We'll all be together. If you just run along and find them for me, when you've finished with that blood."

"We have to do some tests."

"He flew into the drinkski."

"Mrs. Kaminski—"

"It was a flying bomb, dear. It wasn't the Battle of Britain. He got through all that. Do you remember the Battle of Britain?"

"I'm twenty-five. I wasn't born."

"Nor was little Teddy. You'd like little Teddy. I can see it, you and him. But I was the lucky one, I had his father. Not for long. Tadeusz Kaminski. He flew into the Channel. I married a Pole. I didn't mind at all. The Germans invaded Poland. And we'll all be in Poland soon, we'll all be together."

"This is England, Mrs. Kaminski. It's Tooting."

"A flying bomb. He shot it down. He blew it up, then he flew into the sea. That's what they told me. But it doesn't matter now. We'll all be together."

"Nora—"

"They were coming over by the hundreds, nasty buzzy buzz bombs. It was worse than the Blitz. Nothing you could do, except not be under one. Fifty, a hundred people gone in a flash. If they landed on a school. Or a hospital."

"Mrs. Kaminski—"

"Just think about it, dear, just thinkski. If one of them dropped right now on this hospital. I know it's a hospital. You must have a boiler room somewhere. But I'm not here for long, I'm on my way to Poland. Just imagine. If one of them drops we'll all be gone. You, me, doctors, nurses, all gone in a flash."

Dog

His father had once said to him, "Money doesn't buy you happiness, Adrian, but it helps you to be miserable in comfort."

He'd wondered ever since at this equivocal utterance. Was his father saying that his own life had been miserable? Or that life itself, as a working premise, was miserable? These possibilities were suddenly dreadful.

All he'd done—though it had taken courage—was ask for more pocket money. He wished he'd never opened his mouth. Perhaps his father, who was rich and not given to utterances, had felt the same.

His father had died long ago anyway, and he'd heeded the recommendation—if recommendation it had been. He'd made money himself, lots of it. He'd made it when it was possible to make lots of it and he was one of those clever or lucky ones who'd got out before losing it, and put it where it could keep working.

Now here he was featherbedded with the stuff. Which was just as well, with an ugly divorce and an estranged family to pay for. Though all that, too, was now some time ago and all the bills had been settled. So, had his father's words been only wise? And what counsel—the same?—had he given his own children? Hugh, Simon, Rebecca. He couldn't remember giving them any counsel at all. He couldn't remember them ever seeking it. They were all grown-up now.

He pushed the buggy which contained his daughter Lucy, though he was old enough, easily, to be her grandfather, listening to her wordless burblings and knowing that he loved her wholly, that right now he loved her more than anything in the world. She shouldn't really be there, she shouldn't be there at all. He already had, he'd already raised, a family. He shouldn't be pushing a helpless infant still years from articulate speech on a journey to the park. Yet he was, and he loved her completely and loved her burblings as if there were a string running directly from his heart to hers. He loved her as he couldn't, in all honesty, remember quite loving his other, now adult children.

Whenever his new young wife Julia urged him to take Lucy for a buggy ride to the park so that she, Julia, could have some respite, he tended to feign reluctance or even resentment, for the simple reason that he didn't want Julia to know that he really loved doing it. Nor did he want her to know that, though Lucy could sometimes be impossible at home, she instantly became utterly sweet-tempered once she felt him pushing her along.

He loved being alone with Lucy perhaps more than he loved being alone with Julia, though Julia, even after a difficult first pregnancy, was a beautiful slender woman with light brown hair, some twenty years his junior. Why, after all, had he fallen for her, then married her? But he knew (he wasn't stupid) that the question was rather: Why had she inveigled him, seduced him into marrying her? Because she'd wanted a Lucy of course. A Lucy plus security.

And now look.

There was something particularly entrancing, he couldn't say why, about this physical act of steering Lucy in her buggy, about having his hands on the handles and feeling through them the bumps and swerves that she felt through her whole body. These rides seemed to induce in her such a simple infallible delight, she became a kind of living cargo of happiness, and he could sometimes find himself, quite unselfconsciously, echoing out loud her burblings, as if infected (at last, at fifty-six!) with mindless *joie de vivre*.

His father had spoken those disenchanted words. But these babblings! And of course he didn't tell Julia that, while she put her feet up, he was only too keen to push Lucy to the park yet again.

Lucy, of course, had no control. She had no power of decision, and she had no control literally. She relied on him entirely to steer her. The fact that she did so with such delirious trust made his own steps light, and right now he loved her absolutely because her helpless burblings matched, though entirely benignly, the fact that he'd lost all control of his life and that she was the product of that loss of control.

It was a mild day in late February. Spring was in the air. A few innocuous white clouds hung in the sky. Crocuses were poking through by the entrance to the park.

When had he lost control? He hadn't lost control of the business of making money, he'd been a dab hand at that. He hadn't even lost control of the money itself, though he'd handed over large chunks of it. But when had he lost control of himself, of his life, of who he was?

When he was twenty-eight, say, he'd felt pretty much in control. At least he'd felt a good notch surer of himself than when he'd been eighteen or twenty-one—when all doors are supposed to open. He'd even say now—now he was exactly twice twenty-eight—that twenty-eight was actually the age he was inside. He was a twenty-eight-year-old in heavy disguise.

But by the time he was thirty-eight, or certainly forty-five, the sense he'd once had long ago as a little kid—long before that bleak interview with his father—that life and growing up could only ever be about gaining more and more control, a steady upward graph, had deserted him. It wasn't that he was losing control in some ways but gaining it in others, he was seriously and centrally losing control, and he knew it. And he knew that very probably this loss of control would only increase and accelerate for the rest of his life, he'd crossed some sort of dire threshold, till one day he'd be approaching his death in a state of utter and terrifying loss of control, never having—to put it mildly— put his affairs in order.

When he understood this he did what most people do. He ignored it. He had another drink. Was putting your affairs in order the purpose of life anyway? Affairs! A poor joke of a word. It was his affairs, having them, that had got him into this mess. Once, when he was twenty-eight—or was it thirty-five?—he'd thought that having affairs and their rather thrilling disorder was actually the stuff of life, if not maybe its purpose. He was, he'd have to confess, quite good at it.

Did anyone put their affairs (other sense) in order? People said, didn't they—people not like his father—that you should seize life, grasp it while it was there? Which sounded like taking control, big-time. But it also sounded exactly like what he did when he toppled—dived—into another affair. It was taking control, but it was also like going full-tilt for the complete opposite.

By his forties he'd started to do something he'd never done before. He looked at people. That is, he studied them and wondered about them, as if he might be the other side of a glass wall. Did they look out of control, did they look as if they all secretly felt like him? No. The amazing thing was that they didn't. They looked as if they were pretty much holding it together, as if they were moving along paths they felt they should be moving along. How did they manage it?

He'd never had this feeling of a glass wall before, he'd never felt he was an observer, not a doer. Though what he'd been doing, perhaps for some time now, had been losing control.

And now here he was pushing a buggy along a park path—an act of control and calm purpose if ever there was—with a child in the buggy astonishingly remote from him in years yet to whom he felt closer than anything else in the world.

It was a Sunday morning. The sun, with a real warmth to it, seemed to be seeing off the clouds and the park was doing good business. There were other people pushing buggies, like him, either towards or back from the little mecca of the play area, with its brightly coloured attractions, that had opened recently and been an instant success. On Sunday mornings it could heave. It was hard to tell if adults or small children dominated. There were buggy-parking issues. There were multiple-child buggies. You understood at once one of the principal local activities: it was to breed and to do so with a certain public self-congratulation.

But there were also joggers, in Lycra, with headsets. There were people with dogs. There were also people—they were professionals—with lots of dogs, whole packs of them, because their owners were too busy, even on a Sunday, or too lazy to walk them, so they paid someone. Money, the things it could do. Even some of the buggy-pushers would be hired live-in nannies, speaking foreign languages. Nannies! He'd had a thing once— he'd lost control—with a nanny, called Consuelo. It hadn't lasted long, not long enough even to call it an affair. Now, spotting the nannies, and even though Julia wasn't around to catch him looking, he wasn't even tempted.

There were about as many dogs as buggies. And—setting aside the nannies—not a few of the buggy-pushers and dogwalkers had a similar appearance. They were men, otherwise unaccompanied. They weren't young. They were often rather chubby, jowly or flushed of face and their hair was receding, if they weren't in fact bald. If they'd had looks once, they'd lost them. Yet for all this, they didn't appear out of control. Far from it. They were in charge of a buggy or a dog after all. Some of them even had a pretty lordly air and issued, to the dogs, bellowing commands.

In other words (though he refused to acknowledge this outright) they looked like him. And sometimes, in the case of the buggy-pushers, the age of the child or even children they were pushing told the whole story. It was a bit like his story.

But he was pushing Lucy. No one else was pushing Lucy. In a little while he'd unstrap her from the buggy and place her with a father's tender care—a quite experienced father's care—on one of the contraptions in the play area. She wasn't old enough to be more than placed briefly in this way, but the mere contact with the colourful apparatus seemed enough for her. It gave the buggy ride its goal, but he felt that for her as well as for him it was the ride itself that was really the thing.

All the time she was out of the buggy and just perched on one of the bits of equipment his hands would hover close to her, his whole body would want to shield her, as much from the roughness of other children and the intrusions of other parents as from any other form of harm. He'd keep guard of her and would think while he did so, as he would at other times of such close vigilance, of what would become of her in later life, of how her life would be when he was gone, of the possibility, which was not at all unreal, of his being gone before she was a woman with whom he might have a grown-up conversation. He'd feel a punishing stab. But he had her burblings.

They approached the play area. But the whole park, with its tree-lined paths and expanses of grass, its peeping bulbs and its joggers, dog-walkers and buggies, was like a play area, and on this smiling Sunday morning was the very image of communal well-being. It was the serener broader version of the kids' place, without the latter's tendency (he could see that this morning it was thickly patronised) to teeter into stressful frenzy. In truth, he didn't greatly like the play area, but Lucy wasn't able to say to him, understandingly and exoneratingly, "It's okay, we don't really have to go there."

The dog came from nowhere. If it was one of the many dogs

he'd been loosely holding in his view, it still seemed that it hurled itself from a different place, as if through some unperceived screen, and there it suddenly and loudly was. And it was one of those breeds of dog that weren't supposed to be let off leads, or even to be owned by people, or even, possibly, to exist at all. But there it was, and it was mauling—no, it was attacking—a child strapped in another buggy on the edge of the play area. Another little girl of less than two, with pale blonde curls, only yards away. With a father and mother who appeared to be momentarily paralysed.

It seemed that he too was suddenly on the scene, like the dog—that to others looking on it would seem that he too had sprung without warning from nowhere. It seemed so even to himself. Who was this man? He was suddenly grasping, grappling with a vicious snarling dog (whatever its behaviour had been just seconds ago), a dog that, but for his action and the sturdiness of modern buggy accoutrements, might have had in its mouth, in its claws, a helpless defenceless child.

The little girl was screaming and the dog must have been making a terrible row. People all around must have been yelling, but he didn't hear them or care, and he didn't even care, for some reason, if this dog was about to savage his own flesh or claw out an eye. He was *going to stop it*.

For a moment it writhed in his weird embrace, he felt the uncontainable spasm of its muscles—yes, it was going to bite his face off—but he wrenched it somehow from the buggy, then, as it shot from his clutches, it lost its balance and he was able to kick it, kick it *hard*, in the ribs, in the head, in its skidding legs, he didn't care. He'd won the battle, he knew, it had been a matter of seconds. Were people cheering? But he kicked it, and kicked it again.

He knew too, even as he did this, that the outcome of this episode would be that the dog would be put down. A dog that attacks a child. No arguments. It was what would happen. He could already picture the child's father—galvanised now into action—speaking righteously into a mobile phone, gathering a circle of witnesses round him. This is what would happen. And he would be a principal witness, and in some people's eyes a hero. And the dog would be put down. Professionally.

But he kicked it as if to save them the trouble. He kicked it even when it was beaten. He didn't care about its owner, who must be somewhere. The owner of a dog like this wouldn't, or couldn't, entrust it to a dog-walker, and the owner of a dog like this would only own it in order to feel a vicarious power. Yes, that was why people had dogs (he'd never had one), in order to have the illusion of mastery and control.

It was all split-second stuff, but he kicked it more than once, enough for him to imagine that when people later discussed his daring action they might add, "But did you see the way he kicked it?" Enough for him to think (and this was perhaps what made him stop): What would Lucy think, of her father furiously kicking a dog? Would she grow up with this whole scene indelibly imprinted on her? Her first and enduringly scarring memory of her daddy.

But of course it was for *her* that he'd done it, it was because the child in the buggy might so easily have been—

Lucy in fact, he realised, was bawling, screaming. Some well-meaning bystander was seeking to comfort her. Other buggy-bound infants were also in a state of howling terror, or else of white-faced shock, at what had happened to another of their kind, and thus at what could happen—it was plainly possible—to them. Lucy wasn't concerned with the gallant actions of her father, she was concerned with her own appalling vulnerability, and she was particularly concerned with the fact that her father had taken his hands off the buggy, thus abandoning her to such horror.

He quickly went to her, to place his hands back on the handles, and almost at once, as if some electric current of safety and assurance, or of something deeper, had passed between them, she was calm again, she was almost her untroubled self again.

"It's okay, Lucy, everything's okay. I'm here."

In a matter of moments she even began a subdued, speculative version of her customary burbling, as if this encounter with a dog, from which her father had come off visibly discomposed (he realised he was shaking a bit), was already moving out of her mental compass. She seemed, in mere seconds, almost to have forgotten it—never mind bearing the image of it for the rest of her life. Her father, wrestling with a dog! This rapid shift both relieved him and disappointed him.

"It's okay. Everything's okay."

They had to hang around for some time while the matter was dealt with—while a parks policeman (so parks policemen had a purpose) arrived and notes were taken and calls made, and while he tried not to listen to comments being uttered about him. "He was amazing . . . Just think what might have happened, if he hadn't . . . Just think what might have happened—you know—to that little kid . . ."

He could have done without it all. He had never in all his fifty-six years heard himself being called amazing, but he could have done without it. All the while he kept his hands very tightly on the buggy handles, except when he stooped to pat and stroke Lucy's head. His place was with Lucy. He wasn't even interested, now, in the poor child he'd rescued—had he been told its name?—whose life he'd quite possibly saved. That wasn't so farfetched. It wasn't every day that you, possibly, saved a child's life.

He wasn't interested in the sudden paean he was getting—distress turning to relief and almost hysterical gratitude—from the child's mother. "How can we ever thank you enough? How can we ever repay you?" That sort of thing. He actually wanted to say, "Control yourself, woman." He said, "It was nothing." He wasn't interested in his own patent prowess. He'd moved like lightning. Younger men around him—twenty-eight-year-olds!— had stood rooted to the spot. He didn't have any of these feelings.

And he wasn't interested in the dog, least of all. He knew it was done for.

He wanted to get away. He wanted just to be pushing Lucy again. There was no question now of spending any time with her in the play area, where all activity seemed suspended anyway. He knew that she wouldn't feel let down by this. It was the buggy ride that mattered.

Eventually, with anxious looks at his watch, he excused himself and edged away. He had his own child to look after—clearly. Her mother would be wondering. No one seemed surprised that he said "child" not "grandchild." It wasn't a rare phenomenon. And anyway he'd just behaved with the speed and agility, not to say sheer ferocity, of someone half his age.

He pushed Lucy back the way they'd come, alone with her again and totally in love with her, listening to her burblings resume their joyful commentary. It was as if nothing had happened. He very much wanted it to be as if nothing had happened. He envied his daughter's eclipsing amnesia. He didn't want to tell Julia about any of this. He looked at his watch again. Allowing for the time they might otherwise have spent at the play area, they wouldn't be unduly late back, so he need say nothing.

But of course word about the incident, in which he'd played such a central and dramatic role, was bound to get around to Julia, and pretty quickly, through the local grapevine. And there was the simple obvious fact that he himself bore the immediate evidence of something. Though his hands were firmly guiding the buggy he knew he was still shaking, he was shaking in fact quite a lot. He needed to grip the handles to stop it. There was a big streak of mud down one of his trouser legs, there was a tear at one knee, and if his face and hands seemed, remarkably, to have come away unscathed, his jacket was in several places snagged if not actually torn. That was all right. You could replace clothes, with some money. He hadn't wanted any money from that child's mother, though she'd offered it, she'd offered to replace his entire wardrobe. She was blonde and totally at his service. It seemed that she might offer him anything.

You could replace a jacket. But the claw marks themselves—yes they were actually claw marks—and his general appearance of having been in some fight, of being a bit of a walking catastrophe, he hadn't the slightest idea how he was going to explain away these things to Julia.

Fusilli

He pushed the trolley round the end of the aisle, ignoring the stacks of boxed mince pies.

It would be Christmas Day in just over two weeks' time, but he and Jenny had already agreed, without really talking about it, to abolish Christmas. They couldn't go through with it. The calendar would be different this year. Remembrance Day had come and gone, but it would be Remembrance Day on Christmas Day. Even that was going to be terrible.

On Remembrance Day itself they'd adopted, without ever talking about it either, a sort of double position, both to mark it and to ignore it, they couldn't work out which way their superstition should go. But he remembered now—how could he forget?—coming here about a month ago. It was just days before Remembrance Day. The clocks had gone back, it was dark outside. He remembered pushing the trolley then.

How he wished it was still then.

There'd been little boxes of poppies, with plastic jars for coins, by the entrance. He'd wondered whether to buy one. Yet another one. Whether to tip in all his change. But the bigger thing, already, was Christmas. Christmas stuff, Christmas offers. It was Christmas before it was even Remembrance Day. A sudden wave of anger had hit him. It had been Halloween less than a fortnight before. The shops had been full of pumpkins and skeletons.

No one saw his anger, it stayed inside. He wasn't even sure if it was anger exactly. He'd pushed the trolley in the normal way, his list stuck in one hand, his mobile in his top pocket in case of problems.

"Shop patrol to base. No fresh ginger, Jen. What do you reckon?"

That sort of problem.

He did the weekly supermarket run—his duty, or his regular volunteering—and for several months now not a time had passed when he didn't think: And what are Doug's little problems right now? His tricky two-for-one choices?

He'd never forget how his mobile had rung—right here in the rice and pasta aisle—and it had been Doug. In Afghanistan, in Helmand. That sort of thing was possible now.

He was talking to Doug. And Doug had phoned *him*. So he couldn't say, "I'll get your mum." (Why did he always say that anyway?) Doug had phoned *his* number.

Shit—was it something bad? Was it something he should know first?

"I'm in Waitrose, Doug. By the pasta. Doug! Doug! How's it going?"

What a stupid way of putting it: "How's it going?"

But Doug had wanted to know all about his shopping list. He'd seemed tickled by the picture of his father pushing a trolley, holding his list, dithering by the shelves. And while Doug was so keen on the situation in Waitrose, he hadn't wanted to ask his son about the situation in Afghanistan. His anger, if that's what it was, had dropped away.

"You should stick with dried, Dad. Fresh is a scam." Doug had said this in Helmand. "Try the fusilli for a change. The little curly ones."

A November evening, days before Remembrance Day.

But Christmas was coming apparently. Doug had called from Helmand.

He couldn't think about it now. He couldn't not think about it. He could hardly enter Waitrose again. It was almost impossible to go now—though he had to—to the spot, in the aisle, where it had happened. Where he'd spoken to Doug and looked around at all the others with their trolleys and baskets and thought: They don't know, they don't know I'm talking to my boy in Afghanistan.

He and Jenny would never eat fusilli again, that was for sure, they'd never eat those things again.

And had it been anger, just before Doug called? Anger was sometimes supposed to be a substitute for fear, so they said. Or grief. Had that surge of anger, or whatever it was, been some sort of advance warning? If he hadn't had it, if he hadn't got angry, then would nothing have happened? But then if he hadn't had it, would Doug have called, just then?

Everything, now, was a matter of mocking superstition.

But Christmas before Remembrance Day! And now it was almost really Christmas. The aisles were crammed and glistening with it. He couldn't bear it. The only good thing was not to think. The only good thing was to ignore, ignore. But he couldn't.

He pushed the trolley. He couldn't even bear to think of Jenny. Maybe she took the opportunity while he did these supermarket trips just to sit with her head in her hands, tears trickling between her fingers.

He couldn't bear to think of calling her to ask, like he used to, about the rice. "What sort, Jen? Regular? Basmati?" Such things. It couldn't be done, it just couldn't be done any more. Their little foodie fads, their fancy cooking. Their being nice to themselves and splashing out—Waitrose, not Tesco's—now the lad had left home.

Puy lentils, Thai green sauce. That sort of shit.

He couldn't bear to think about how thinking about Jenny only half a mile away was the same as thinking about Doug three thousand miles away. He wasn't here, he was there, but you could talk, just the same, on the phone. Now the simple words "here" and "there" confused him utterly. Doug wasn't here, but he wasn't there. He wasn't *there* at all.

Or—and this is where it got really terrible—Doug *was* there. Doug was in a mortuary in Swindon, pending a coroner's decision. They couldn't have Doug yet. It was pretty clear now that they couldn't have Doug before Christmas, maybe even for some time after Christmas. All they wanted for Christmas was Doug. But Doug would be spending Christmas in a mortuary in Swindon. And anyway Christmas wouldn't happen this year.

"Christmas is coming." He remembered when he was a kid how the words had excited him almost more than the word Christmas itself, the idea that it was on its way. At Christmas, or when it was coming, you made lists, you dropped hints. He wanted to remember now—but at the same time didn't want to remember—every present they'd ever bought Doug for Christmas, every one.

Had they ever bought him any kind of toy gun? If they had, then it could have been another of those signals, those things that become real. So they must have done. If only they hadn't. Or if only Doug had been a girl. If so he'd have been called Natalie and the list of presents would have been different.

He tried to think, while trying not to think, of all the presents. But it wasn't so hard to remember being the man, in years gone by, in the days when Christmas was coming, looking for a gift to give his son. Not to remember being that man was the harder thing.

Fifteen, twenty years ago. Wars on TV. But there were soldiers to do all that stuff, and he'd never thought it was wrong or unmanly of him to be traipsing round Mothercare with Jenny and Doug—"Dougie in his buggy"—while there were wars going on. He felt it was the right thing to be doing. And it had never occurred to either of them that one day Doug would get it into his head . . .

"Stick with dried, Dad."

Why had he been so interested in pasta? Was that what they got out there? Dried stuff. Not stuff in tins. Pasta, all the varieties. Had it been a soldier's advice?

Before him suddenly was one of those floundering young mums with a loaded trolley, two small kids swinging from the sides, using it as a jumping-off point for marauding charges up and down the aisle.

Nothing, once, on these shopping trips used to get his goat more than these bawling little bastards, these kids their mums or dads seemed unable to restrain, Doug never having been a noisy, out-of-control child. He'd been proud of that. He'd been proud of his soldier-son too. But now these screaming brats in front of him simply made him stand stock-still. They were kids. There was their mother. They were, all of them, both there and here. The kids were only doing what kids do. He looked at the mother's strained, about-to-burst face. He thought: She doesn't know how lucky she is. He wanted to look hard at her, to catch her eye, so she would see something in his.

But beyond her was the pasta section. He couldn't go there. He had to go there. They were out of pasta, he'd checked. They weren't interested in food any more, but they had to eat. They were out of even basics now: pasta, rice. Fuck mince pies.

He'd told Jenny, of course, about the phone call, of course he had. Should he have kept it a secret? It was why they'd eaten the things, that same evening—with a tomato, garlic and basil sauce. A bottle of Sicilian red. They'd been Doug's "choice." They'd never eat the fucking things again.

He had to go there, yet he couldn't. And now anyway this losing-her-grip mother was blocking his path. She was standing exactly where—

Everything was like this now: a reason for, a reason against. He was suddenly furious with this useless hopeless mum. Was it anger? What was it exactly? He understood how violence gets done. He pushed his trolley forward, in a no-swerving, no-yielding way, as if to smash into her trolley. Did she catch his eye? Did she see something in it? She was probably thinking: Bastard of a man. She moved in any case, she got out of his damn way, so did the screaming brats. And he was suddenly there, on the spot where he'd spoken to Doug.

His mobile had rung. He'd thought: What now? What had Jenny forgotten to ask him to get? It was the last time he'd heard Doug's voice. It would have been the middle of the night in Helmand.

He saw them, in their little clear-plastic bags, alongside the lasagne and the tagliatelle. He even knew what the word meant now. Had Doug known? He picked up a packet. He knew that it wasn't for them to eat. It wasn't even for Jenny to see, to know. He had to do it. He held the scrunchy packet. He'd put it separately somewhere, he'd hide it. He grabbed a big pack of spaghetti and tossed it into his trolley anyway.

"Fresh is a scam, Dad. The dried lasts for ever."

He clasped the fusilli close to his chest. They'd never get eaten. He'd put them somewhere, God knows where. Under the seat in the car.

Christmas wouldn't happen this year. No presents, no lists. But this was his gift for Doug, or it was Doug's gift to him. He didn't know. Everything was this and that. The woman had gone. He'd somehow even cleared the aisle. He felt the pieces of pasta beneath the shiny plastic like the knobbly, guessed-at things inside a Christmas stocking long ago. The little curly things.

I Live Alone

~

There was a moment, as Dr. Grant spoke, when he didn't see Grant's face at all. He saw Anne's face, streaming with salt water. He saw her wet arm held out to him, as if she herself had delivered this news. It made it strangely bearable.

It didn't otherwise help to know that he was the victim of a rare disease, with some foreigner's name—as if the rarity, so Grant seemed to be suggesting, was some kind of compensation. He didn't feel privileged to have been introduced, in this intimate way, to this Dubrowski or Bronowski or whoever he was—as if he too might have held out a hand across Grant's desk. He saw his wife's hand. Anne's hand, Anne's face.

He saw, but in a different way and more vividly than ever, what he'd never failed to see every day for ten years.

He stopped listening to what Grant was saying. There was only so much you could take in after the announcement of such a basic fact. He was trying to take that in—along with his vision of Anne. He was trying to take in the fact that his life was no longer the indefinite thing of which he'd always been the subject, it was a closed thing, a finite thing, an object.

And he suddenly remembered himself, distinctly, at primary school, aged perhaps ten, holding a cricket ball. It had been a matter of some debate—he remembered this—whether small boys should be allowed to use proper hard cricket balls. But this was the school team, it was serious grown-up stuff, and they were playing St. Michael's. Astonishingly, he remembered even that. He saw himself in the outfield on the off side, picking up a cricket ball struck in his direction. He saw the dry summer grass beneath him, the flattened dandelions. He saw the ball he'd grabbed, its scuffed red surface, felt its solidity.

His life was now like a cricket ball.

But he saw himself, too, fling back his arm and hurl this same ball, with inspired force, not just towards the wicket keeper, but directly towards the stumps. Saw it shatter the stumps long before the running batsman—or batsboy—even with bat outstretched, could gain the crease. Saw the wicket keeper lift his gloved hands in jubilation. Saw everyone lift their hands.

It was a spectacular throw, perhaps thirty yards, and perhaps his only moment of sporting glory. And the strange thing was that he'd *known* it wouldn't miss. He hadn't thought about it in decades, but he saw it now, in Grant's consulting room, as clearly, as triumphantly as yesterday. He saw the ball, with its dense red weight, briefly clutched in his hand.

After leaving his office he'd taken the bus across the city and by the time he'd entered the now familiar private hospital and sat in the waiting room he'd set out in his mind three possible outcomes for this visit and given them each a percentage. One was that Grant would say the latest tests had revealed nothing of further importance and, though they should keep it under review and meet again in, say, a couple of months, there was really nothing to worry about. Thirty per cent. Second, Grant might say there was now a clear diagnosis, but the problem, though significant, could be treated. Sixty per cent. Third, Grant would say that unfortunately the diagnosis was that he had a rare incurable fatal disease. Ten per cent.

He'd considered these options to be fairly weighted, if anything rather tilted against him, and he'd believed in them like a superstition. Of course he'd hoped for option one, if not exactly for an "all clear." Though he was technically prepared for it, he hadn't believed in option three, but to have left it out would have been tempting fate.

Yet he'd known from Grant's face, even before Grant began properly to speak, that option three was actually the one.

There'd come to him the absurdly calming notion that since Grant was a doctor and he was a lawyer a certain professional comportment should be maintained. The roles might be reversed. As a lawyer he'd often had to give clients grave disquieting news or maintain a quasi-clinical detachment while they exhibited signs of distress. He couldn't complain if it was now the other way round. He should handle himself properly. He should look Grant in the face. He did.

But he saw Anne, he saw her arm. And seeing Anne was really the thing that saved him, not his professional decorum. This was what kept (these very words came to him) his head above water and made it look to Grant perhaps that he was taking it rather well, he was taking it like a man.

He told himself: I deserve this, I'd even wanted it. This too was the other way round. Ten per cent.

So then.

Then the notion of his life as some small separate finite object, like a cricket ball, had rushed towards him.

He told himself (he actually had the sense of standing outside himself to do so): And anyway it's hardly unfair. I'm fifty-nine. Many will live to a much riper age. But many, many—though, above all, Anne—have died long before.

And with that supremely balanced thought there'd entered his head—no, it seemed that they *themselves* had entered Grant's room—the actual roster of all those he'd known but who'd died before him. They appeared with remarkable clarity and in remarkably organised reverse order, taking him all the way back to the very first of their kind he'd known.

Yes, he remembered now. It popped up from some sub-merged place as if it had only been waiting for this moment. The very first had been little Howard Clarke. Now he remembered even the name—and remembered the other thing too. Howard Clarke had been the wicket keeper, his small hands encased in monstrous gloves, the wicket keeper whose skill had not been needed when he'd made that legendary throw. The wicket keeper who'd raised his exultant arms.

The point being that Howard Clarke, aged ten yet already marked out as a wicket keeper, had gone off as they all had for the summer holiday, but had never returned. It had been somehow conveyed to them, early in September, that he was never going to return. A brain tumour, someone said, whatever that was. A brain tumour, perhaps as dense and undeniable as a cricket ball, inside his head.

Grant continued to speak, but he didn't listen or couldn't focus. It was enough—surely enough since it was everything—to have to take in the main thing. He'd already asked the question that he'd never thought he'd hear himself ask, the question people only asked in films. And Grant had answered, though through a sort of fog. Had he said six months or eighteen, or that it could be anywhere between the two? Grant was now speaking of what might be done to "maximise his quality of life" (had he heard that phrase?). But he wasn't really listening. Oddly, given the crucial nature of it all, he wasn't concentrating.

Again, he knew this sort of thing from the other side. How many times, after telling clients some urgent sobering fact, had he watched their faces glaze over as he went on to explain the repercussions? They were still digesting the main thing. But what could you do except carry on? It was your professional obligation.

But mainly he couldn't concentrate on Grant because of the way Grant was crowded out, in his small room, by these others, by these ranks of dead ones, or of living memories, going back as far as Howard Clarke. They were far more important than Grant. Grant was being replaced by them—he'd even for a moment turned into Anne—so that his voice seemed to become increasingly feeble. It even seemed—but was this another confusion with Anne?—that Grant was the floundering and struggling one, the one in difficulties, and he felt a great gush of pity, mixed with something like wise seniority, for this man placed in the awful position of having to make the announcement he'd just made.

Grant, he supposed, when he wasn't being a physician, was a family man with a wife, and children perhaps now in their teens. He would go back to all that this evening. Which meant that he belonged, unquestionably, to the freely living, to those whose lives were not closed and finite. Whereas he, now, was of the other sort, the minority. He was not now of the same kind as Grant, though he had been moments ago, before entering his consulting room.

Yet he'd always been—or had been for the last ten years and those ten years had become a sort of "always"—a man of a different kind of minority. Of a kind who'd sometimes say, by way of giving a general, guarded account of himself, "I live alone."

Had he said it at some point to Grant?

It had become his watchword. He said it to clients, particularly clients he was guiding through the troublesome process of divorce, and he could say it with a judicious ironical tone, even a crinkly smile. So they could never tell what he really meant. An expression of sad fact? Or of proud resolution? An explanation, or a recommendation?

Grant, he thought, was speaking, in his flailing voice, with the strange loquacity of the living, with the gabble with which one might speak about all the detailed necessary arrangements for a wedding while somehow forgetting the main thing, that two people were about to commit themselves to each other for life.

Except this wasn't a wedding.

Yet he saw himself clearly for a moment (no longer a small boy on a cricket field) at his own wedding, nearly thirty years ago, and all the other people at it, several of whom were now dead and thus among this muster here in Grant's room. It had been a thronged lavish wedding because Anne came from a large and wealthy family, while he was just a suburban boy who'd landed on his feet. West Ealing to Winchester. The Sixties song had lodged in his brain. *Win-chester Cathedral* . . . Would they have to get married, he'd joked, in Winchester Cathedral?

How strange to have had such a packed wedding when he was now a man who said, "I live alone."

And he remembered how before the wedding he'd gone with Anne down to the jetty at Lymington with two bottles of champagne clanking in a bag. And they'd rowed out to where the *Marinella* was anchored. It was theirs now. It had been in Anne's family for years, but it was officially theirs now, a wedding present, though the sort that can't be wrapped or hidden. And before they climbed aboard—to drink the second bottle and make ceremonial waterborne love in the cabin—Anne had smashed the first bottle, with a fine flourish of her arm, against the bows, saying, "I name this yacht the *Marinella,* the yacht of our marriage. May God bless all those who navigate and copulate in her."

He'd never thought he could become (with Anne's instruction) a sailor. That, with Anne, he could sail the *Marinella* to Jersey, Guernsey, Brittany, Portugal. He was a provincial lawyer, a decent fish in a smallish pond, whose only act of physical prowess had been that amazing throw at primary school, Howard Clarke's leathered hands raised high.

. . .

"I live alone." Fewer and fewer people now knew, or remembered, why he said this. One of them was Janice, the receptionist, the veteran uncomplaining Janice, right now guarding his office.

Why had Janice, who was not dead, sprung suddenly into his mind?

Because, he realised, she'd almost certainly be the first person, not counting Grant himself (who was still wittering on), he'd have to confront after having received this news.

And then . . . and then he'd have to confront Mrs. Roberts, whom he'd never met. Mrs. Roberts: 5:15. Mrs. Roberts who was on the brink of that troublesome process, or precipice, known as divorce.

Why was he thinking of his office—in Grant's "office?" "Eliot and Holloway." He pictured it for a moment like some distant light seen in a dark forest. Why was he thinking of Mrs. Roberts whom he'd never met? But he knew now. He knew now why he'd kept his 5:15 appointment, despite Janice's puzzled and concerned gaze. "Why don't you get me to move it?" she'd almost said. He'd read her thought: Why, if your appointment's at four, don't you just take the afternoon off? A fair question. But he'd insisted. "I'll keep my 5:15."

"I live alone." Would he say it to Mrs. Roberts? And in the same cryptically smiling way as ever?

I live alone. Did that fact, too, save him, come to his rescue now?

Grant was gabbling on, so it seemed, like a man put on the spot. And he was listening to him, hearing him out, like some silent patient judge. It came to him that what Grant was saying might be a fabrication, a ruse. He knew it wasn't. Little Howard Clarke had proved it. Nonetheless, the idea was somehow to be seized. There also came to him, in this meeting of two professional men bound by rules of confidentiality, the phrase he sometimes used, with a certain solemnity, in his own profession: "Nothing need go beyond this room."

He saw the cubicle of a room he was in like some locked vault in a bank. It was a very important room—it was the room in which he'd learnt the most important fact of his life—but nothing need go beyond it.

Except himself. He saw that it was vital that in a moment he should get up and leave and in passing through the door, crossing the waiting room, signing out at the desk, then exiting through the glass doors be absolutely no different (though he absolutely was) from the man who'd walked in.

And he *was* no different. How could he be different, even to himself? He was the same creature, with the same legs beneath him, the same mobile, thinking, breathing vessel that contained all he was.

He did get up. It wasn't difficult. He didn't totter. It was 4:25. He may have shaken Grant's hand. He may have shaken Grant's hand in a way he'd never shaken anyone's hand before. He may have looked him in the eye and nodded obligingly in response to some further reassurance on his part about "what should happen next."

But what should happen next was that he should put one foot in front of the other. That was the most important thing. One foot in front of the other. He walked, feeling the extraordinary exactness of his steps, to the desk in the waiting room. The nurse smiled at him. She couldn't possibly know. It was an ordinary smile. But the fact that she'd smiled so simply must mean that his own face looked ordinary. So—Janice was not, quite, the first and he'd proved that the thing could be done.

There was a name tag over the nurse's left breast: "Gina." He noted this fact and the smooth skin of her throat.

When the glass doors slid open and he emerged into the cold

and darkening air of a November afternoon it was a sort of shock, but also a kind of cancelling continuity, to know the world was still there.

He began at once to walk, buttoning his coat: across the forecourt, through the main entrance, turning left onto the pavement. One foot in front of the other. He knew this was the walk of his life. He knew he could have picked up one of the taxis that dropped incoming patients by the glass doors, or just got the bus. He'd got the bus on the way and now he knew why. The company of other, living people. But now he knew he must walk.

Across the city, beyond the cathedral, to his office. There was time. He knew he must walk, to prove he was healthy and alive and able to place one foot in front of the other. And to give himself time, while his legs worked beneath him, to cement and seal up inside him the great secret he'd just learnt. If the secret could be successfully hidden from all but himself (and Grant) then it would be as though the secret—even perhaps to himself—might not be real.

Win-chester Cathedral . . .

He walked. It would take half an hour, perhaps a little more. He wouldn't disappoint Mrs. Roberts.

Dry leaves scurried along the pavement like small alarmed animals. The lights of passing traffic glared. He couldn't drive any more, of course, because of his mysterious blackouts, and he'd supposed it was a temporary prohibition. Now he knew it wasn't. So he should sell the car perhaps. But what did it matter now to sell it or not? Six months? Eighteen months? Scores of practical considerations and decisions, as if he were being a good solicitor to himself, suddenly rose before him, then scattered meaninglessly away like the leaves at his feet.

He'd sold the *Marinella* quickly enough. That hadn't been a protracted decision. It had come with the force of a gale behind it, if not like the gale—but it had been more than a gale, it was a mad murderous whirlwind brewed up by a gale—that had smashed through the sea around them that afternoon, ten miles off the Needles, and picked up the *Marinella* like a toy boat and tossed it over. And tossed them out of it.

Hours later, close to freezing and like a drowned rat, he was winched up on the end of a wire, clutching a man in a helmet who'd said, "Hold me, hold me," like a lover.

This was something also that he'd never seen himself doing, or having done to him, in his life.

But Anne was never winched up. The last he'd seen of Anne alive, as a huge wave lifted her then took her sweeping away, was her face and outstretched arm—as he'd seen it in Grant's office, as he'd seen it countless times. Hold me, hold me. But she'd been too far away for holding, even reaching. Then she was gone.

He'd sold the boat, after the salvage team had brought it in and the damage was repaired and paid for. He'd never stepped in it again, would never sail again. He'd been a sailor once, to his surprise, a lawyer and weekend sailor, a solicitor and occasional marine adventurer, but he'd never be those things again, except the solicitor, and he'd never know again the joy of being married to Anne and of riding with her, in the boat of their marriage, the high, astonishing seas.

"I live alone." Some who heard him say it understood. After all, the thing had been in the papers.

And now he'd never even drive a car again. Though, in any case, now he must walk. Now he must feel beneath him his own motor efficiently propelling him forward.

And so he did. He crossed the city, here and there taking short cuts he knew through back streets, away from traffic, so that he could even hear the rasp of his breath and steady scuff of his footsteps. Even now, there was the feeling like a patent disproof: look, there's nothing wrong with you.

Win-chester Cathedral . . .

He seemed to be walking back into all the previous bodies—which were only this same body—that had once been his. His younger stronger imperishable bodies. So that at one point the legs beneath him even seemed to be—he could feel them there again—the little stick-like but superbly alive legs he'd had when he'd once hurled a cricket ball and had, soon afterwards, resolved that Howard Clarke, who had similar stick-like, immortal legs and who'd so spontaneously applauded his spectacular throw, should become—perhaps when they all returned after the summer—his friend.

And as he walked he couldn't help noticing, within this body, this fifty-nine-year-old motor that was himself, the central pulsing component that kept now thumping out its rhythm as never before. He could feel it, hear it. Surely others must hear it. How was it possible that he'd carried this same beating thing inside him all this time, since he was a boy with stick legs? How was it possible that it had kept up its persistent and so often unappreciated beat all this time, as if it would never stop?

He reached his office. It was now completely dark and the lit-up windows and railed frontage—a fine Georgian centreterrace converted, like others in the row, into offices—struck him, as it sometimes did but now more than ever, like a stage set, like a doll's house. "Eliot and Holloway." He seemed to see, through the windows, the swallow-tailed and crinolined folk who'd once inhabited it.

Janice knew, of course. Janice knew what "I live alone" meant. Janice had been there when . . . Janice had watched and known ever since. And Janice had been there some nine months ago when he'd had that first extraordinary, and extraordinarily embarrassing, blackout in his office. She was there beside him— he'd never seen her knees so closely—with a glass of water, looking down at him on the office carpet as he came to. She'd called an ambulance. Janice was there, and he'd recognised her face, among the others (Alan Holloway looking a bit white) pressing round and looking down, before he'd even recognised who he was himself.

That's Janice. What on earth is she doing? And then he'd seen rapidly disappearing from Janice's face, but not so rapidly that he couldn't notice it, her horrified conviction that he was dead.

Janice looked up at him now as he walked in. He knew that how he looked back at her and how he spoke to her was of the utmost importance. Even so, he wondered if she could see—surely Janice must see—through his gaze and his words.

"Nothing new, Janice, don't even ask."

Did he sound sufficiently disgruntled?

"Same as last time. More tests. Honestly, I sometimes wonder if they know what they're doing."

When Janice kept looking he said, "I walked. I walked all the way back. Did me more good than going there."

He eyed his watch. Ten past five. He took off his coat. Alan had closed shop for the day, so it seemed. Good. Well, Alan would be ruling the roost before long. He peered into the open door of his own office as if into a room that some other person had left.

"So, Janice, we have . . . er . . . Mrs. Roberts."

As if Mrs. Roberts hadn't become his unexpected lifeline.

Even as he spoke a figure in a black coat and red scarf entered where he'd just entered, a woman of forty or so, not unattractive, but etched by an anxiety she was clearly trying to hide.

Was it so difficult then, to wear a disguise?

"Mrs. Roberts?" he said and, when she said yes, held out a hand and smiled. "David Eliot." How strange his own name sounded. "And this is our receptionist, Janice. You've caught me on the hop. I've just returned from an appointment of my own." She only blinked at this. "So then—"

And now he extended an ushering arm, in exactly the same way, he realised, as Grant had done at his consulting-room door, just as all professional people habitually do.

He'd quickly made his assessment: Well, she's not one of the hard-bitten ones, out to grab all she can. She's one of the ones (he seemed to see this more clearly than he'd ever done) who thought this sort of thing could never happen to her, not to her—that her marriage, her life was all soundly, safely in its place. She's putting up a good front of businesslike poise, but really she's lost, she's all at sea. She's looking out over a gulf which was never meant for her and which she has no idea how to cross.

They sat down. He made some lawyer's small talk. He looked at her, at the notes he had. Then he leant back patiently and attentively in his chair.

"Now, in your own words, in your own time, tell me all about it."

Articles of War

He had the wretchedest of coach journeys, a grey relentless drizzle shrouding everything, clogging the roads when they should have been at their firmest and denying him any farewell visions of apple-hung orchards or golden stooks. Harvest time and every field sodden. And all the while the familiar desolation claiming him, like some awful return to school.

They changed horses late in Totnes, and night had fallen when they arrived. It had been falling all day. So, he would have to wait now till dawn. It was always some small relief when you first saw the ships. He saw a distant twinkle of lanterns, through the gloom, out on the Sound.

So, he must wait. And then no doubt—he must wait. It was his experience that you sped upon their lordships' bidding only to languish indefinitely pending further orders. His chest was taken into the Bell. He had intended making some better arrangement for his shore quarters only to fall back on the known devil. It was convenient. It was convenient to say, "I am at the Bell." He had no money for grandeur.

He was shown to his chamber. He knew it—or one like it. He had been confined here before, as had God knows how many others like him. It was strange that it felt so immediately incarcerating when it was bigger by far than any pitching cabin.

He took off his hat and cloak and at once felt chilly. He

inspected the supply of candles. There was a meagre fire that appeared to have been unwillingly lit. It was only just September after all. September, 1805. In August, three weeks ago, he had passed his twenty-fifth birthday. So—he would not have to note it solely to himself at sea. Was it noteworthy?

He removed his gloves. He resisted an attack of the ancient urge to chew his fingertips. He pissed into the chamber pot. It was too early to sup, and if he supped—then what? He would sit by this skulking fire with this cheerless companion who was himself. He would commence the melancholy business of writing letters—letters as if written on the eve of sailing, though the eve of sailing might be three weeks hence.

If he made himself visible and if he were lucky (or unlucky) some other soul in blue and gold might hail him and invite him to dine. This might allay or aggravate his dejection. "Wives and sweethearts—may they never meet." But he had neither. He was the Navy's wholly. So (he always told himself) he was spared the much-sung pangs. He had only these other pangs that came from some deep and solitary place within him.

Or, not to mince the matter: he had his mother and his two older sisters, Emily and Jane. His two older brothers, Arthur and George, moved in spheres beyond him and were both of an age, it sometimes seemed, to have been his father. And then there was his father . . .

He was, in short—and he would only dwell on it in these dire intervals before embarkation—the youngest: the late and unexpected addition, the afterthought (though no thought could have gone into it), a plaything for his sisters, a thing of no account to his brothers and a conundrum to his parents.

Yet to the womenfolk at least he would write his fond, unmanning, still shore-bound letters—disguising his real misery—as if he were still the weeping schoolboy who had forgotten to pack his handkerchief. My Dearest Emily . . . My Dearest Jane . . .

How little they knew how their pet rag-doll could rasp out

an order. He had sea legs (if he were allowed to find them) and sea lungs to go with them. And of what should he write to them now, long as it was since he had last beheld them? Of a perilous expedition by coach from Bridgwater?

One day his father had summoned him to the library and had spoken to him as if from an immense and patient height. It was so that he would be told the modest nature of his allowance, but it was also so that he would be given words of general advice. He had trembled before this seldom-seen figure as he would one day tremble before admirals. He would remember—as he remembered now—how his father's face briefly softened as if in recognition of his discomfort.

His father had said, "My dear Richard, you are a member of the Longridge family. You are neither a king nor a commoner. You will understand all you need to know for your conduct in this world if you understand these words: know your place." His father's features had hardened again and his eyes had seemed to probe him, as though behind the words, clear and implacable enough, were some other message.

The library clock had chimed, painfully, the morning hour. So distant had he felt from his father at this point that his father might as well have been a king and he himself the lowest of commoners. Or his father's bastard child. It had dawned on him afterwards—gradually but with a nagging lucidity—that, though the matter was apparently being charitably concealed, this might indeed be the truth of it. It was not in his interest to question anything. It was in his interest to conspire in the deception and be grateful—to write milksop letters to his mother and sisters.

He was perhaps, though it was not in his interest ever to verify it, what his schoolfellows had called a "fitz."

He prodded the disobliging fire with the poker. He recalled his mother's once constant refrain to the maid, like some further, if unwitting, piece of parental advice: "A feeble fire, Betty, is worse than an empty grate."

He saw again his schoolfellows, remembered their plaintive names. Ashmole, Palgrave, Wilkes . . .

Since he had not, even with the advantages of education, overcome by his own ingenuity the problem of his essential superfluity, it came down to the Army, the Navy or the Church. He preferred blue to red, and preferred either to the black-and-white absurdity of being a parson in a pulpit.

He hadn't thought much, strangely, about a thing called the sea. He was acquainted with it now. And he hadn't known that service in the King's Navy, even when he was commissioned and sea-seasoned (even more so then) would involve these vile periods of limbo and of dismal self-exposure—a creature neither of land nor sea, caught between a dubious homesickness and three or four days, depending on the course and the weather, of actual vomiting.

There was no evil in the world but uselessness and no good but its opposite. This he understood, if he would never, precisely, understand his father's words. He knew that his present disease could only be cured by a series of remedies. It would be eased, a little, by the first sight of his ship, then, more so, by first stepping upon it, but it would only be fully purged (and only then with much retching and wishing to be dead) once that ship had drawn up its chain. Now he was denied even the weakest of those medicines. He did not even know if his ship was at anchor.

He might have enquired at once of the innkeeper, he might enquire of anyone, but he did not want to suffer the naval indignity of having to ask the whereabouts of his vessel. He went to the window and, craning his neck, saw the lights across the water. He imagined himself foolishly asking, "Is any one of those the *Temeraire*?"

He would surely know at dawn anyway by the evidence of his own eyes. A Second Rate would be unmistakable. And the sight of it, the pride of it, even under veiling drizzle, would surely chase away this malady. He had never served before in anything so mighty. Even his sisters had understood. And the fact that their lordships had assigned him to a ship of the line must mean that he had not gone entirely unnoticed and was deemed to have some worth. It might even be the preliminary to a captaincy and a frigate.

But he had heard of the *Temeraire*. The name itself was an audacity. Quite so. A French name when they were fighting the French. Napoleon himself might be styled *"téméraire."* More to the point, and as everyone knew (even his sisters knew and forbore to mention it), mutiny had been committed on this ship. Men had dangled from its yardarms. And for all its guns and its belligerent name, the *Temeraire* had never seen action. Its timbers had been damaged by storm and dishonoured by sedition, but never been struck by shot.

Well, it was like him then. He had not seen action either. Action: it was the very word of validated existence. He had received such promotion as he had neither by grace and favour (perhaps the whole fleet knew who, or what, he really was) nor by exploit. Their lordships must have dispatched him to the *Temeraire* because of his competence at gun practice. What else was there to do on the blockade? Gun practice, and more gun practice.

Now he would command a bigger battery of guns on a bigger gun deck. But as a proportion of the ship's sum of guns his command would be less than what it had been on a Fourth Rate. And on the same gun deck, commanding the other battery, might be another lieutenant—call him Lieutenant Lanyard—and Lieutenant Lanyard might be a squeak of eighteen, and have seen action.

But the *Temeraire* had seen no action save mutiny.

Why, every time, must he suffer these forebodings, like Jonah going down to Joppa—and now be posted to a ship accordingly?

He turned from the window back to the fire. He might go out into the dripping lamp-lit darkness, to stretch his coach-cramped legs, to breathe at least the salt-flavoured air, to soothe his spleen. But he did not want, for some reason, to walk, as he would have

to, among seamen, though he would walk among them continu-
ally soon—let it be soon—on a heaving deck. He had noticed,
even as the coach rolled in, that there were many of them. He
had not before seen Plymouth so crowded, nor felt—but this was
some sixth sense and not a matter of the eyes—the place so pregnant with preparation. So, it would not be so long perhaps.

His reluctance was not from any cocked-hatted nicety. They
would of course make way for him and touch their temples, and
should he wish (but he would not) to snap at them they would
jump. As sailors ashore they were not technically under the full
articles of war, but it was not in their interest not to look lively.
Everyone minded their interest.

It was more that such contact, or non-contact, might only
make him think of his hidden respect for them, or even—and
this was mutinous thinking indeed—his kinship. Aboard ship it
was different. You acted within timber bounds and iron laws. A
sea creature? More a sea mechanism. You did not think. This was
precisely his affliction now. He was thinking.

But it was one thing the Navy had taught him, or confirmed
in him. He was not, essentially, different from them. Mutinous
meditation indeed. Perhaps his competence in the matter of gun-
nery, his quality of leadership in this regard, his ability at least to
achieve what others achieved, but without threats of the lash or
other fulminations—with only firmness of voice and no other
tyranny than that of his pocket watch—owed itself to this inad-
missible fact. Again, boys, and again! And yet again, till you are
but part of your guns. As if, as he commanded them, he were
really proclaiming: Know your place, know your place. Neither
God nor man will find any other place or use for you than this. It
is what you are for.

But he had not known action. He knew about noise and
smoke and hissing steam that became as great as the smoke. He
knew about powder in the mouth and nostrils. But he did not
know about splinters. He trusted that, should the occasion arise

and they were flying about, he would not lose his power of command. He would not lose his voice. He would not flinch or duck or wish to cover his face, not just because this would be unexemplary, but because he had been led to understand that whatever you did it made no difference.

He had not seen action, but some other sixth sense—a seventh sense—told him that this time might be the occasion. He trusted, simply, that he would do his duty. As he had done his careful, grateful, unmutinying duty to his father and (if such she was) his mother.

My dearest Mama . . . My dearest . . .

He stabbed the fire. All boldness and lustre had fled from his heart. He chewed his fingers savagely. He was himself like one of his mother's empty grates.

Temeraire. It was a mocking name, it was an inglorious, ill-fated ship.

Saint Peter

It embarrassed him now, so many years later, to say he was a vicar's son, that he'd been raised in a vicarage. It was like saying he'd been raised in some cosy cottage in the country—even if the vicarage had been in one of the less appealing suburbs of Birmingham. It was an ordinary house with a bay window. If you stood by the window you could see the church a little way along the road on the other side. "A stone's throw" was what his father always said, they were a stone's throw. It was a common enough expression, but when he was small he always used to picture someone actually lifting their arm and tensing their back to throw a stone. He'd wonder whether the throwing was from or to the church. He was troubled by the idea of anyone throwing a stone at a church, or even from one.

He could still summon up now, though it was long ago, his father's keen but gaunt face. His father had died when he was still small, so it was always the same unageing face that he saw, while his own face in more than fifty years had changed immensely. There was something about that time, when he was only eight and when his father, though no one knew it yet, was dying, that was imprinted on him. He couldn't picture nearly so clearly, though he'd actually known him for longer, the face of Peter Wilson, his stepfather. And he'd never known, though the question remained, if when his father had been dying Peter

Wilson had been just his mother's friend and a friend of the family or something more, even at that time. And if his father had known it.

It was like picking up a stone and trying to guess its weight. And not knowing, even now, which way to throw it. His mother knew, but had never said. Why should she? And now that she was old and frail and losing her memory he had even less reason to press her. He could only wonder if it all still pressed upon her anyway.

His mother hadn't met him in any case, that afternoon, at the school gates. He was eight years old and he didn't need his mother to meet him. The school wasn't much further away than the church. But she was one of those mothers who'd still turn up, perhaps because she was the Vicar's wife. And he was one of those kids who, though he might have preferred his mother not to turn up, was secretly glad that she did.

But this time it was his father. It was a cold grey day in March. A mean buffeting wind was blowing. It was also the last day of term before the Easter holiday, and he wondered, though there was no logic to it, whether it was because of this that his father and not his mother had come to meet him.

He certainly hadn't known then that his father would be dead by Christmas. Nor could his mother have known, nor even his father himself. He wasn't well and he looked tired, standing by the school gates, but not especially ill. He'd been clearly able to manage the walk to the school, something that would prove impossible soon. He'd been told by his doctor that he shouldn't overdo things, at just the time, around Easter, when his duties were particularly demanding, but he'd made a joke about this. There was a deputy vicar lined up to take at least some of the services, and since "vicar" meant deputy anyway that meant there was a deputy-deputy.

It had disappointed him to be told that a vicar was only a

209

deputy. It seemed like a mark of unimportance. And he'd been troubled by the idea that a doctor could tell a vicar what to do.

They'd walked back together. He felt that his father had come to the school gates in order to tell him something, to have his exclusive attention as they returned home. But something—perhaps the evil wind, constantly sending up clouds of dust and grit as they walked—had forestalled this.

It was anyway only when they got back that he realised his mother wasn't at home. He'd assumed she'd simply indulged his father's whim, but now his father said, "Mum's sorry she couldn't meet you, but she'll be home any moment." It was said in a way that made him understand he shouldn't ask why. In any case, almost in the same breath, his father said, rather strangely, "Easter is coming." It was hardly necessary to say it, everyone knew Easter was coming, but since he'd said it so quickly after what he'd said about his mother it made him think that Easter was like a person too who'd turn up at any moment—from wherever it was that Easter went.

His father put the kettle on and cut a thick slice of bread which he plastered with butter, then with strawberry jam. This was his regular reward for coming home from school. His father was doing exactly what his mother would normally do, though he was doing it, sleeves rolled up, with his sinewy arms, which for the first time he'd thought were not like a vicar's arms, but just like any man's arms.

They took their tea, and the bread and jam, into the front room. They used their front room regularly. A lot of people seemed not to do this—they reserved their front rooms for special occasions. Perhaps their own case was different because the house was a vicarage and because from the front room you could see the church. From where his father now chose to sit he couldn't have seen the church—you had to be close to the window—but he sat so that he was nonetheless looking out, at their gate and the privet hedge juddering in the wind. It was clear that he wanted to say something.

It was St. Peter's Church and it was only a coincidence that it was Peter Wilson. There were lots of Peters. His own name was Paul. There was a St. Paul too. Since his father was the Vicar of St. Peter's, he'd absorbed a few facts, even when he was very small, about St. Peter. That his symbol was the crossed keys. That these keys represented the keys to heaven, since St. Peter was the keeper of the gates to heaven. That Jesus had once said to St. Peter that he was the rock on which he'd build his church, since the name Peter was also just an ordinary word meaning "rock." It had seemed to him that, with all these attributes, Peter must be the best and most important of all the saints. So he'd been proud and glad that his father was the Vicar of St. Peter's.

But his father now said, with the tiredness in his face showing in the light from the window, that St. Peter had once been no kind of saint at all. It was like his remark about Easter. It came from nowhere and seemed to be heading nowhere, but he said it with some emphasis. He said it was important to understand this. St. Peter had once been no saint at all. Then he said, and this was a rather shocking remark, that it was important to understand too that there had once been no such thing as Easter.

It became rather difficult to eat his bread and jam. It felt wrong while his father was pronouncing such things. It had been wrong perhaps of his father to prepare it for him. But his father had only been doing, decently, what was expected, what his mother would have done. And, until moments ago, he'd been a hungry boy, home from school.

He'd remember always that slice of bread—it was rather thicker than his mother would have cut—that he wasn't able, even with an effort, to finish. His father must have seen his struggle, but, caught in a quandary of his own, been unable to say anything. He was talking about St. Peter.

He'd remember always his challenging bread and jam, the blue-orange glow of the gas fire, which his father had turned on, and the noise behind him, through the window, of their gate knock-knocking in the wind.

"Can you imagine that?" his father had said. "Can you imagine when there wasn't any such thing as Easter?"

He couldn't. Easter was something that came round every year, like birthdays and holidays, like Christmas. Then his father had told him the story that, even at eight, he probably mostly knew, and even knew mostly from his father. But his father had never told it like this, as if it were a story that had never been told before.

It was important to remember that there'd once been no such thing as Easter. It was important to remember that when Jesus spoke to Peter on the night before Good Friday it wasn't the night before Good Friday, because Good Friday didn't exist then. There was no such thing. And Peter wasn't a saint either. He was just Peter. But this was nonetheless the night, the real and actual night before Jesus was put on the cross, if no one but Jesus understood it. Peter didn't understand it, and didn't believe it when Jesus said to him that before the cock crowed in the morning he, Peter, would deny him three times. Peter didn't know what was happening. He was only Peter.

Jesus had gone to a place to pray, and though he knew what was to come he'd begged God to spare him. He'd said, "Let this cup pass from me." All through the night Jesus had stayed awake and prayed, but the three disciples who were with him had just slept in a huddle close by. Despite what their master was going through, they'd just slept. One of them was Peter.

More than once Jesus had woken them, but they'd just slept again, even at such a time. Because their eyes were heavy, his father had said, and they were only human. They didn't really know what was happening. Jesus had already that night named the disciple, Judas, who would betray him, but he'd said to Peter too those words about the cock crowing. Even knowing this, Peter had just slept.

His father had said all these things not like a vicar speaking in church, but as if they were being said for the first time. Some of his father's words were just words from the Bible and perhaps, even at eight, he knew this, but he felt them, saw them, like real things. He felt the weight of the disciples' eyes. Saw that cup, though it was only a cup in Jesus's mind. Felt the passing of that long night and the stern exactness of those three times.

He couldn't finish his bread and jam. It was what his mother had said, almost immediately, when she came in: "You haven't finished your bread and jam." She'd noticed very quickly the little remnant of bread with the small half-moon shape in it of his mouth. But she must have noticed too that there was an atmosphere inside the house. An atmosphere. She must have noticed it more than the piece of bread.

Let this bread and jam pass from me.

It was only a story. But he lay awake that night, listening to the wind and feeling somehow that he should stay awake the whole night, he should do this, for his father's sake. But he'd slept too, despite the story. He'd simply fallen asleep. He was eight years old and he slept deeply and sweetly and when he woke up it was bright daylight and he knew that he didn't have to get up to go to school. He could shut his eyes and go back to sleep if he wished. It was a delicious feeling. For a moment he hadn't remembered his father speaking to him or anything about the previous day. Then there was a sort of shadow in his head. Then he remembered.

Outside, the sky was clear. The wind had stopped. It was Birmingham, and no cocks crowed. In a while his mother would come in to see if he was awake. She would stoop to kiss him.

Sometimes, so as to enjoy her kiss, he'd pretend he was still asleep and that it was her kiss that had woken him. He wondered if she guessed this. It was a little like wishing she wouldn't come to the school gates, but being glad, inside, that she did.

He'd surely have remembered if his mother had kissed him that morning.

Peter Wilson was a teacher at the primary school. Peter Wilson had once taught him. He'd become a friend of the family, as teachers can become, perhaps a particular friend of his mother. He'd been Mr. Wilson, then he became Peter. Then he became his stepfather.

If his father had known that Peter Wilson was something more than just his mother's friend, then he'd have known, when he became more seriously ill, that if he died it would give her her freedom. And if he'd died knowing—or even wishing—this, then that would, surely, have been not unsaintly. In any case, being a Christian, a vicar, his father would have known that he'd have to die without anguish or bitterness, accepting that it was God's will.

When his father died—it was early December and now it was Christmas that was coming—his mother hadn't cried, or not much, or not in front of him. But then she too had to behave with composure, like the wife of a vicar. But she cried a lot, and in front of him, when Peter Wilson, many years later, left her, just suddenly left her. It's more uncomfortable, perhaps, for a mother to cry in front of her twenty-year-old son than in front of her eight-year-old son—setting aside which is more uncomfortable for the son. But she cried anyway, uncontrollably, as if she were crying two times over on the one occasion. He'd hesitated to embrace her.

What's in a word? Words aren't things. Cup, stone, rock. He didn't really believe, even at eight, though his father must have believed it, that St. Peter had a pair of keys that opened the gate to heaven. How could heaven have a gate? How could heaven have the same arrangement as his school, or even their front garden? People say of themselves, it's the commonest excuse, and he must have said it of himself more than once in his life, "I'm no saint."

He's no saint. Or: She's no angel.

Could he have thought it, of his own mother, as she stooped like that to kiss him in the morning? She's no angel.

His father had said that it had all happened just as Jesus had said. Those who came to accuse and arrest him accused Peter too—of being a follower of Jesus. Three times, in fact, Peter was accused and three times he said that he had nothing to do with Jesus. Even though he'd been told by Jesus that this was just what he'd do—which should have been the severest and most unbreakable command not to do it—Peter had gone ahead three times with his denials.

His father didn't say about this that it was because Peter was only human and he was afraid. He just said it was what happened. Peter had slept because his eyes were heavy. Now he made his denials, three times. Immediately after the third time the cock suddenly crowed. Then Peter had wept.

First on the Scene

⌒

Nearly every week now—more often if he could and if the weather was good—Terry would catch a train to the country and take a walk in one of the places where, not so long ago, he and his late wife Lynne used to walk together. They'd discovered these places and the appropriate train timetables when he'd had to give up driving because of his Parkinson's, and because Lynne had never learnt to drive. In just an hour or so from town they'd be stepping out into quiet countryside with good walks, fine views and maybe a handy pub. It was all a lot better, in fact, more free and easy, than driving somewhere. They'd never have discovered these places in a car. It made him less miffed about not being able to drive, even about his altered state of health.

He'd always thought that, with his Parkinson's, he would go first, but it was Lynne.

Now Terry went on these same walks, caught exactly the same trains on his own, because it was the nearest he could get to being with Lynne and enjoying it. At home, in the house they'd shared for years, the same theoretically applied, but it wasn't enjoyable, it was the opposite. He needed the countryside, the trees, the open air, the familiar paths.

On these walks he'd sometimes say to himself: This is as good as it gets. It was something he'd never have thought of saying to himself when he was young, it would have seemed foolish, but there'd come a point in his life when he began to say it quite often, like a reminder. He used to say it to himself nearly every time he walked with Lynne. But he said it also now. It was important. It wasn't true now, because when he'd said it to himself while walking with Lynne everything had been so much better. But it was also true now. It was true and it wasn't.

When Terry took the trains for these walks he would look at other passengers as if he were a complete outsider, as if he might be invisible. He'd listen to their chatter. All of this wasn't an uncomfortable feeling, in fact he sometimes felt a strange tug of warmth, of soothing fascination for these creatures he was no longer one of. He couldn't have had these feelings driving in a car.

It might have been that on these walks he would have just felt lonely, but it was the opposite. It was only on these walks that he felt totally free to imagine that his wife was walking beside him, that he could be uninhibited about talking to her out loud, not even in his head. He couldn't do this at home, it would seem like the first sign of madness, but on these walks he'd initiate and conduct whole conversations with his wife, and, yes, as he spoke or even as he just walked he'd sometimes really believe, turning his head quickly to check, that she was there.

It might have been, too, that, wrapped up in this process, Terry wouldn't have been so attentive to the countryside around him, to the pleasing views, to the observation of nature. Yet it was all the more important to notice these things, to point them out to his wife, to see the butterfly, or the woodpecker, like a speck of paint, against the tree, or the kestrel quivering in mid-air. These things were alive.

So, in fact, he was all the more observant. He'd sometimes be drawn, with a surprisingly tender concentration, to just a cluster of primroses or a clump of moss. He'd notice things even at a distance.

So he noticed very quickly now, through the ferns, the patch of bright colour—bright red—up ahead.

There was a place where if you left the main path and struck out through the undergrowth you emerged onto the brow of a hill. There were bramble bushes, a thick bank of ferns, then a small clearing of grass and more ferns. Then the woods encroached again. It was a semi-secret place and, with the grass and the view and the enclosing bushes and ferns, a perfect spot in fine weather just to sit for a while and rest before walking on, or walking back. Or (with Lynne) to have had a small picnic—to have got out the thermos and the plastic box of stuff he'd carry in his backpack. He'd sat here with Lynne many times and, surprisingly, they'd never found it occupied by anyone else.

He thought that this might be the case now and that he should stop, back-track into the woods and circle round. Too bad, that the place was taken. But the red patch, though it seemed like a patch of clothing, didn't move and there were no sounds. He concluded that it was something left by somebody, and this at first annoyed him. How could anyone leave behind anything so glaring?

After a few more steps and without yet emerging from the narrow gap through the ferns he saw that the red patch was indeed an item of clothing. It was a woman's red T-shirt and it was being worn by a woman in her mid-twenties, and the woman was alone and very still and dead.

He knew this at once and for certain, without ever drawing close: the woman was dead. She was lying on her side in a curled-up position, in what is known as the foetal position, but she wasn't asleep, she didn't stir. She was dead. If he were questioned—and he soon realised that he would be—as to how he knew the woman was dead, it wouldn't be easy to explain. He'd never come across a dead person in a clearing before, but some ability in him that perhaps all humans come equipped with, to recognise another human who is dead, instantly asserted itself. Perhaps he possessed this ability more keenly now that Lynne was dead.

There was nothing else in the clearing and the woman appeared unmarked, but she was dead. There was the unavoidable impression that she'd lain there for some time. There was a total immobility about her and a sense that the passage of hours, the weather and other, more mysterious processes had worked on her to claim her as just an inanimate part of the surroundings.

Apart from the red top, she wore blue jeans and lightweight, stylish trainers—clothes for a summer's day, but not for sleeping outside through a summer's night. This thought was merely technical. The thought that she would have been cold was irrelevant. The clothes seemed attached to her in a way that was not the usual way of clothes. Her hair was strangely tangled about her face as if the hair and the face were only incidental to each other. There were tiny bits of vegetation, things that might fall from trees or be blown about the air, dotted all over her. A small leaf was lodged in her exposed upturned ear.

He was no expert, but he didn't need to go any further to verify that she was not alive and had lain there like that, without stirring, since at least the preceding evening. He was sure of this, if he was sure of nothing else.

It was now not long after ten on a warm Sunday morning. He'd taken a fairly early train.

He stood still. He didn't want to emerge from the screen of the ferns. He peered carefully around. There was only the innocent sunny aspect the scene would have had if he were the only one there—which he was in a sense. Or if nobody was there. Indeed the absurd phrase came to him: "first on the scene."

In all his life—and he was sixty-nine—he'd never been first on the scene. Was this remarkable, a sort of achievement, or just the norm? In all his life with Lynne, in all their walks, they'd never been first on the scene either. It had never even occurred to them that it might happen. But he was now, for the first time, first on the scene. He was the one who "while out walking" . . . It was another phrase that came to him.

He stood and looked. He also shook. But this was his Parkinson's, his occasional and really not so violent tremor. It was another virtue of his solitary walks that this sometimes embarrassing symptom no longer mattered. It was anyway the lesser of his plights. He was so constituted now as to have from time to time a condition usually associated with strong emotion—and now he was under the sway of strong emotion his body had no separate way of signalling it. But he wasn't sure what the emotion was. Was it fear? Or rather anger?

Whatever else this sight before him signified, it was something that had brutally interrupted—swept away, cancelled—his much-needed conversation with his wife, his being still with her though she wasn't there. It had desecrated the memory of being here, in this same grassy clearing, with her in the past. It had made it impossible ever to walk this way with her (though without her) again.

It was hardly the appropriate emotion: anger. Yet he felt it. He would never tell anyone about it, though he understood that he'd have to tell people about other things. It was an inescapable consequence of his being here right now that he'd have to explain things and carefully answer questions. He'd have to justify his actions.

What were you doing walking in the woods? Why were you there?

She was in her twenties. If she were alive (and since he was sixty-nine) he might have called her a girl. The trainers were pale blue and white and had red laces to match her top. There was something impossible about the small swell of her ankle bone.

"Stumbled upon": that was another phrase. In all his life he'd never stumbled upon. He understood that his role in all this—though it was not as if he'd been assigned a role—was minor, incidental, the result of the merest chance, yet at the same time it was critical and would involve him a great deal. He might have walked another way, he might have caught a later train, he might not have come for a walk at all. This encounter might have been entirely someone else's, but it was his.

If he gave an honest answer to why he was walking in the woods he might at once be thought to be a little peculiar. Why are you trembling? It's Parkinson's disease. I have Parkinson's disease. Anyway, why shouldn't he tremble? Who wouldn't tremble at such a thing?

As the first on the scene, he might automatically—this possibility suddenly hit him—come under suspicion himself. Automatically and provisionally, yet almost definitely. A young woman, a girl. A retired man, a widower, with a tremble, walking alone in a wood . . .

What would Lynne think of this predicament he'd walked into? Suppose it had happened while he'd been walking with her. But he couldn't now turn to his wife and say, "Lynne, what should I do? What should we do?" Lynne, who just moments ago had seemed so assuringly to be with him, had now totally disappeared.

And that was really the worst of it all.

A great temptation came over him: to make the hypothesis, the other, not realised possibility be true. He might simply retrace his steps, go back into the woods, rejoin the main path. He might never, after all, have forked off through the undergrowth to this spot that only he, he and Lynne, and perhaps just a few other walking folk knew. He might just carry on with his walk. He might contemplate nature. There would be a story, a news story, which he might not even hear about, which would have nothing to do with him.

But he knew he couldn't do this. It was true that he hadn't gone near the body, let alone touched it, he'd only stood here and looked. Yet he felt that his presence, the path he'd taken, brushing aside twigs and stems, his tread on the ground beneath him were as indelibly imprinted as any scent an animal might pick up. There was something irrevocable about his being here. It was so much the case that the emotion afflicting him was perhaps neither anger nor fear but a sort of contaminating, trapping, but unjustifiable guilt. And he wanted to cry out suddenly to Lynne, who wasn't there, to be his witness, his alibi.

The woman was not in any way like Lynne. She was not even like Lynne had been when she was, say, twenty-four. Except, of course, she was like Lynne in one fundamental way.

The trees, the ferns all around him were trembling, shaking in their way too. It was just the summer breeze. It was only for entirely extraneous reasons, an unlucky gene, that he was trembling himself. And yet he made a determined and futile effort—as if it were something both vital and within his power—to stop doing so.

Then he saw the whole truth of what must ensue, of what he and no one else must inescapably instigate, the truth of what was embodied before him—setting aside the immense riddle of why it was there at all. This was someone's daughter, someone's . . .

He reached for his mobile phone. It wasn't easy. Mobile phones aren't designed for people with Parkinson's, but he still carried one, even on solitary walks, and would have said that it was in case he got into difficulties, in case of emergencies. And this was certainly an emergency. Even before his symptoms had appeared he hadn't been a great user of his mobile and had called it his "walkie-talkie" because he used it almost solely for communicating with his wife. Walkie-talkie: he should never have used those mocking words. When Lynne died he wished he hadn't recently deleted all her inconsequential voice messages. But how should he have known?

It took time and was a struggle, with the shaking of his hand. But then others in his circumstances, without his condition, might have found this to be the case. He had no choice but to remain here, to be fixed to this spot. He even resolved not to budge from his position among the ferns, to stay as still as possible (setting aside his tremor), as still as that woman over there. Look at the ferns, the green ferns. Look at the butterfly, the woodpecker. Look—

He looked at the woman in her red top and saw, almost with a longing, the absolute absence the dead have even as they are there.

A voice crackled in his ear. He hadn't a clue how to begin. He hadn't a clue how to describe his situation or to pinpoint exactly where he was. What a terrible thing it can be just to be on this earth.

England

He came over the familiar brow and saw at once the red lights of the solitary vehicle, perhaps half a mile ahead on the otherwise empty stretch of road. It wasn't moving, it had pulled up. Then, as he drew closer, he saw the odd angle. Its nearside wheels had lodged in one of the treacherous roadside gullies where the tarmac stopped.

It was not yet five. His watch began at 5:30. Only minutes ago, while Ruth still slept, he'd eased the car, in the dim light, from the garage. At this hour the straight stretch of road, the only straight stretch in his short journey, was normally all his own. He seldom rushed it. It was so starkly beautiful: the mass of the moor to his left and up ahead, in the scoops between the hills, the first glimpses of the sea. He told himself, routinely, not to take it for granted.

It was dawn, but overcast, there was even a faint mist—a general breathy greyness. The sort of greyness that would burn off, to give full sunshine, by mid-morning. The weather was in his professional blood. Fair weather, calm seas, late July. But it was the busy season.

He looked at the dashboard. He could spare perhaps ten minutes. He slowed and pulled over—not too far over, taking his warning from the car ahead. In it he could see a solitary figure in the driver's seat, who must be amply aware by now that help was at hand. It was a blue BMW, but of a certain vintage, not a rich man's car. Exmoor, these days, was full of rich men's cars. Every species of plush four-by-four. Well, it was four-by-four territory. The joke was that since they drove the things around Chelsea, then here, surely, they should use their dinky little town cars. He didn't quite get the joke, never having been to Chelsea.

He stopped. He could, in theory, have driven on. He was under no obligation. But how could you? In any case rescue was in his professional veins too. He understood at once what the situation might look like—he was even wearing a dark uniform. It must be why the driver didn't open his door and, back turned, seemed almost to be cowering.

He walked forward, inhaling the cool air. A thin dreamy envelope of sleep still clung to him. There was the tiny cluck of water in the gully. A stream, barely more than a trickle through the grass, came down off the hillside and, in the slight dip, cut away at the edge of the road. It was a dodgy spot.

The driver's window was down. He was met by a sudden blast of the foreign.

"Fookin' 'ell. Fookin' 'ell!"

The driver's face was black. He had, in silently noting the fact, no other word for it. You might say it wasn't deep black, as black faces go, but it was black. This was not a place, an area, for black faces. It was remarkable to see them. There was, on top, a thick bizarre bonnet of frizzy hair. It looked cartoonish in its frizziness.

"Fookin' 'ell."

"It's okay," he quickly and pacifyingly said, "I'm not a policeman. I'm a coastguard. It's not a crime to be stuck in a ditch. Can I help?"

"Co-ahst-guaard!"

The man's voice had changed in an instant. The first voice (the normal one?) had a strong accent which, nonetheless, he couldn't place, because all northern accents eluded him. The second voice was a foreign voice in the sense that the accent wasn't English at all. He couldn't place it exactly either, just that it was broadly—very broadly—Caribbean. But the man had slipped into it as if it were not in fact his natural voice. It was turned on and exaggerated, a joke voice.

On the other hand, since both voices were alien to him, both voices were like joke voices. That wasn't a fair-minded thought, but he knew that people not from the West Country made a joke of the West Country accent all the time. It was one of the standard joke accents.

"Where de co-ahst, man? Where de co-ahst? I is lookin' for de co-ahst. You guard it, you tell me where it is."

He felt at once compelled to comply.

"It's over there." He actually lifted an arm. "You're looking at it."

The man wrinkled his face as if he couldn't see anything.

"I is lookin' for Ilfracombe, man." Then he pronounced the word at full-pitch and with declamatory slowness, as if it were a place in Africa.

"Il-frah-coombe!"

Then the voice broke up into little screechy, hissy laughs. He couldn't tell if it was nervous laughter, panicky laughter or a sort of calculated laughter. Or just laughter. It was like a parrot. He couldn't help the thought. It was like a parrot laughing.

"Ilfracombe is over there." Again he felt the ridiculous need to raise an arm. "You're in the right direction. You'll need the thirty-nine, then the three-nine-nine. An hour, at this time of day."

The man peered, putting a visoring hand to his eyes. "I no see it, man. I no see no three-nine-nine. Ilfracombe, Deh-von. We in Deh-von, man?"

"We're in Somerset." (He almost said, "We in Somerset.") It surely didn't need saying, but he announced it, "This is Exmoor."

"*Ex*moor! Fookin' 'ell. *Ilkley* Moor, that's me. Ilkley Moor bar tat. Ilkley Moor bar fookin' tat."

The voice had completely changed again. What was going on here? He was used—occupationally used—to the effects of shock and exposure. He was used to the phenomenon of disorientation. To gabble, hysteria, even, sometimes, to the effects of drug taking.

He wanted to say a simple "Calm down." He wanted to exert a restorative authority. But he felt that this man, stranded in what seemed to be, for him, the middle of nowhere and talking weirdly, somehow had the authority. He peered into the car's interior. He saw that on the not unroomy back seat there was a grubby blanket and a pillow. It was five in the morning. He got the strong impression that this man, going about whatever could possibly be his business, used his car as at least an emergency place of overnight accommodation. Having just affirmed that he wasn't one, he felt like a policeman. He felt out of his territory, though he couldn't be more in it. He knew this road like the back of his hand. But he was a coastguard, not a policeman.

The voice changed again. "I is in de right direction, man. But I is goin' nowhere."

"No. I can see that. What happened?"

"Fookin' deer." It was the other man—the other other-man—again.

"What?"

"Fookin' deer. Int' middle of road. Joost standin' there."

"You saw a deer?"

"Int' middle of road. Five fookin' minutes ago."

He looked around, over the roof of the car. It was Exmoor. There were deer. You saw them sometimes from the road, especially in the early morning. But there was little cover for them here and he'd never, in over twenty years, come upon a deer just standing in the middle of the road. If they stepped on the road at all, they'd surely dart off again at even the distant sight of a vehicle. This man had come from—wherever he'd come from—to see something he'd never seen in decades.

He had the feeling that the deer might be another symptom of disorientation. A hallucination, an invention. Yet the man (the other one again) spoke about it with beguiling precision.

"A lee-tal baby deer, man. I couldn't get by he. I couldn't kill he. A lee-tal baby Bambee."

He looked over the roof of the car. Nothing moved in the greenish greyness. It was just plausible: a young stray deer, separated and inexperienced, in the dip, in a pocket of mist, near a source of drinking water. It was just plausible. He was a coastguard, not a deer warden. He asked himself: Would he have had any sceptical thoughts if this were just some unlucky farmer?

"I see his lee-tal eyes in me headlights. I couldn't kill he."

The man was behaving, it was true, as if he were being doubted, were under suspicion, as if this were a familiar situation.

He saw, in his mind's eye, a deer's eyes in the headlights, the white dapples on its flank. A small trembling deer. It was a startling but magical vision. That alone, on this routine journey to work, would have been something special to talk about.

He tried to give his best, friendly passer-by's smile. "Of course you couldn't kill it. You didn't hit it?"

"No. He hop it. I the one who end up in de shit, man."

It might shake you up a bit, nearly hitting a deer.

The man changed voices yet again. "Fookin' deer." Then he said, in the other voice, "I is a long way from Leeds."

So it was Yorkshire. He was from Leeds, but he was on the edge of Exmoor, at five in the morning. Which was even more bewildering perhaps than a deer in your headlights. He felt a moment's protectiveness. He wasn't sure if it was for the lost man, or the lost deer, the little Bambi. He'd helped to return many a lost child, over the years, to its distraught parents. It was one of the happier duties. Now was the peak time for it.

"So. Let's get you out of here. You've tried reversing?"

"I've tried reversing." It was the northern voice, but with no manic exaggeration.

He stepped round to the back of the car. Either he'd reversed clumsily and the back wheel had slipped into the gully or it had gone into the gully in the first place when he'd braked and swerved—for the phantom deer. He'd got stuck anyway. And what were the chances—they were remote, extraordinary and barely believable too—that in such circumstances help would come along, uniformed help, in a matter of minutes?

The man got out to inspect the damage for himself. He didn't look like a man who'd have regular roadside-assistance cover. He was shorter and slighter than he'd supposed. It was the hair, the two-inch hedge of it, that made him tall. But he had a strutting way of carrying himself. The gait of a cocky, belligerent York-shireman? No, not exactly.

In the dampish dawn air—his own sidelights lighting up the gully—they assessed the situation. No harm done, just the misplaced wheels.

"If we do it together," he said, "we could just lift her so the back wheel's on the road again. Then you can reverse. I can push from the front if you spin. But you should be okay."

"You tell me, skipper."

This was no doubt a reference to the looped stripe on his sleeve. It was a perk of his job occasionally to be mistaken for a ship's captain. But he'd said, and noticed it even as he said it, the nautical "lift her."

"We lift her arse, skipper, nice and easy." The man even crouched, ready to take the bumper, like a small sumo wrestler.

"Wait."

He went round to the left-open driver's door. He checked the position of the gear stick. Then he took off his jacket and, folding it, placed it on the passenger seat. He felt chilly without it, but he didn't want to arrive on duty looking as if he'd been in an accident himself.

The man watched him and said, "That's righ', man. We don't wahnt you messin' de natty tailorin'."

The man's own clothes might have been natty once, long ago, in their own way. There was a faded sweater—purple and black horizontal stripes—over which there was a very old, perhaps once stylish full-length leather jacket. It hung about him like a droopy black second skin, which was an unfortunate way of thinking of it. The clothes looked anciently lived-in.

He rolled up his own crisp white sleeves. He walked round to the gully. There were some convenient small stream-washed rocks and he jammed a few against the stricken front wheel. He surreptitiously checked, as if trained for it, the front of the car—for dents, for possible bits of deer. There were none. That is, there were many dents, but they were old.

He walked back. He now felt, if it was only fleetingly, in charge, as if the man had become his appointed junior.

"Okay." They crouched. "You have a hold? On 'three' then."

"You give the word, skip."

The man seemed calmer, less disoriented—if that was the proper diagnosis—even appreciative and submissive. The mere fact of doing together what couldn't have been done by one man alone seemed to have put everything into a complete and, if just for a moment, composed perspective. Around them was Exmoor being slowly unveiled by the dawn. Except for a few sparse, travelling lights in the distance on the main road up ahead, they were alone in the landscape. There was a tiny, seemingly stationary light in the further distance. It was the light of a ship in the Bristol Channel. It would be in the station's log.

"One—two—three!"

It was simply achieved. A heave, an instinctive sideways thrust to the right. The back wheel was returned safely to the tarmac. The boot can't have contained anything heavy. No dead deer, for example.

"Fookin' champion!"

What was it about these voices—both of them? But the man seemed genuinely elated, as if wizardry had just occurred.

"You have to reverse her out yet."

Again he'd said "her." They both went to the front. While the man got in and turned the ignition, he continued to the nearside front wing. In another situation he might have said, "*Reverse*, and gently." Fortunately, his own car—engine off and lights on—was parked at a comfortable distance.

There was no difficulty. There was a slight skittering, but the gully wasn't deep and the back wheels hauled the car entirely onto the road again. His own bit of effort on the front bumper was almost superfluous. He looked at his watch. Five minutes had passed. The man cut his engine, yanking on the handbrake, and the sudden returning silence made the brief grinding of reverse gear seem almost like some effrontery.

The man got out.

"Fookin' champion!"

He came forward, hand extended. Like everything else about him, the extended hand was like an act, it was like something not quite as it should be. But he took it and shook it.

"I've got a thermos inside, man. Black coffee. Want some?" The voice was normal now—normal with its Yorkshire tones.

He'd had coffee at home, minutes ago, and there'd be more at the station. But it seemed wrong not to accept the man's gesture of gratitude. There had to be a gesture, a little ritual. Besides, he was curious.

"Okay." He looked at his watch.

"I know. You have to—clock on."

"Be on watch," he said, a little stiffly.

"Aye aye."

He vaguely allowed for the fact that in Yorkshire, so he believed, they said "aye" for "yes." All the same.

"A cup of coffee," the man said. "Tain't every day, is it?"

He had to agree, even give a yielding chuckle. "No, it's not every day," he said, not really knowing exactly what the man meant. But, true, it wasn't every day.

The man groped inside the car, first graciously producing the folded jacket from the passenger seat, then a thermos. He shook it, judging the contents, close to his ear. He unscrewed a pair of cups, one inside the other.

"Black coffee. While I'm driving, to keep me awake. Same as you, I suppose, when you're—on watch."

Like the rest of the world, the man had a picture of a coast-guard as a solitary figure, eyes glued to the horizon, telescope to hand, maintaining a sentry-like vigil. It wasn't quite like that. It was a big station. A huddle of white buildings, with masts and dishes, beneath the tower of a decommissioned lighthouse. There was a rotating watch of staff. At any one time there'd be at least two on duty. There was an array of monitoring and com-munications equipment.

Never mind. It was a coastguard station. It was an out-standingly beautiful, dramatic section of coast. People came at weekends and for holidays. He was there all the time. He was exceptionally lucky, in his work, in his life. Ruth, the job, the two kids who'd made him, twice over, a grandfather—though they were still kids in his mind. The only cloud, it seemed, was retire-ment. Having to stop it all one day. He was fifty-three. The man was—what? He sometimes seemed young, then not young at all.

"Yes," he said. "Coffee helps."

"Black coffee," the man said. "I never know whether to make a joke. And I never know whether to make a joke out of the black or the coffee. See my face, man? Black or coffee?"

He tried to look obtuse and passive. But there was something he genuinely didn't understand.

There was a pause while Exmoor reasserted its presence. Then the man cackled. It was the shoulder-shaking, oddly engag-ing parrot-laugh.

"I'm a joker, man. My business. I'm a comedian."

That in itself seemed a possible joke, a possible trick. I met a strange man today, he was quite a comedian.

"A co-me-di-ahn!"

And now the man—or one of his personas—was back at full frantic tilt again, even while pouring not very warm-looking coffee. He had no choice, nor did Exmoor, but to listen.

"Ah coom all the way from Yorkshire, from fookin' West Ridin', just to get rescued by a coastguard, a fookin' *coastguard,* on Exmoor. Serious. *Exmoor.* What's a *coast*guard doing on fookin' Exmoor? Ilkley Moor, me. Ah never knew you 'ad moors down 'ere an' all. Ilkley Moor bar tat. Ilkley Moor bar mitzvah! Ee but ah do luv Ilfracombe. Il-frah-*combe.* Ave ah said? Ah *combe* from Yorkshire. Ee bah goom! But ah tell yer what they *do* 'ave on Exmoor. Apart from coastguards. Fookin' deer. Did yer know? 'Erds of fookin' deer, and 'erds of fookin' coastguards. Ave ah told yer me deer joke? It's the one where ah tell it and yer all go, 'Dear oh dear oh dear.' "

It was astonishing. It was a performance, an unabashed performance—in the middle of nowhere. It was utterly disconcerting, but now, at least, he understood. And, actually, he was laughing, he couldn't help it. A comedian.

The man saw that he understood. He slowed down, became near-normal again. He grinned. He held out his hand once more, as if he had to introduce himself twice.

"Johnny Dewhurst," he said. Then, grasping his coffee in one hand, he slipped the other inside his jacket and pulled out a card. It said "Johnny Dewhurst, Comedian and Wayfarer." Underneath, in smaller print, were the words "All Engagements Gratefully Appreciated." And to one side there was a picture of a clown, a standard circus clown—big feet, big nose, made-up face. The picture bore no resemblance to Johnny Dewhurst (if that was his actual name). On the other hand, you could see that, with the topiary of hair and mobility of face, not to say voice, he could play the clown if needed—if he wasn't doing it already. And who knows what comic paraphernalia might be stored in the boot of his car?

He laughed his parrot-laugh again. It seemed like a laugh of conspiracy, of complicity now, because his audience had laughed too.

"Il-frah-coombe!" The personas switched again. "Tonight I play Ilfracombe. Then I play Barnstaple. Baahrn-stable! I sleep in de barn or I sleep in de stable? Barnstable not very far, I tink. Then I play Plymouth. That far enough for Johnny. That like Land's End. I next play Verona. No, that different gig. That *Kiss Me Quick* or someting. By Cole Porter. Wid name like that, he must be *black man*! Night before last I play Yeovil. Yo-Ville! I say, 'Yo brother, this my kind of town, this where Johnny belong.' But they don't understan' me, they don't clap very much. Then they send me on to Taunton. They send me to *Tawny Town*! I say, 'This some kind of a *joke*? This some kind of a *rayssiahl* ting?' "

He couldn't help but laugh, whether or not he was meant to. But at the same time he felt that it didn't matter whether he laughed or not, since he understood it now—it was rather like the worn-smooth wrinkled leather coat—the man was inured to the reactions of audiences, be they friendly, hostile, hard-to-please or indifferent. Or perhaps absent.

But the man laughed too.

"How you going to be my straight-man, man, you keep laughing like that? You have a name? You save my life, you haven't told me your name."

"Ken," he said. Now he too held out his hand a second time, but with concealed caution. He desperately wanted to avoid giving his second name. It was Black. He was Kenneth Black. Lots of people are called Black, but he shuddered to think of the comic repercussions.

"Johnny Dewhurst and Kenny—Coastguard. I see it, man. I see it!"

He hid his relief. "Is it your real name, 'Johnny Dewhurst?' "

"Hey, you tink I's a liar, man? You tink I gives you joke name? I have a card made up with some joker's name?"

The shoulders shook, he hee-hawed and he was off again. It bubbled out of him. It was hard to see where the one thing stopped and the other thing began. He'd always supposed that comedians (was there truly a section of humanity called comedians?) were really hard-nosed crafty individuals. There was a gap between the act and the person. But with this man you couldn't tell. There even seemed to be something wished-for in the confusion.

"Johnny Dewhurst, it no joker's name, it a butcher's name. I say, 'First Johnny tell de joke, then—he get butchered for it!' "

He reached inside his jacket again, pulled out a folded slip of paper and handed it over. It was a flyer, a flyer for a tour—"The Johnny Dewhurst Tour." It was a list, a remarkably long one, of places and dates. The places criss-crossed and circumscribed England. The tour began—or had begun—in Scarborough, then had taken in several northern locations, then worked circuitously south. It had networked the Midlands, then struck southwest. It had touched Lincoln, Nottingham, Derby, Shrewsbury, Rugby . . . as well as towns he couldn't exactly place. The first date was in late June and there was still over a month to go. It had still to track the length of the south coast and to reach such venues as Lowestoft and Skegness. It was a list of theatres, corn exchanges, seaside palaces and pavilions, and indeterminate halls. And it must be a very ambitious list, because he'd never heard of Johnny Dewhurst, though he'd met him now, and at many of these places, some of them even having a faint hint of glamour, Johnny Dewhurst must be very far from star billing—"on tour" as he was—he must be a very short spot a long way down the programme.

And now he was stranded, or he was rescued, on Exmoor.

"Johnny Dewhurst wish he were back in Leeds, man. Johnny Dewhurst wish he were back in Dewsbury."

He seemed to speak from the depths of his soul. But you really couldn't tell.

A moment had come. They both upended their thermos cups, both making the same, mutually accepted, grimace. They shook out the dregs, roadside fashion. It was a piece of perfect mime. There was no one to see it.

"You come to my show in Ilfracombe, if you like. Il-frah-coombe! Bring your Missis Coastguard. I don't have a bag of money to give you, I don't have any free tickets. But you come if you want. Johnny Dewhurst entertain you."

A challenge? A genuine invitation? A forlorn hope?

"Then I know I have an audience?" He screeched and hissed and pistoned his shoulders again.

Then, by more mutual, resigned understanding, they turned to their cars.

"You go first, Mister Coastguardman. Johnny Dewhurst have to water Exmoor. Three-nine-nine. I remember. I see it, man! I see it up in lights!"

He couldn't think of anything witty or memorable to say, but then he was the straight-man, apparently. He said, "Take care now." It was what coastguards said when they put some foolish member of the public right. Take care now.

He started his car and drove slowly by with a final wave, then continued along the straight, gradually rising road. He didn't speed. He would make it. He also needed to think. Now he was back in his car, with his lights on, it seemed that dawn had retreated, it was semi-dark again. He looked in the rear-view mirror. The other car remained stationary.

How did someone decide to be a comedian? He'd wanted to be a coastguard since he was small. It was no more than a boy's yen, perhaps, for the seaside, for things maritime, though he hadn't wanted, clearly, the perils of the open sea. He'd wanted perhaps the taste of adventure, but with a good measure of its opposite. He'd never wanted to be a sailor, a soldier—or even a policeman. He'd seen himself, yes, with a vigilant stare and a mug of cocoa. It was a commendable, if not necessarily a courageous thing, to guard the nation's coastline. He'd wanted, if he were honest, to be a preserver of safety, while having—and perhaps the one thing conferred the other—a large slice of safety himself.

Was being a coastguard courageous? No. It was ninety-five per cent not courageous. There were incidents, some of them nasty, there were rescues. You were in the business of rescue. Was rescue courageous?

But it was certainly courageous, it was unfathomably coura-geous to do what Johnny Dewhurst did. Could he, a man from Somerset, possibly go to Leeds (he'd never been to Leeds, he'd only twice been to London) and, with his West Country voice, his joke of a voice, get up in front of a local audience? And make them *laugh*. His knees buckled at the thought of it.

He looked in the rear-view mirror. The car hadn't moved. It was just a distant twinkle. The poor man had hundreds of miles yet to drive. Did he really sleep in it? What the hell would he do in Ilfracombe at six in the morning? But what the hell was he doing anyway, there, at five?

He hadn't done enough, surely, not nearly enough, just to lift him back onto the road.

But, as he mounted another ridge and the car behind disap-peared, it seemed somehow that its existence and everything that had happened, from the ghostly deer onwards, became obscure and doubtful too. Had it really all happened?

He should now be eagerly working out how he'd tell the story, to his colleagues, his fellow coastguards, and then, later, Ruth. You'll never guess, you'll never guess. On the Culworthy road, at five in the morning. I met a comedian.

But the more he reflected, the more it seemed impossible. How to begin, how to be believed? How to convey every impor-tant detail? It was a story he didn't have the power of telling. So, better not to tell it. It was one of those stories you didn't tell. He wondered, already, if he believed it himself.

He reached the main road, which he would briefly follow before turning off again. There was the conspicuous sign: "Barnstaple, Ilfracombe." The man could hardly get lost. To his right now were bigger, broader pockets of sea, touched, as the land wasn't yet, by rays of pink-gold light from the east. It was the Bristol Channel. It was also the Atlantic Ocean. It was, at this point, a satisfying expanse of water. Swansea lay beyond the horizon, further away than Calais from Dover. Ships, he knew, had once sailed up the Bristol Channel with cargoes of sugar. On the way out they'd made for Africa. Then sailed west.

He took the familiar right turn, the narrow twisting road. In a while he'd see the white buildings with the lighthouse. On some mornings it could still take his breath away. And if you arrived at sunset . . .

It wasn't a head-in-the-sands job—if that wasn't a joke in bad taste. There was bad stuff. There were suicides, washed-up bodies. But he could never go to Leeds. And it was a job, by very definition, perched on the edge and looking out. It was also, by definition too, mainly stationary. A coastguard station. He thought of Johnny Dewhurst's amazing itinerary.

Was it true? Was it really a story to be told? He patted suddenly his breast pocket, containing the flyer and the card, as if even that hard evidence might have been mysteriously whisked away from him.

Should he take Ruth to Ilfracombe? Tonight. Should he explain, and should he take her, even under protest? I think we should go. But would that risk having his roadside encounter hurled outrageously back at him—and at Ruth? Have you heard the one about the lost coastguard? On Exmoor. That's right, missis, a *coastguard* on Exmoor. Would he risk discovering that he'd now become "material"—in Ilfracombe and all points to Skegness?

He thought of that double-act that was never going to happen. Kenny Coastguard—or Kenny Black?

No, he'd tell no one. Not even Ruth. In time even Johnny Dewhurst, like that questionable deer, might start to seem like a hallucination.

The familiar tower of the lighthouse appeared before him, its topmost, no longer functioning section nonetheless touched with pink glinting light. He sat on the edge of England, supposedly guarding it, looking outwards. He knew a bit about the Bristol Channel, its present-day shipping and its history. He knew a bit about Exmoor. But Exmoor wasn't England—much as you might want it to be. Brand-new shiny SUVs nosed around it like exploring spacecraft. He knew what he knew about this land to which his back was largely turned, this strange expanse beyond Exmoor, but it was precious little really. He really knew, he thought, as he brought his car to a halt again, nothing about it at all.

A NOTE ABOUT THE AUTHOR

Graham Swift lives in London and is the author of nine novels, including: *Waterland*, which was short-listed for the Booker Prize and won The Guardian Fiction Award, the Winifred Holtby Memorial Prize and the Italian Premio Grinzane Cavour; *Ever After*, which won the French Prix du Meilleur Livre Étranger; *Last Orders*, which was awarded the Booker Prize; *The Light of Day*; and, most recently, *Wish You Were Here*. He is also the author of one other collection of short stories, *Learning to Swim*, and *Making an Elephant*, a collection of non-fiction pieces. His work has been translated into more than thirty languages.

A NOTE ON THE TYPE

This book was set in Scala, a typeface designed by the Dutch designer Martin Majoor (b. 1960) in 1988 and released by the FontFont foundry in 1990. While designed as a fully modern family of fonts containing both a serif and a sans serif alphabet, Scala retains many refinements normally associated with traditional fonts.

Typeset by Scribe, Philadelphia, Pennsylvania

Printed and bound by R R Donnelley, Harrisonburg, Virginia

Designed by Soonyoung Kwon